Permission Slips

Permission Slips

A Novel

by

Jerry Sander

The Way It Works Press
Warwick, New York

The author is grateful for permission to include the following
previously copyrighted material: Excerpt from "Many a Mile
to Freedom" by Steve Winwood & Jim Capaldi
©1972 FS Music Ltd. And Freedom Songs Ltd. (Renewed)
All Rights for FS Music Ltd. Administered in the U.S. &
Canada
by Warner-Tamerlane Publishing Corp.
All Rights for Freedom Songs Ltd. Administered in the U.S.
& Canada
by Universal – PolyGram International Publishing, Inc.
All Rights Reserved. Used by Permission.

The Way It Works Press
Warwick, New York
www.thesandsoftime.net

THE WAY IT
WORKS
PRESS

Library of Congress Control Number: 2005922294
ISBN 0-9766127-0-4

Special Thanks To:

Lauren, Bonnie, and Jackie.

The Warwick/Monroe Writer's Group, for their continued
support and laughter.

The Skaneateles Police Department.

My colleagues: the teachers, psychologists, social workers,
counselors, aides, and administrators who do their intensely
challenging jobs with dedication, professionalism, hope, and
humor.

Mike Levine, for meeting at the Monroe Diner years ago with
a Writer's Group of one.

Michael, my roommate and brother on the trip to WR's
outdoor shower shrine.

Miki Frank, for her fierce, no-holds-barred embrace of life.

Nancy Aronie, for her inspiration during those beautiful
summer days at Omega.

Philip, Frederick, David, Jim, & Ann for writing with fire
from one century to the next.

The Skyline Drive/Blue Ridge Parkway.

Shasti, for the wake-up call.

Peggy Gavan, for the meticulous reading, and Diane Tinney
for design assistance.

Melissa Browne, Rachel, Jessie, Nathan, and Micah, for
surrounding me with love and patience and making it possible
for this book to come into the world.

With honor and respect for
all the teenagers who talk.

For Maurice Sander

"The nature of reality is this:
it is hidden, and it is hidden, and it is hidden."
—Rumi, Sufi Poet, 13th Century

In the Tank

Alison Gepner sat in ninth-period Global Studies on the first day back after Spring Break examining her arm. It was almost seventy degrees outside. Global warming. Like that movie. Next thing you know the Statue of Liberty would be under a hundred feet of snow. It could happen. A teacher-voice droned in the background. She wondered why—if everything was warming—there would be snow. It was because it was all interrelated in some way. Heat and snow. Yin and yang. Except in Hadleyville Falls. There was just pollen and mold. Humidity, pollen, and mold, actually. The leaves looked good in fall, though. Japanese tourists came up in buses, just for that. That and the shopping at the outlets. Which weren't even that cheap. Cheaper than Tokyo, maybe.

Her skin itched. Her arm most of all. The Neutrogena Body Wash might have aggravated that bug-bite thing that everyone-said-probably-wasn't-Lyme on her upper left arm. It looked buggy. Her hair was starting to frizz. You couldn't see it yet, but she could feel it. It was about ten minutes from being visible. It was a good thing it was ninth period.

She wondered what her upper left arm tasted like, whether it had been a sensual experience for the bug. She wondered if it died after tasting her.

Nothing important was being said, or even thought about, by anyone around her. Especially not by Mr. Peckwirth, who seemed to have run out of steam in January. He had resorted to a lot of videos and handout reprints from *Newsweek*—never a good sign—as if any of her classmates cared. She remembered back to the summer before, when ninth grade was still the big-show-to-come, when she got her schedule in the mail in late August. "Pacelli, North, Peebles, and Peckwirth" for her major subjects. Not exactly like winning the lottery, her brother told her, but she could have done worse.

She wondered how much worse it could have been. True, "Freshman Friday"—when you were welcomed by the older kids by getting your head stuck in a toilet and flushed—turned out to be a myth. But ninth grade had been the pits. She had done well academically—oh, wow—and had remained utterly invisible to every male in the building, other than the jerks around her who punched each other in the arm all the time and called each other "faggot" every chance they got.

It wasn't true that this was the fate of all ninth-grade girls. There was the "Sluts-'R-Us" crew, who could be seen after school zooming around Hadleyville Falls in their senior boyfriends' Camaros. Probably en route to the Clinic, to take care of a "little problem." Whoops—have to miss cheerleading for a few weeks.

It was late April. The year was basically cooked. Kids were cutting left and right. After another two weeks of classes came "Final Review." Then finals. Then the Regents. They gave you four years to pass the Global Regents. It was insulting. Anyone who couldn't pass it the first time around deserved twenty years working in the food court at the mall. As if there were consequences to this stuff.

Her hair was definitely starting to "boing."

If every year were like this there was no sense to any of it. She would run away and join Ani DiFranco or some other women's alternative-rock tour and stay with it until she was sixty. She would run Righteous Babe Records until another opportunity presented itself. Then she would buy a horse farm. First she would learn to play an instrument. Or sing, or something.

"Let the bell ring, let the bell ring, let the bell ring."

Her arm really itched now. She thought Neutrogena was supposed to be "hypo-allergenic." Maybe it was "hyper-allergenic."

Maybe she was losing her mind.

Claire was halfway through a mouthful of the school's sixth-period lunch-sludge ("Sizzlin' Salisbury on 7-Grain Sesame Wedge") when Tina walked into the cafeteria. Claire could sense the friggin' attitude one hundred and fifty feet away. She had better lose it by the time she came over to this half of the cafeteria or Claire would dispatch Carly as an intercept. Claire had gotten a 23 on a Social Studies quiz ("...some crap about the Middle East...like it matters?") and was in no mood.

Tina was looking like she didn't know where to sit but Claire wasn't buying it. "She is not allowed within ten feet of The Court of No Appeal today," she told Carly, referring to their lunch table. "Ten feet. Measure it and enforce it."

"I need a yardstick. Wait...ten meters or ten feet?"

"Ten feet, Carly," Claire said, sneering. "It's always been ten feet. Y'know what? For her, make it fifteen feet."

"Why?"

"Because regular rules don't apply to blonde bimbos."

Carly was silent. She brushed a lock of her own blonde hair back.

"I don't mean all blondes, Carly. C'mon…It's not like a racial thing. I mean, do you go running around making up lies about people humping cars and stuff?"

"No. But you did tell me you were lying on the car, right?"

"That's not the point. She had no business spreading rumors."

"But if…"

"It's a rumor if the person telling it didn't see it. And it's not forgivable if a blonde-bimbo-skank is talking about you behind your back to all the people you were friends with first. I mean, c'mon, Fat Mike and I were in kindergarten when he was Little Fat Mike. She's known him for, what, ten seconds, and he's supposed to come to the little tart's rescue anytime anyone speaks harshly to her?"

"Ummmmmm…."

"I'm sick of it. She thinks she rules the school because she's the first one to spread her legs at every party and…"

Carly cleared her throat loudly and pointed.

"What?! You're annoying me."

Carly pointed, meekly. Claire whirled around, nearly knocking Tina down. Tina was close enough for Claire to smell her J. Lo Glo perfume. "I'm sorry. Do you have some business with me?" Claire asked, affecting an air of professionalism.

"I don't want this to become like a 'thing,' or look like we're clashing, but I don't want to cover it up," Tina said.

"I wish I knew what you were talking about, but I'm not sure I really care." Claire turned and glared at Carly. "Thanks a lot, Carly, for the fifteen foot thing." Carly looked down.

"You'd care if you heard what people are saying about you," said Tina with a snarly smile.

"If anyone is saying anything about me, Tina, it's because you put the words in their mouths."

"No. Not even. I just think it's fair that you know what people are saying."

"Oh, right. Like you're my friend. We're best buds. You're my right lung. 'Pop a squat and let's catch up, yuh?' C'mon, Tina, you want to know what, like, ninety-eight percent of the school is saying about you?"

Tina turned red, but it didn't look like from embarrassment.

"I heard the only two guys who haven't seen your naked butt, like weekly, are the two gay guys in Advanced Computer class who upgrade the school's Web site fifteen times a day."

Tina reached past Carly's face to her plate, grabbing a handful of Jell-O Jewels and quickly slamming it against Claire's head. Claire rebounded, with her right hand shoving Tina's nose to the left just as Tina's second handful—this time a soggy cup of Fruit Medley—came flying toward Claire, a half-grape momentarily lodging in her right nostril. "C'mon, bring it, bitch!" she screamed, her voice somewhat more nasal because of the grape.

"Parking Lot Pussy, and you fight like it, too!" shouted Tina.

The kids at the tables around them started immediately hooting and laughing. "Fight! Fight! Fight!!"

Claire grabbed Tina's blouse and pulled. The upper left shoulder ripped. Claire reloaded, with a handful of Sizzlin' Salisbury. "I'm going to beat you like a red-headed stepchild!" she screamed. Before Claire could unload it, a hail of raisins nearly blinded her. She let the steak wail, but felt Tina's sharp claws ripping at the shoulder of her blue-and-white peasant top. Unbelievably, and unfairly, Tina successfully pulled down Claire's blouse two full inches below her right boob. The boys hooted at the sight of her boob bouncing in its beige bra. Claire recovered, with fury, fixing her blouse and slamming a handful of mashed potatoes onto Tina's nose. Claire followed this up with resourcefully pulling a Game Boy out of her backpack and knocking Tina in the head with it. Two double-A batteries went flying, one of them landing in Alison's applesauce.

Both girls were suddenly lifted upward and back—Claire by Security and Tina by Fat Mike. Three minutes later they sat in the principal's office.

"You're both out. Five days. There is no excuse for this," the principal boomed. "And, by the way, Claire, we've spoken to your group home and that Game Boy, the one you hit her with, was reported stolen yesterday."

"I know that. I was returning it as a favor."

"Where did you get it from?"

"If I told you it would violate confidentiality."

"What are you talking about?"

"O.K., what had happened was…let's just say that I know who took it and I know who it belongs to and I would have gotten it back to them today, by three-fifteen, if this slut hadn't started with me."

"Enough. I don't want to hear it. From either of you," their Principal declared, rendering a verdict. "You're both going to do counseling."

"You can't make us," offered Claire.

"You want to see me try? You can do it in school, or on your own expense."

"It would just be a waste of time," volunteered Claire.

Their Principal thought carefully before he decided to say nothing.

———◦◦◦———

The fat retarded boy stumbled off the bus, slinging his knapsack quickly over one-half of his right shoulder, jabbing at his glasses with stubby fingers, high-tailing it off of Bus 26 at warp speed. His butt wiggled rapidly as his backpack was flung from side to side. Zach breezed off the bus behind him, the only kid not in a raincoat or carrying an umbrella in the cold rain. He wasn't wearing a coat at all, but a turquoise "Surf Naked" t-shirt. Raindrops immediately pummeled his hair and saturated his shirt. Alan could hear him from sixty feet away.

"I'll cut you a new asshole, you wanna fuck with me, nigger...you wanna go? What's the matter? What's the matter now? Cuz I don't fucking care...get it? I don't care...I'll put you down...and what are they going to do? What?"

"ZACHHHHHH!..." an old lady's voice screamed, puncturing the moment. The teacher aide glared at him from a distance. "Language! You want a bus write-up?"

Zach turned and soft-shouted, "Fuck you!"

"You're going to get a write-up, young man!" she said in an almost-loud voice.

He rubbed his hands together, rearranged the contours of his crotch, and strutted toward the high school.

Alan didn't have to watch the kids come off the bus (contractually), but he always liked to. This was where most of the traumatic action of the day took place. His office would soon be full of victims relating what other victims had done to them on the bus ("when no one was looking"). You could see the guilty ones a mile away, as they always were laughing.

JERRY SANDER

Having survived six years with a children's psychiatric center, Alan now worked for a good school district. What a thought: escaping to a high school. Most people escaped *from* a high school. Hadleyville Falls was, apparently, The Great Reward. Alan Mitchke was late-thirties, twelve pounds overweight, single/divorced, had borderline high blood pressure, but he was alive. His job, as a School Social Worker, was to try to track and "support" the influx of "inclusion students" who had previously attended an all Special Education center a few towns over. The kids were, often, nightmares to regular-ed teachers and the administrators were ready to throw out the kids on the slightest provocation. Only the Director of Special Education and a few noble special-ed teachers—who looked like stragglers from the seventies— were pulling for the kids. Alan's job was a balancing act; he was allowed to see the "regular-ed" students for counseling purposes, but wasn't supposed to provide therapy, only "supportive, school-based counseling." To assist him with this, the school contracted with his old boss—the very State Mental Health system he'd escaped from—for monthly "supportive supervision" with a supervising psychiatrist who had never worked in a public school, had poor command of the English language, and was burdened with administrative paperwork which no longer applied to Alan. It didn't make much sense, but the job would pay him well and he'd have summers off.

How any of this would fit in with the School Psychologist's or Guidance Counselor's jobs was anybody's guess. Complicating matters was the unusually high number of teachers in the building over sixty-four years old. They were supposed to be nearing retirement, but no one seemed to have told them that.

Alan watched as a scrawny blonde girl, Tina, emerged from behind Bus 28, and began screaming loudly to Zach.

"Zach, you bastard! You were supposed to call me!"

"I did!"

"You did not, you friggin' liar!"

"I did!"

"You did not. I was home."

"You weren't home!"

"I was home!"

"Well, you weren't when I called."

"Maria says you never called."

"Maria's a slut."

"Yeah, well...what-EVER...."

"That's the one who was suspended," Alan heard one teacher aide say to another one. "Some mouth on her, huh?"

Walking the halls before the buses arrived felt like something in between sleeping and waking. The building stank in an already-familiar way. Something of hot dogs, sauerkraut, Tater Tots, and human waste. The smells of the bathrooms seemed to mingle with the smells of the cafeteria and classrooms to the point where they were indistinguishable. Everyone walked around smiling before the kids arrived. It wasn't even 7:15 yet. It was as if he and everyone he saw were somehow afloat in a warmly-heated large bathtub, bobbing past each other, waving, smiling, and ignoring the smell. No one would drown, no one would age, no one would ever leave. Nothing could pull you down. Everyone was in the tank. Every two weeks scraps of paper with hundreds of dollars written on them would float by to be pocketed eagerly with a grin. There were "50/50" raffles, Super Bowl Betting Pools, and opportunities in Tupperware. They stayed, they floated, they treaded water, and the years passed.

Tina walked closer to Zach, wearing her "Cute But Psycho—It All Evens Out" t-shirt.

"Did you see Carlos?" Tina asked.

"Nah," Zach replied.

"He got busted at the mall."

"For what? Stealing Timberlands?"

"Nah, he, like, went up to Richie's car and started kicking the shit out of it."

"Out of the car?"

"Yeah, he was, like, wailing on the driver's side door and busted one of the mirrors off and he cracked the windshield."

"So, what'd they do?"

"He gotta, well, wait, they took him down, vright?, and he's gotta make an appearance. And he's probably gotta do restitution."

"The fuck…?"

"Yeah, he's gotta do restitution."

"Oh, yeah…"

"The thing was, Mike was there just around the time it happened. And he was—"

"Wait…wait. Which Mike?"

"Fat Mike."

"Yeah."

"And he was like all jealous, because Claire had been hanging around the car, and joking around and like…lying on it?"

"Claire?"

"Yeah," said Tina. "The Group Home loser bitch with Dumbo ears who started with us."

"I thought Claire was going with Ninja Dave?"

"Yeah, well, they were…they were, vright? And they were supposed to meet at The Mall? I dunno. I can't keep it straight. I don't think we have enough time to…"

"Yeah, well, I gotta go," Zach blurted out. "So…does he want to talk to me?"

"Who?"

"Fat Mike."

"I thought you meant Carlos," said Tina.

"Fuck Carlos. I don't even really know Carlos."

"But you thought he'd be stealing Timberlands?" asked Tina, looking at Zach earnestly.

"Tina, I'm talking about Fat Mike. Where is he?"

"He's at his aunt's."

"He didn't come to school?"

"No."

"Tell him I got a dime bag for him," said Zach.

"I ain't gonna see him."

"Why are you telling me all this, Tina? It gets me aggravated…"

"I didn't want you to hear it from someone else. I wanted you to get the facts."

"Yeah, later. Whatever."

In the hallway, Zach checked out the new Art teacher. Very red-haired, very slim, very sexy. She was the kind of sexy that dressed like she was trying to hide the fact. Probably wearing a thong. Like people wouldn't be able to tell that she was real proud of her body if she wore loose-fitting clothes. Zach took her in, like a long sip of Pepsi from a Big Gulp. He could feel his dick stir.

Suddenly a huge smack propelled him five feet forward and off balance. He didn't have time to stop himself from smacking into Alison, sending her books flying. It had to be Fat Mike. Only Fat Mike was allowed to touch him like that.

"The fuck?" Zach asked, pushing off of the startled girl in front of him, head arched back, taking in Mike's gargantuan frame.

"You owe me a dime bag, or what?" Fat Mike asked.

"Not here. You don't have to push me. What's wrong with you? I thought you weren't here anyway. Tina said…"

"Tina?!"

"She said there was…"

"Tina is lucky I don't kill her…"

"Why?"

"Tina was supposed to set me up with her girlfriend, at The Mall, only she was so friggin' nosy that she has to go get involved with Carlos and this other…it's hopeless, man…you don't want to know…you don't want to know… So where's my bag?" asked Fat Mike.

"Fourth period. Fourth period."

"Your locker?"

"No, what do you think, I'm stupid? I don't keep things in my locker…I'll have the stuff."

"Where we going to meet?"

"Health," said Zach. Meet me outside of Health class."

They parted. Alison stared at the two of them. She was kind of stunned from the feel of Zach's half-hard, um, "maleness" and muscular frame pressing up against her from behind. Even if just for a moment. "Wassup?" she thought, almost blushing. She didn't say anything, but she smiled in Zach's direction.

NO LOVE LOST

Alison found most of the boys in her grade boring. They tried hard to hang out with the girls (after three years of pretty much not talking to them at all), but that just made it more pathetic. It wasn't all physical—though some of them looked quite dumb, caught in that in-between stage where their legs were long enough and they wore the right jeans but their faces looked goofy and…well, like Goofy. Some of them slapped on cologne even though they didn't seem to have to shave much yet. The worst was "Polo," which smelled to her like the stuff her father had used to remove paint from his hands after working on the shed one day.

Ahhh, the shed. The musty, almost spooky shadows the first time she had been in it, holding her dad's hand tight. Huge cobwebs draped over old wooden and metallic boxes and tools and copper rusted things. The air smelled of oil and gasoline. She knew she was in another land. It was the land of her Grandfather. The whole house, including the shed, had been Grandpa's for about fifty years before Grandma and Grandpa moved to South Florida. She figured she had to have been around three years old the first time she was in the shed. She now thought of it as the best part of her house—maybe because it wasn't in her house.

Alison's house was very clean with a lot of brightly colored wallpaper and "thoughtful attention to details," as her mom's magazines liked to say. Her mom had carried on Grandma's tradition of assuming that you had to be ready at all times for a stranger to walk in and be able to see any room in the house without embarrassment. The way some of her friends' houses looked just before Passover Seder is what her house looked like year-round. It was nice, but also really annoying. It was…embarrassing. Her mother never asked for her thoughts about this. She just nagged her a lot to keep it clean.

Alison felt okay about being Jewish. She couldn't understand kids from Youth Group and Hebrew school who didn't want kids from "regular school" to "know." It wasn't like you could fool people much anyway, because the parents of most of the Jewish kids were either doctors, lawyers, teachers, social workers, computer experts, or business owners in town (all right, a few were cops), where a lot of other kids' parents had different kinds of jobs. It wasn't like she could make believe her parents were farmers or factory workers, so why should she try? It was dumb to be a wanna-be-poor-person just like it was dumb to parade around in new clothes all the time, like Natalie Pinsker from Hebrew school class who tried so hard to look seventeen at age twelve.

Every now and then Alison would see a swastika around school on someone's notebook. Or she would hear jokes about "the Jews." It hurt. She knew that people who did this were ignorant but there was something really creepy and disgusting about joking around just a few years after millions of people like her had been murdered. It no longer surprised her that the world didn't care about this or that she could only talk about this stuff with other Jews. Or that the world thought that the deaths of two thousand or so Palestinians, over fifty years of fighting about land, was the equivalent to the deaths of six million people. It made her really sad to think about it for more than a few minutes, so she didn't, and didn't like it when they made you talk about it in Hebrew school, because it seemed too much to even talk about.

Her brother—in his "Super Jew" phase, just before heading off to Cornell—once shocked and amazed her in the way she had come to rely on him to shock and amaze her—late one night when she had Robin Wedner (whose dad owned Wedner's, the farm equipment supply store in Galesville) over for a sleepover. Alison couldn't remember how they got started, but she remembered Jeff sitting on the edge of her bed lecturing as she and Robin sat cross-legged on the floor. (She could have predicted that Jeff would come into her room to get a good look at Robin in her light blue Powerpuff Girls pajamas.) Jeff had been smitten with Robin ever since their families had gone to Jones Beach together and Robin had worn a dark blue bikini. Robin liked blue. Big woof. But Jeff must have asked Alison a dozen times or more if all girls wore belly-button jewelry with bikinis and whether her ankle bracelet was, in fact, "a coded message."

"Saying what?" Alison had asked him.

"I don't know. That's why I'm asking you. You're a girl."

"So...?"

"You speak their language," said Jeff.

"But you think you know what it might mean?"

"Yeah."

"Well it probably means the exact opposite," said Alison.

Alison's brother held the floor, the two girls in pajamas before him. "You know when Christians will understand the Holocaust? After *they* have been rounded up, burned, and killed *because* of being Christians. When the government does door-to-door searches for them, killing one in four of them randomly, just to send a message. Would that be what it takes to feel another people's pain? Them having to read, every day, of how wonderful the world will be when there are no more Christians around? And then to have them start disappearing? When even Mel Gibson can't help them? Maybe then they can relate?"

Robin was staring at him, but probably not with whatever feeling he was hoping for. (Lust and admiration were Alison's guess. Instead Robin was giving the "watching-a-car-crash" look usually reserved for sitting in Global Studies watching the teacher go off on a tangent about a decade no one cared about.)

"Hey–let the healing begin," Jeff continued. "After the smoke settles. Send in Oprah, Al Sharpton, the New Age bimbos, send in the Pope. Then Jews and Christians can comprehend each other. Until then, no. It's just 'sensitivity.' Garbage. Worse than garbage. Humiliating. Let *us* be the ones with 'compassion' for their losses. 'The Christians have had *such* a hard time over the ages, haven't they? What a plucky little people! Let's hide them in our attics.' We can even set up Commissions and areas of academic study to try to understand their pain. There could be whole departments of 'Christian Holocaust Literature.' They could raise enough money to have museums, with entire floors showing what pre-Holocaust Christian life was like. They could have a whole 'American Christmas' floor. But–let me ask you both something: If they did this, do you think there would be a single exhibit in the museum about the original Holocaust? The one that so-called Christians perpetuated? I don't think so. I believe theirs would become the Only Holocaust, the Original Authentic Holocaust."

Alison and Robin had just finished listening to The Beatles' "Abbey Road" moments before this. Alison was shocked and amazed—she knew that a very beautiful, popular Christian girlfriend had dumped Jeff not five months ago—but she hadn't known he had given it this much thought. The month after getting dumped he had rented

"Schindler's List" four times—which seemed excessive to everyone in the family—and had accumulated a large body of books about the Holocaust. No one seemed to have the guts to tell him to just start getting over Colleen O'Malley, though. Alison and Robin agreed, afterward, in hushed tones: she wasn't *that* good-looking, talented, smart, or nice. Robin thought the likely scenario was that Jeff was just on the verge of getting some nooky from Colleen when Colleen dumped him. Neither of them could figure out what else might motivate such murderous fantasies. It certainly didn't come from Hebrew school, which emphasized some vague "remembering," lighting a few candles, perhaps some crying, but little else. There was nothing in Judaism that would support Jeff's wondering about killing most of the population of the country just because one Catholic girl wouldn't go all the way with him. Not even Al-Qaeda would support that.

Jeff needed a good Jewish girlfriend, thought Alison. The problem was, however, that he was a major pain-in-the-ass quite often. Smart, but arrogant, confident, but obnoxious. He needed a confident, assertive Jewish girlfriend. The type he never found attractive.

Alison didn't know what was making her think about this stuff now, except that they were riding past the street that her temple was on, on the way to the Thomas Henry Hawthorne House in nearby Renwick, New York, which was supposed to be some kind of historical site. Field trips in general were dumb, unless they were to New York City. The only excitement came from seeing who was going to sit next to whom and whether there was going to be any making out on the way home. It wasn't that Alison had ever done the making out, but she was able to watch, through quick backward glances, at Danielle (who got hot-and-heavy on the way back from the Metropolitan Museum of Art with Carlos) and Tina, obviously tongue-kissing some Italian guy in their grade whom Alison had never seen before. Tina seemed to be in the habit of sitting on guys' laps a lot with her arms wrapped around their necks as she squirmed and giggled and said things like, "Stop it!" Tina was the kind of girl who said she didn't like other girls. The feeling was mutual.

Once, coming back from the Museum of Broadcasting, there had been a really cool surprise ending to the trip. Coming over the mountain, after Route 209, Carlos had put his usual moves on a girl three seats from the back and the girl had punched him in the face so hard that his nose bled. The bus had to be pulled over to the side of the road and she was later suspended for three days. Her name was Claire.

The inside of the Thomas Henry Hawthorne House was really boring. She tried to picture an average day in the life of a Colonial American, as her teacher had suggested, and she…kind of drew a blank. She wasn't able to picture what these people did all day long. She wondered if any of them dreamt of the twenty-first century.

There were times when Alison felt really deep. She knew it would surprise most of the people around her to know that she felt that way. Entire weeks would go by, sometimes, where she would want someone around her to know how many different levels she worked on at once without her having to tell them.

The ceilings on the bedrooms were really low and the tour guide explained that everybody was really short then. It kind of shot the image that she'd had of Colonial Americans (tall, muscular pioneers of the wilderness) and she started thinking about how it was possible that they were actually short—and maybe even mean—people. It was a funny thought: short Puritans walking around, talking weird, yelling at each other all day long with nothing to do. The book said they had "...quilting bees, corn-huskings, and house-raisings." You had to dig a little to find out that they also had witch-burnings. Whatever.

Unless you were a witch.

She imagined the witches as tall and wearing slinky black dresses. They wouldn't look like Samantha on "Bewitched." They would be able to change themselves into a black cat and back several times a day. They were, no doubt, dangerous but had more exciting lives than the Puritans. She knew there were no Jewish Puritans, but wondered if there had been any Jewish witches. That's what she would have been, she decided: a witch who had been bat-mitzvahed and who could turn herself into a cat whenever she felt like it and who looked down on the shrimpy, weak Puritans with disdain. She'd be Jewitch. And tall.

No. There was no way around it. The whole seventeenth and eighteenth centuries were not good times for someone like her to be.

She was bored, as the tour guide explained another quilt. That is when she first saw him.

It must have been out of the corner of her eye, because he was standing in the back of the low-ceilinged room, several feet back from Danielle, Zach, and some girl. He looked older, more intelligent than everyone in the room, and he had the coolest haircut of the year. It was slightly spiky-looking, but not stupid-spiky, tapering into a really short length on the sides that made you just want to hold his head in your hands and rub it. His eyes were dark and his skin was cocoa. She didn't know who he was.

His silence was, like, a statement. His partial smile was a warm challenge. She had never seen him before. She was almost afraid to breathe, like the way when you see a deer you stop moving to just become witness to a godly moment. She opened her eyes wider. She drank him in.

She listened carefully when they took attendance on the bus. His name was Elijah.

"Amazing," she thought. "He wears wire-rim glasses, just like me."

———•◦•———

Ronald Dubeck sat on the porch, cupped his morning coffee in his shaking hands, and surveyed the late April sights. He had taken to adding some whiskey to his black coffee on cold mornings, starting last December, and there was something to the combination that let him know he was alive.

He didn't know why his hands shook. It wasn't all the time. Mostly when he woke up.

He had seen this town change…the county change, the state change, everything on t.v. change…nothing was better than it used to be.

The county had wasted fifty million dollars or more polluting the landfill three-quarter miles from his house, then wanted fifteen million dollars to do a study about possibly spending another twenty-five or thirty million dollars to possibly clean it up. There had once been country roads up here, winding through tiny hamlets where you knew everyone, because your families knew each other from years back. There had always been hard times, but everybody pulled together and helped everybody else. They lived close to the land. Not anymore.

There had never been many blacks around these towns before the 1960s, before the Jews brought them up. They didn't have one Jew he'd heard of when he was a teenager. Now there were Jewish realtors, Jewish bankers financing low-cost loans, Jewish social workers in the schools teaching kids that everything their parents taught them was wrong, teaching them to have sex with each other like rabbits, teaching them to smoke pot. Mexicans were now found in every town in the country, almost... He couldn't imagine what was next. Maybe Haitians, or entire towns full of homosexuals. Like Provincetown. Guys in hot pants. Thongs.

You couldn't get, and keep, a job if you were white. Every governor of this state for the past sixteen years was either Italian, Irish, or Greek—all Catholics—and in league with the blacks in spending Jew money to import drugs into every little farmland in America. The result was that all the government did now was to tell you what kind of guns you could, and couldn't, own, where you could shoot them, and what taxes you needed to pay.

The whiskey tasted right.

Soon there would be a "bullet-tax," a brilliant idea from their dyke senator, inherited from the Irish Catholic senator before her. What did she know, anyway? She didn't need to arm herself from the blacks with their nine-millimeters, because she had lived behind electric fences her whole life–including at the White House–and didn't have blacks trying to date and have sex with her daughter, because she sent her to some all-white private school where the only blacks wore white gloves and hairnets and prepared lunch to be rolled in on a silver platter.

He tanked up his cup.

He'd send Claire to a private school, if he could. The girl was an alley cat. Claire was still taking ninth-grade classes and had just turned sixteen. She wouldn't listen to him or her mother. He tried to raise her like she was his own daughter. The girl just wanted to run free. Ronald had told her mother she's probably dating niggers, to expect a half-nigger baby any month now, but her mother wouldn't listen. He'd given up trying to whoop her butt, after Claire threatened to tell the school. He'd finally gotten off probation about a year ago and would be damned if he'd have to go in and answer to that Polish idiot every month again ("When ya getting' a job? When ya getting' a job?"). His wife—well, almost his wife— had dried up and would sit around watching "Survivor" and stupid comedies where they mainly laughed at men. She would eat her packaged snacks, reading her friggin' women's magazines where the articles were always about how to lose weight (with a picture of a brownie in the background, with whipped cream on it, next to articles about having "super sex"), then she'd fall asleep without even letting on that his dick had any rights at all.

No...he didn't have much in the world anymore. Except for his sister in the Carolinas (who he used to visit every year to hunt bear), who now wouldn't talk to him. There was the standing job application at the cheese factory. He had his house (her house, if you wanted to get technical), two deer rifles, and one of the last big modified-for-automatic assault rifles sold before the United States government—acting under instructions from international Jews—legislated it away.

Sure, they'd let you keep it with a "Federal gun permit." But not once it had been made fully automatic. The AR-15 was capable of shooting about 100 rounds in four seconds.

Not only was the AR-15 his, it was the only thing in Ronald's life that was truly his.

———•◦•———

"Tony fucked Tina without a rubber."

"Says who?"

"Carlos."

"When?"

"Thursday."

Fat Mike regarded Richie with caution. He'd heard him go on like this before and ninety-nine percent of it was a bunch of happy horseshit. They stood behind Radio Shack in a little back alley between the Laundromat and the new Chinese restaurant, General Chao's Delight, passing a joint. Zach's weed was up to its usual quality.

"He was there?" asked Fat Mike.

"Yeah, for most of it," vouched Richie.

"Then Tony's definitely got AIDS now."

"Tina is a major slut."

"Duh. How was Carlos there?"

"At the fairgrounds. Tony made believe he wanted to go out with her again."

"Yeah."

"And she says yes."

"To go out with?"

"No, to fuck."

"Carlos saw them do it?" asked Fat Mike.

"No. But he heard all about it after. Tina's living with her mother again, but her mother is working nights at Meatland, so Tina can use the condo."

"That ain't no 'condo.'"

"That's what they call it."

"It's a fucking apartment. And a royal scummy one."

"Anyway, she can fuck anyone she wants to, all night long. Five nights a week, and her mother'll never know." Richie stared off at a plane overhead.

"What was that stuff happening between you and Carlos at The Mall, by the way?" asked Fat Mike.

"Carlos," Richie responded, "is your basic out-of-control youth, okay? He is a lying, burrito-breathed, crackhead gaylord who owed me major money and then says $75 makes us even. In my neighborhood we call that 'crime.'"

"So you pressed charges?"

"Fuckin' A," said Richie. "It was my car he went off on. You don't do that. You want to hit me, hit me. You don't touch a guy's car." Richie passed the joint back to Fat Mike.

Fat Mike inhaled and felt the crackling of a few good brain cells. A deep relaxation kicked in.

"So, who else she do?"

"Who?" asked Richie.

"Tina. At the condo."

"You know that band that played Pine Jr. High?" asked Richie.

"Like I'm gonna go hang around a bunch of preppy jock assholes?"

"I didn't go either. But you know them?"

"The ones that do…"

"…the Led Zeppelin tribute?"

"…where he takes out a violin bow and bows it, with the Marshall amp turned up all the way, like Page?" asked Fat Mike. "Yeah, I saw that."

"Monster guitar noises…down on his knees, with all the lights all weird and shit…"

"Yeah, I know them."

"Well, she did the bass player," declared Richie.

"The guy…"

"…with the hair?"

"…and the headband?"

"Yup."

"You're lying."

"No shit."

"She did him?"

"She blew him on the loading dock. I SWEAR TO CHRIST, you can ask Nick's father, he's a janitor there, he seen it all."

"She did?"

"And then they were out of there like a fat kid in a dodge-ball game and they went to the condo and she did him."

"How do you know?" asked Fat Mike.

"That's what I heard."

"What time does Meatland close?" Fat Mike asked in his best CSI-investigative voice.

"It's twenty-four hours."

"Since when?"

"Week before Christmas, I swear to God," said Richie.

Fat Mike thought it through. It was possible. He reached his decision. "Tina is a fucking whore."

"I know. I'm telling you."

"She didn't used to be."

"Oh, what, when she was, like, five?"

Fat Mike remembered Tina from a fourth-grade field trip to the Energy Conservation Display. She was already wearing stockings. And she'd offered to let him look up her skirt...for no particular reason at all. He agreed. She lifted her skirt, for a half-second, until a parent chaperone came down the aisle. She slammed her legs together and looked out the window, all innocent. Her panties were light blue. The next time he'd been around her, in fifth grade, she'd kissed him, hard, on the mouth, during some game they were all playing with no parents around. His sort-of-girlfriend saw it and nearly tore Tina apart before telling her to never come near Fat Mike again. Fat Mike wondered if Tina had liked him. She wasn't really slutty back then and she listened when you talked to her. Why had she shown him what she did without asking for anything back unless she'd liked him? He was jolted by Richie's voice.

"What, you're saying she's not a slut?"

"No," said Fat Mike. "I'm saying that Tony's a fucking idiot for not using a rubber."

"Well, he is stupid," admitted Richie.

"I mean, the guy is smart..."

"...but he's got no street smarts."

"He's got common sense, but his judgment is for shit."

"In this day and age, when you know she's been around..."

"...with guys from the city..."

"I heard she went with a black guy at Danielle's sweet sixteen," said Richie.

"Forget it."

"She's dead. She'll get AIDS."

"Uh-huh."

"And maybe Tony."

Fat Mike tried to picture Tina dying soon. Suffering like those guys he'd seen on a Barbara Walters special, wasting away with sores and shit all over their bodies. He couldn't come up with it. It didn't register. All he saw was Tina looking away...out the window...with a small smile on her face.

PARKING UP THE WRONG TREE

Hadleyville Falls' High School Principal, Peter Epperschmidt, supposed that there were some who thought it was "cute" that his wife's name was Patrice. He didn't. "Peter and Patty." Life as the top of a wedding cake.

The same morons had encouraged him to name their one and only child "Little Peter." He hadn't.

Being a high school principal was nowhere near as much fun as he imagined it might be when he hated classroom teaching.

Peter wondered if he would have been less attracted to Patty when he first met her if he knew her name. Or knew that years later they would be the middle-aged version of "Peter and Patty." There was something simultaneously sad and embarrassing about it. It was not enough to be caught in mid-level school administration for the past seven years; he had to be part of a "cute" couple, too. The sex was bad (there was no doubt about it). He frequently told himself that it really didn't matter, but he'd have a surge of anger every time he'd pass by a cover of *Cosmopolitan*, with its endless repetition of articles about young housewives having "creative, orgasmic sex" with their husbands at least ten to fifteen times a month. ("Touch Him Here, Then Stand Back!" read April's cover.)

It was not enough that she'd become "born-again." It was not enough that this was public knowledge. The icing on their embarrassing middle-class cake was evident during Lent, when Patty first started telling him that something was

27

happening in her dreams. These were not ordinary dreams, but messages from God.

At first they were images—a small boy carrying a lamb, a woman crying endless tears by the side of the road, an old man blowing a hollowed-out ram's horn—but the images stopped after four days and she began to hear Jesus' voice. At least this is what she thought she remembered. Though she would pay studious attention to every sound and syllable uttered throughout the night she could not recall a single thing upon awakening. Peter listened to her with rapt attention, the first week.

Now she was completely, fully, losing it. She was lapsing into the worst sort of religious babble while staring at him over breakfast, her eyes those of a future mental patient.

"Thus sayeth the Lord," said Patty as if in a trance.

"What?" snapped Peter.

"That's the only part I can remember. Every morning. Just the last line."

Peter shoved a piece of rye toast into his mouth.

Patty went on. "I mean there must be something huge being said. There must be a Revelation. A series of Revelations. Maybe ones that would transform the world. But I can't remember anything. All I can remember is 'Thus sayeth the Lord.'"

"Well, Patty...why don't you just write that down...and see if the rest comes to you," said Peter, rising to gather his coat and keys.

"I really need you to not be mocking about this."

"I'm not mocking. If that's the Revelation, that's the Revelation. I don't know, maybe you're saying...God exists, or something."

"You think I'm going nuts, right?"

Peter looked at her sadly. "No."

"It's all right. That's what they always think."

"They?"

"About Prophets."

"Oh. Yeah. Maybe you are meant to put it in writing, and more messages will come once God sees that you are doing the job." Peter couldn't believe he was talking this way without laughing, but he was. It must have been the part of him that still cared for her.

"You're right. Or maybe you're right," said Patty, tiredly.

When Peter came home that night there was a spiral notebook on the kitchen counter, eighty pages full, titled, "Revelations, 2005/2006." Each line of it was, "Thus sayeth the Lord."

He poured himself a Dewars.

Alan was meeting with Claire for the third time. She was one of the "Group Home Girls." They were all legally registered to attend, even though their parents lived out-of-district, because the girls lived in a "therapeutic residential outpatient facility." No one seemed able to answer for how long they'd be living there. In the meantime, the kids needed a school, as well as a lot of attention during the day. Despite a woeful history in previous districts the girls couldn't be classified as "special ed," because they hadn't been enrolled long enough to show "demonstrated academic failure." Each was hard at work on it, however.

Claire's hair seemed to spread itself out in three very dramatic directions. Still, she hated it and was planning to have something big done to it on Monday. "But only," she said, "if I still have the nerve by then. You know that girl, Judy, with the sweater? You know how her hair is kind of folded around shoulder-length, but under, so that it covers the ears? That's how I'm getting it, only I'm going to keep bangs on top."

Alan squirmed. He didn't know what she was talking about. He wasn't sure he cared. He knew that the real issue was Claire hating her ears. She'd told him that two times already. Last week she'd told him that she'd seriously considered using Crazy Glue to adhere the larger parts of them to her head "so they don't frickin' stick out so much." She had had it. She was sick of people looking at her ears and judging her by them. The only problem was that she had some sort of modern buzz-cut hairstyle that shaved the sides of her head so that her ears stuck out prominently. And she wore enormous hoop earrings most of the time.

"You don't even know what I'm talking about, do you?" Claire said glaring at Alan.

"Yes, I do. A haircut. So your ears don't show as much."

"It's not 'as much'…you don't get it. You all don't get it. I look like *Dumbo*. And I've been telling you people that for six months, or whatever it's been, and NOBODY DOES ANYTHING TO HELP ME."

"You've only been here three times," said Alan calmly.

"The point is that no one listens. I don't even know why I bother anymore. You all say that you're supposed to be here to help people, and then I ask for help and DO I GET IT? NO! 'Go to your room, we'll talk about it tomorrow…'"

"Who says that, Claire?"

"Everybody."

"No…Claire…I've never said that to you."

"That's because you don't live with me. If you lived with me, you'd say it too."

"I've let you down? I've betrayed you?"

"I don't even want to talk about it."

In the pause that followed Alan thought about how very unfulfilling the snack-size salt-free V8 had been twenty minutes ago. He remembered the brownies from the deli with love. What would happen if he ate them more than two or three times a week? What would happen if he gave in to more pleasure?

"Like right now," said Claire. "You're not even listening."

"Yes I am."

"What did I just say, then?"

"About how things would be if we lived together."

"WRONG."

"Then…what?"

"I don't…FORGET IT, all right? Just forget it."

"Claire…"

"No, don't 'Claire' me. I've had it with people who say they're going to help you and when the time comes they don't lift their finger, or if they do it's just because they're getting paid to do it."

"How do you want me to help you with your haircut?"

"It has nothing to do with my haircut."

"What does it have to do with?"

"I told you."

Alan looked at the clock. He was actually hoping that some sort of buzzer would go off or something, indicating that whatever this confused event was had to stop for today. Hopefully by the time it was resumed it would be completely transformed into something which more closely resembled a meaningful exchange. The minute-hand on the clock seemed frozen.

"I'm sorry," said Alan. "Maybe you told me something I missed."

"Damn right. You all missed it. I should be dead or something and not MAKE ANY MORE DEMANDS ON ANYONE and then no one would have to 'miss' anything."

"Don't you think I would miss you? Claire?"

Claire stared down intently at her knee. Her foot started bouncing up and down the way it usually did. She tightened her jaw, then released it. She looked up at the clock, then down at her feet. Silence.

"Don't you think I would miss you?"

"Honestly? NO."

"Really?"

"No one would miss me. Especially those squids at the Group Home. Frickin' Debbie with her always telling me what I should do...when to do homework, when to take a shower, when to turn out the light...like it's some kind of prison camp or something...I'm TIRED OF IT, and I'll tell her that. I'm tired of it. Her attitude is like she thinks she's GOD or something. I swear, I'm gonna go off soon—I think it might be tonight—if she doesn't learn to keep her frickin' opinions to herself. Walking around like she's got the 'authority,' all because she kisses Larry's ass. Well, I DON'T KISS ANYONE'S ASS and if I have to suffer just because of that little fact, well, too bad then, that's the way it has to be. If they want to get rid of me, if they want just LIARS and WHORES in the house, then they're parking up the wrong tree with this person, because I'll get a gun and kill them before I let them ruin my life. Because it's my life and I'm sixteen and I'm tired of being treated like a baby."

"Who is it who is always telling you to go to your room?"

She took a gulp of air, whirled her head around to respond in a flash, then stopped. "No...forget it. I don't want to talk about it. It's not worth it."

"Claire...you're already talking about it."

"No…It's just that frickin' Beverly can do ANYTHING SHE WANTS in that house and have NOTHING HAPPEN TO HER and if I even fart it's two weeks of grounding. No phone, no visitors, no shopping. Even if I just ask a question. But Beverly can admit she did something wrong—like putting ammonia in Diane's plant and killing it—and they say, 'We appreciate your honesty.' And if I look at them the wrong way they say, 'Two weeks.' That ain't right."

Claire's knee bounced up and down with fervor as she continued.

"And…wait: who did I hate? Oh yeah, Beverly, she's been saying she's taking me out shopping with the quarterly money—two hundred dollars which, c'mon now, doesn't buy you more than a blouse, a belt, and MAYBE sneakers—and now suddenly it's like 'When can I find the time to take all the girls out to Wal-Mart in the van?' 'ALL THE GIRLS' and 'IN THE VAN' when it was supposed to be me and her in her Firebird and NOT to Wal-Mart. How am I supposed to trust anybody after stuff like this?"

"I heard someone was going around spitting on the doorknobs last week," Alan offered.

"That's right, and IT WASN'T ME! I'm not gonna say who it was, but it definitely wasn't me. But WHO DO THEY COME LOOKING FOR, AND ASKING QUESTIONS OF?"

"You?"

"Right. Where Beverly ate the leftover meatloaf at two in the morning—which was supposed to be the next night's dinner—and left the refrigerator door open so everything was all wilted by the morning. I tell you, if *I* did that, staff would be frickin' dancing on my liver."

———•———

Fifty-nine miles to the southeast, ten hours later, Angel Rivera stood on the corner of 103rd Street and First Avenue wrapping the knife in his Tommy t-shirt, then throwing it into a sewer pipe. The short, Dominican teenager walked briskly, having just stabbed a six-foot-two black man named Five-Dollar Bill in the heart with a 007 knife. The crack vial, falling to the ground, would have only Bill's fingerprints on it, not his. Angel threw his cap into a dumpster behind the bodega. 1:20 a.m. No heat. He kept walking. He put on the Bulls jersey as he walked. It had been where he left it— beneath two stones at 102nd. He continued south, circling back to 103rd, but this time on Broadway, instead of First. No cap, different shirt, no weapons, no one who would say a word, no problem.

Five-Dollar Bill had been scared of him for years. Bill's sister, Estelle, was a loyal crackhead, if there were such a thing, but had told Angel so much. Tiger, the seventeen-year-old Dominican junkie whore, working the corner at 1:00 a.m. on a Monday—the only witness—turned white when Angel whispered to her, "I know where you live."

Putty in his hands.

Yeah, he had stabbed the lying hoodrat. Supplying dummy-crack for Angel to sell put Angel's own life on the line. It was more or less an automatic death sentence. It depended on how generous, or stupid, the dealer felt at any given moment. Or who he was trying to impress.

Angel was happy to let the 007 blade decide for him. He'd stab the guy in the chest; if he died, he died. If he lived he knew Angel would kill him if he snitched. Now or later.

On the street, in the joint upstate somewhere, sooner or later. If he lived he had to accept the stab as the cost of business.

Ninety-eighth Street. There were still no cops in sight. Not on foot, not in cars. *What is this city coming to?* Angel wondered to himself.

He stopped at the pay phone and put in some coins. "Pray to God" was scratched into the bottom of the phone.

"...'lo? Rasheeda there?" Angel mumbled.

"No. You know what time you calling?" (*Shit*, he thought. *It's her mother.*)

"Where she at?"

"Is this her little Spanish boyfriend calling? And you wondering where she at after midnight on a weekday night, huh?"

"Yo, put her on."

"I told you, hon, she ain't home."

"Where she at?"

"Hmmmmm....I don't know, Mr. Latin Lover. Ricky Martin...Mr. Ricky Ricardo. Mr. Fucking Mambo King hisself."

"You don't know where she's at?"

"That's what I said now, isn't it? And maybe if I did know, I wouldn't tell you. How long has it been, anyway, since you seen her? Three weeks? I know it ain't been since her 'friend' was due, cause then you would have known why she leavin' you to go get some sense in her head 'stead of jes thinking like one of them babies-havin'-babies-projeck-bunnies over in your neck of the woods...y'know, gettin' all ready for a life of screamin' at the kids and servin' you them refried beans and burritos and tacos and shit and cleanin' for you while you out scoring some new teenage pussy and maybe once a year if they get lucky you take them all to Six

Flags/Great Adventure, y'knowwhatI'msayin? Cause my girl is jes not that way. She takin' some time off... She upstate."

"You put Rasheeda upstate?" Angel asked, not quite believing his ears.

"She put herself upstate."

"That place you threatened her with?"

"Mmmm-huhh...I tole her—I don't make threats. Jes promises."

"They take her pregnant?"

"They don't know."

"She gonna have it?"

"Well...gee...you soundin' all CONCERNED all of a sudden. I don't know. I forgot to ask her. She probably run away by then anyway. I give her two weeks there."

"You her real mother, anyway? You a sorry-ass super-skanky excuse for one, y'know that? You more like a natural-born BITCH, if you ask me."

"Ain't nobody asking you, baby. Oh, and one thing you should know: They have a picture of you up there already waitin' and an Order of Protection keepin' you away from her place. Jes in case she still there."

He slammed the phone down three times in a row. He tried to rip the cord off. It was metal and it only stretched.

He saw a female cop walking into Broadway Donuts. A fat, dark-skinned one with glasses. Look like she could run a mile in forty-five minutes, if it were downhill.

He considered grabbing her gun and shooting her.

He walked on.

He would find Rasheeda. Upstate, downstate, in another state. In whatever white-bread town they tried to hide her in. Angel might leave the bitches, but bitches don't leave Angel.

RASHEEDA DREAM

Alison was sitting next to the new guy, definitely from New York City and definitely some kind of Hispanic. A lot of Hispanic kids had come up the last few years and most of them lived in Stephens Manor, the low-priced condos near the power lines and the Jiffy Mart.

She would have rather been sitting near Elijah. He wasn't even in this class.

She didn't have anything against Hispanics, except when they talked Spanish. There was a group of them at lunch who sat at a table all together and acted like they thought they were better than the whole school. They were loud and played like they thought a camera from a reality show was filming their every dramatic move. A couple of times there had been fights in the hallways and girls like her had ended up being called "funky-farmer bitches" by people like him.

Not that Alison believed in making generalizations about people.

The kid next to her—Angel Rivera—was real quiet. He looked sneaky, but she doubted that you'd ever find anything on him, because he also looked smart. She had heard the stories about the Barrio Lords and other gangs that kids said had three hundred members in towns near her, ready to take out any enemies at a moment's notice. All it took, she knew, was a phone call. You didn't have to have a reason and you didn't have to give an explanation. You could say, "I want Alison Gepner jumped" and she'd be jumped by three o'clock that afternoon. She heard that in the city they had calling cards and they'd beat you up, cut you, spit on you, and throw a calling card on you. Then they'd leave and no one would ever complain. You didn't go to your principal about the Barrio Lords.

One girl she had heard of, from the Group Home, was said to be able to stash a single-edged razor blade in the inside of her mouth (in her upper cheek) and not get cut or reveal it while eating a bagel.

Up in the front of the classroom, Mr. Peckwirth had a map pulled down and was saying something that sounded like he had been repeating it two or three times already.

"Mr. RIVERA…would you be kind enough to share with us your thoughts as to three possible vital interests which led the United States to participate in the original Gulf War?"

The Hispanic kid next to her just stared at him.

"Two vital interests will do, Mr. Rivera."

There was a long silence.

"Do you know which war I am talking about? Do you know what century I am asking about? Do you know what part of the world is illustrated on the map behind me?"

Peckwirth was old but a good teacher, Alison thought, because you could tell he really cared about what he was talking about. She didn't know, at the moment, what he was talking about, and she didn't particularly care today, but it was nice to see a teacher who really cared. There were a couple of teachers like this in the building. Alison felt sorry for them. It wasn't right how kids made fun of them and, in one case, let the air out of his tires and "keyed" his car on the Friday before Christmas vacation. It wasn't the teachers' fault that a lot of kids were stupid.

On the other hand, teachers could get really annoying. They didn't understand things like really having to talk to a girlfriend about what happened yesterday, or what might happen if Richie gets that note that Carol said she was going to write about Alison thinking he was "hot in a weird way" and making it sound like she wanted to do everything with him. First of all, it wasn't accurate (mainly). Second of all, she had no right, because that was a private conversation and if Alison wanted Richie to know she would have told him herself because she wasn't one of these little girls who played games with in-between-friends carrying messages. Third of all, everybody would say she was a slut. You could get called a slut for absolutely no reason at all, even for thinking about doing something. Guys, on the other hand, could sleep with everybody, everybody's sister, and everybody's pet dogs and somehow still be okay. Guys would throw up their hands and say things like, "I wasn't thinking, all right?" and you were supposed to not only forgive them, but somehow feel bad yourself. She wondered if there was a school that guys went to, like in summer, or on early Sunday mornings, that teaches them how to use their eyes to look all hurt and confused and sad to go along with saying, "I wasn't thinking, all right?" so that by the time they were done talking you just wanted to throw your arms around them, buy them jewelry from the mall, and lend them your CDs.

Alison had really gotten into appreciating guys' bodies (though their wieners were likely to be overrated, she imagined), starting with those old Obsession ads, when they would show like the chest going down to the top of the underwear band and it would make you want to run your hands all over them and smooth in some creamy Obsession After-Bath Lotion on, slowly...

"Ms. GEPNER! Three reasons for U.S. involvement in the first Gulf War!?" Peckwirth's voice boomed from out of nowhere.

Whoa. *Relax*, she thought. "What war?" she asked. "Ummmmmmm…could you repeat the question?"

"No, I'm not going to repeat the question."

Suddenly there was a deep silence in the room. She prayed, prayed, prayed for a fire-drill or for the bell to ring. *Please, please, please, I'll do anything. I'll take the garbage out, I'll do the dishes, PLEASE RING, RIGHT NOW.* She looked up at the clock. The bell didn't ring. The class still had twenty-six minutes to go. She hated saying, "I don't know," because that's what all the dumb kids automatically said to any question.

"Well…the United States is a world leader…," Alison began haltingly.

"Yes. Is that all?"

"And…world leaders have to stick up for themselves."

"Alright," said Peckwirth, "…so by your line of reasoning the United States should send troops to India, Ceylon, Ireland, El Salvador, Columbia, Indonesia…"

"I thought we had troops in all those places already," mumbled Randy, a burnt-out Deadhead in a dancing teddies t-shirt.

"If you wish to be recognized, please raise your hand," said Mr. Peckwirth. "Ms. Gepner, by what criteria is the U.S. a world leader?"

Oh, no, this wasn't fair. She should have just come up with three bogus answers to the other question.

Suddenly the Hispanic kid spoke up. "She told you, man. She told you already."

"What did she tell us, Mr. Rivera?"

"Respect," said Angel. "When you are a leader, not everything you do has to be right. It just has to be respected. That was the whole reason for the War in Iraq, the one that just happened, right?"

There was a silence before Peckwirth moved forward, leaning on the desk in front of him, speaking to Angel directly.

"So it doesn't matter, Mr. Rivera, what you do or who gets hurt as long as other people think you've done something powerful?"

"Those are your words."

"How would you determine if something is right, then?"

"You know. In your heart," said Angel.

Peckwirth finally had the eyes of everyone in the class on him. "It would be nice to have you attend class on a more regular basis, Mr. Rivera. Is that a possibility?"

Angel didn't answer, staring straight ahead, almost through him. He was thinking about Rasheeda. And the baby son she would give him.

Angel, Jr. No doubt.

———•·•———

The three-quarter acre front lawn of Hadleyville Falls' only School Psychologist rolled gently from the porch to the asphalt lip of the shady street. There was no denying the lushness of its pine-green wave. The soothing curve of healthy, loyal green blades, reaching skyward in two-and-a-quarter-inch unison, stood in significant contrast to the lawns of the small, yellow one-bedroom Cape on the left (which had never taken down its "Bomb the Bastards" sign in front) and the mock-Colonial-of-the-family-that-fights off to the right. The authentically Colonial two-storied structure (with attached two-car garage) seemed to rise proudly from the soothing ocean-mat before it. Thirty-two Plum Tree Lane simply had a lusher, deeper, and more pleasing lawn to it than any of its neighbors.

41

Dolores Solomon loved coming home to the clackety-clack of the automatic sprinklers (set into motion at the peak of the unusually hot late-April day). *CLACK (swish, swish)…CLACKETY-CLACK…(swish, swish, swish)…CLACK (swish, swish)…CLACKETY-CLACK (swish, swish, swish)…*

There was only one vaguely off-color section of the lawn that gave Dolores pause—three square feet near the curb, at most—and she was reasonably confident that the aberration would be imperceptible to most.

Two Italians from Porterville had resurfaced the driveway last spring and—while Dolores had been disgusted by their boorish language and primitive manner of relating—she noted with satisfaction that they had done an excellent job. The high-quality performance rubber of her aquamarine Volvo Cross-Country station wagon always made a satisfying rolling sound on the asphalt as it drew to a halt. On a sunny day such as this, Dolores asked herself, could there be anything more gratifying than arriving home, disembarking, briskly shutting the car door, and hearing the solid richness of the premium lock engage? She savored the moment, as the squirrels scampered.

Dolores took athletic strides toward her handcrafted-in-Maine mailbox. *This is a lovely setting*, she thought to herself, pausing at the mailbox to gather up the local newspaper at her feet. *Most important*, she thought, *this is not a sweaty, commuting "suburb," with its all-too-predictable housing and lifestyles. This is "exurbia."*

Dolores enjoyed a deep breath before starting up the steps to her porch. "The Wonder Years" was in reruns on Nickelodeon tonight, she reminded herself. It was amazing how a television show could capture with such accuracy the give-and-take of early-adolescent peer relations yet miss the pivotal role diet (and particularly sugar) played in the development of all sorts of emotional disturbances.

———

"I wanna know one thing," demanded Claire.

"Okay," said Alan.

"One frickin' little thing, okay?"

"All right."

"Okay?"

"Fair enough."

"And that is...how come I've got to come—every week— to talk to a 'therapist' (no offense)—and all those other size-one-psycho-bitches and losers in the school get to go home, have ginger ale, eat brownies, and spend time IM'ing everyone without anyone looking over their shoulders at all? They can just be losers. And I'm supposed to come here and think about everything...or...whatever. I don't even know what we're supposed to do here."

Claire and Alan looked at each other.

"What *are* we doing here?" demanded Claire. "And don't you dare ask me 'What do *you* want to do here?'"

"They don't let you use the computer unsupervised?"

"No! Like we're two years old and in frickin' Pampers."

"Claire, most two-year-olds aren't on the computer."

Claire's eyes got steely. "Why do you always do that to me?"

"Do what?"

"Mock me; exaggerate what I'm saying, just so it makes me sound stupid."

"I don't..."

"Yeah, well you did. And you do it a lot. You might want to look into that. Ever consider that you might have a problem with women?"

Alan shut up and Claire resumed.

"I'm not sayin' I'm perfect. I know I'm not perfect. That's why I'm here. But...y'know...nothin' for nothin', but...why are you here?"

Alan went blank. He felt a lump in his throat. A stupid, emotional lump that wasn't supposed to be there and which he couldn't identify.

"I mean, do you actually enjoy listening to people's problems all day? Do therapists get off on it? I don't mean 'get off' like sexually....that's like, ucchhh, I don't know, I'm not even going to go there...but...why do you do this? I know when people talk to me it generally bugs the crap out of me. It doesn't bug you?"

"I'm usually pretty satisfied with my days," said Alan.

"Like what does that mean?"

"It means most people don't really annoy me."

"Yeah? Are you sure?" asked Claire.

"I'm sure."

"Then maybe that's why I'm seeing you. Because they annoy me worse than getting chewed to death by thousands of little fleas. And I tell them that. I'm sorry, but if anyone disrespects me, they're going to hear it and if they do it again—oh well—I'll put my foot up their ass and that'll make them think twice, I have found."

"There are other ways."

"Bullcrap there are. Is that what we did with the Iraquians? 'Find other ways'? Hell, no, we kicked their ass."

"And whose ass do you want to kick right now?"

"Right now? No one. I'm just talking. Well...actually there's this one girl. 'Alison.' Total goody-goody. Always in school, stays after for extra activities, probably doesn't have to study to get nineties, doesn't have to diet—and she flaunts it, completely, I'm sorry, like, 'Hello, I'm not even on a diet...' I had a dream last night, she was pigging out on Ring Dings and cheesecake and turned into a size eighteen. She was walking around in school in tight jeans like a little short elephant and her ass had the words 'Phat Ass' written across it in script, so it bumped up and down when she walked and people were laughing. Then I woke up and she's like this effortless size four. So what does that mean?"

"What does what mean?"

"The dream."

"The dream? It seems like outside appearances are still very important to you..."

"Yeah, but do you think it means that I have a chance?" asked Claire.

"A chance for what?"

"To get her boyfriend interested once he comes to see her as ugly?"

"I have no idea. I think the dream is about you having to learn to love yourself more first."

"Therapy with you is really...limited, you know that?" Claire said directly.

"You think it would be better with someone else?"

"Quite possibly, yuh. But to tell you the truth, I don't feel like starting all over from the beginning with someone else."

"Why not?"

"Because I'm not really into this too much in the first place. No offense, but talking about this stuff with an adult sometimes seems really stupid. Like you're a...nice dentist or something. Would you talk to your dentist about your personal problems?"

"No," said Alan.

"Even though he's nice, right?"

"Right."

"Exactly. That's exactly my point."

They looked at each other.

"But I'd trust him to fix a broken tooth," said Alan.

"I have a question for you, and you have to answer it honestly."

"Okay."

"Do you promise to?" asked Claire.

"I'll do my best."

"You see, that's the kind of response that really pisses me off."

"All right, I'll answer honestly."

"What is it with therapists that you have to work to get them to be honest?"

"I don't know. It's the way we're taught to be. Not dishonest, but just not saying everything like in a conversation."

"So is this a conversation right now, or something 'else'?"

"I don't know," said Alan. A sizable silence followed. "How's school?" he asked.

"School? Who wants to talk about school. School is ridiculous. You know what I have to do for English?" Claire asked.

"No, what?"

"A sonnet. Shakespeare, from the year fifteen-something. Do you know what that's like to do? To stand up there in front of your class and recite it? A room full of ninth graders?"

"What is it like?" asked Alan.

"I feel like a fat lesbian or something, saying that stuff."

"Lesbian?"

"Yeah. 'My mistress' eyes are nothing like the sun; Coral is far more red than her lips' red; If snow be white, why then her breasts are dun'…Who speaks like that?"

"And you're thinking a fat lesbian speaks like that?"

"About a chick's breasts? What do you think?" asked Claire.

"I think Shakespeare was a man."

"Yeah, well I'm not, and Shakespeare doesn't have to stand up there and recite it in front of the whole ninth-grade world. It puts a damper on things."

"Did the teacher assign it randomly?" Alan asked.

"No, I chose it." Claire said, holding her gaze with Alan steadily. "Because I liked it. But more to myself, not out loud." There was another silence. Claire broke it. "All right, this is my question for you, from before. Can you honestly say you would be talking to me and trying to help me if you weren't getting paid a lot of money to do it?"

The question hung in the air and echoed through Alan's brain. He didn't speak.

"Yeah," said Claire triumphantly. "See, now that's honest!"

"I didn't answer yet. I need more time."

"Well, take the time and you think about it. We can talk about it next session."

"You sound like a therapist."

"Maybe I am. I could do this for a living, huh?"

———

Rasheeda sat up in her institutional bed in the middle of the night, half-whispering, her breath coming fast. Letitia— her hair pinned-up funny—listened with huge eyes. She was upstate—she knew it, in some facility, just like her mother had threatened.

"Sham-Guard and Malik came up to me in my dream and Malik hit me in the face for no reason at all. And I say, 'Dag…why you doggin' me awla time?' and he point in the direction of Witch Mountain and say, 'There go your mother.'

"So I go, 'Your mother…' and he say, 'I ain't kiddin', your mother was right here lookin' for you and Sham-Guard say you ho-hoppin' the boys' cottages and you up on Witch Mountain with Charles.' And I tole Malik that that's a lie, cause Sham-Guard knows I been iggin' Charles for eight days now because he stole Maurice's crack outta his room and tole Ms. Redmond me and Becky did it.

"And Raymond tole Kayesha that Charles still likeded me anyway, but I don't pay him no mind. I don't mess with these niggas up here, and my mama knows this…particularly no scraggy, nappy-headed ugly ones like Charles. That boy strike out so much, he called 'Projeck Hope' when he be workin' on gettin' a girl. Even the skeezers rejeck him.

"So—still in the dream—I go up to Witch Mountain, only I'm floatin' like I got wings, and the sky is like bright red, and I get there and instead of it bein' itself, there's like a lake there, or somethin'. And suddenly it's like eight-forty-five at night and there are two rowboats out there with lanterns. And Charles comes up and say, 'There go your mother. She's out there,' and he points to the middle of the lake.

"So I step on the stones barefoot and go to swim out there, but the water starts havin' tin-can tops and metal in it. And I start swimmin' anyway and Charles go, 'You better hurry up,' and I swim faster, at the boats, but all of a sudden there's big hunks of broken glass in the water—like big mirror-size—floating on the water, all sharp, coming at me like razors and Charles go, 'You better hurry up, bitch!' and I can't swim forward because of the glass and suddenly he say, 'Forget it, she dead.'

"…And I saw they draggin' her into the boat.

"And I say, 'Momma!'

"And then—the next thing I know–suddenly Ms. Redmond is in the room screamin' at me—okay, this is real, right?—'You no-good black-assed whore! Didn't you momma teach you nothin'?' And I say, 'Ms. Redmond, what do you mean?' And she say, 'I mean this!' and she points to Sham-Guard and Malik who are really in my room, and Becky is laughin', cause she had hid 'em under her bed, but Redmond thinks I did it. And they run out, holdin' their dicks and puttin' on their pants and Becky says, 'We didn't know, Reddie…honest!'

"And Reddie said somethin' about my momma again, so I say, 'Shut the fuck up before I get my step-brother up here to tear you up and fuckin' kill you', and she slap me. Twice.

"And I didn't do nothin' to her.

"I ain't stayin' in a place like this. This place is sposed to help you."

Four hours later, when Letitia woke up again—the morning light playing through the red, green, and blue jars of hair gel and shampoo—Rasheeda was gone.

Father Mark O'Connell sat in his usual booth in the Galesville Pizza Hut. It was 5:20 on a Tuesday night. He wore his collar. He ordered the personal size Meat Lover's pizza.

Father Mark wasn't known to any of these people. And that was fine with him. He wouldn't have to minister to them. It was good to take some time off.

Father Mark took in the people. A crowd of four enormously fat guys came in, ordered something, and bellied-up to the salad bar. Two were wearing NASCAR t-shirts. One wore a stark black-and-white t-shirt that read, "Don't Know, Don't Care."

How could he begin to explain to these individuals—even if he wanted to—that they had already been saved? That their loneliness didn't have to be met by food binges alone?

They were gone...gone.

But not their sons. Their sons were still strong. Their sons could still be the muscular servant army for Christ. Sustained battles required men with fires in their bellies. Backs which didn't break. That is why he spent so much time working with the junior and senior youth groups. That is why he pushed so hard for the youth retreats.

His pie arrived.

When he had been back in the seminary, a priest-professor once asked him if anyone else had ever told him he had eyes like a shark's. No one had.

There were a lot of weirdos in the seminary.

PROMISES

Alison couldn't figure out a way to approach Elijah. She had dreamt three times about his cocoa-colored skin and his wire-rim glasses. It felt exceptionally stupid. And then he had transferred into her upper-level Math class. He was a classmate. Class Mate.

Alison considered asking Robin to somehow relay a message that Alison found him intriguing. She loved that word: "intriguing." It was so him. She was in the middle of staring at him in the only class which they shared when he looked up directly at her. She forced herself, with every molecule, not to turn away. She forced herself to smile and commanded her face to not turn red.

He smiled the most natural smile she had ever seen. Ever in her life.

She carried it with her for the next two days, replaying it in slow motion, fast forward and—best of all—pause. She almost didn't want him to talk to her.

Unless it could be better than that. She dreamed it could.

She was thinking about him all the time. She hated that.

When Robin Wedner called and asked Alison to come hang out at her younger sister's soccer game, where Robin could get paid for sort-of-babysitting her moderately annoying sibling, Roberta, while the older girls sorted through life and romance, Alison jumped at the chance. Robin and Alison could talk for hours but they hadn't factored in the reality of the soccer fields. The soccer fields were...the soccer fields. Lots of blonde-haired "Wendys" and "Blaines" with their over-involved parents screaming from the sidelines (if you were lucky enough to actually get them to stand on the sidelines and not on the field). It was by no means a given that the most insane ones were men. But on this day, the most insane one was.

He was standing five feet to the left of the line that was meant to separate players from lunatic parents, and he was pointing to something that obviously had him enraged. He alternated shoving his finger at some imagined spot on the field, where something had either happened or not happened just a few moments ago. He directed his thoughts to his daughter's coach.

"An offsides, Coach, and it's not called? Like no one notices? Going to do something about that? What are we teaching them? You want me to say something to the Ref? You want the girls to close their eyes to it? You're setting them up for this in the future, you knowwhatI'msayin' Coach…They gonna call it??"

Never mind that his daughter was six. And that the oldest player on the field had turned seven a week ago. There were about three girls on the field, out of sixteen, who didn't have their parents screaming ferociously from the sidelines.

"Downfield, Nicole! Kick the ball!! Give it some foot! C'mon, Nicole—DON'T WAIT! You wait you're gonna lose it!…All right…Stay with it, stay with it, TAKE IT AWAY FROM HER. C'MON—WHAT ARE YOU DOING?? THAT'S YOUR BALL. IT'S YOUR BALL, NICOLE, FIGHT FOR IT! C'MON!! Whose side are you on, Nicole? Attack the ball! ATTACK THE BALL! All right, all right, wait for them to come to you, there you go, wait, wait now TAKE IT, Nicole. Get it out of there…cross field! No! Take it left, not right…not in front! NEVER IN FRONT, NICOLE. All right, all right, o.k.….all right. Nicole, where are you! Get your foot on it...get in there...don't wait! Take it away from her. Get in there! Kick it! KICK IT!!"

Nicole's opponent kicked it to a really fast short girl who kicked it in for the other team's goal. Nicole's team was now behind, 1-0.

"Nice work, Nicole. You gave it to them. You gave the other team their goal. You should get an 'assist' on that from them, right, Coach?"

Nicole walked off the field without asking anyone. She sat down, grabbed her water bottle and refused to look at him.

"If you talk to me like that I'm not gonna play," said the six-year-old, glaring at her father.

"Jesus Christ," the big man muttered, walking away, his hands in his pockets, face flushing. "Are you here to play soccer or you wanna go home and play with your dollies?"

He approached the coach now, without invitation, looking at his feet.

"I'm going to put her on defense for a few minutes, let her calm down," said the coach.

"Yeah, well, just don't let her con you with the 'I feel TIRED' stuff, y'know. You have to push her a little, y'know? Otherwise, she'll be there to the end of the game. She's lazy. She'd be perfectly happy to stand there and watch the whole thing go down around her, y'knowwhatI'msayin'?"

"Yeah, well, it's pretty hot out there today. About seventy-something on the field, probably."

"Let me tell you a thing about girls, Coach. They're...like...girls. And if you leave 'em like that, you let 'em do their thing, that's the way they stay. But if you train 'em and give 'em a little push, they can be ATHLETES. Lookit golf, lookit hockey...Take hockey. It's played by athletes. They didn't wake up knowing how to play the game. They needed to be taught it. The same way as these girls."

53

"Uhh-huh."

Nicole glared at her father, then looked away when his eyes met hers.

"I'm putting you in on defense," said the coach.

"Okay." Nicole got up and ran into position.

"Just do a little better than you did on offense, huh, Nicole? For everyone's sake?"

Alison was waiting for Robin to exhaust the topic of Wayne, some new guy in her life. Robin went on about Wayne's new haircut, Wayne beeping her, the five notes Wayne wrote her in one day, Wayne's intention to meet her mother someday, the girl who thought Wayne was cute but who he didn't write back even though he could have, what Wayne wore last Saturday, the car Wayne was going to buy next summer, and the concerts Wayne was considering taking Robin to.

After a long time, Robin asked Alison, "So…what about you? Anything out of the ordinary?"

Alison thought of Elijah's smile, the texture of his cocoa skin, the way he seemed so tall. Cargo pants fit him just the way they did guys in The Gap and Target ads. She guessed that he knew how to ride a horse. And that he would be really good to the horse afterward, giving it an apple and patting it down and saying things like, "There, girl…" Alison would run away with him and live on an island where they both would sleep until noon and stay up until the darkest part of the night past and the embers of their campfire crackled into silence, leaving them too thrilled for sleep, touching.

"No," Alison told Robin. "The usual."

———·•·———

54

Claire laughed the first time she had seen the article in *Cosmopolitan* (under the heading "Juicy Reads!") called "Sexual Awakenings: Ten Twenty-Somethings Remember Their First Times." Her own "awakening" had been her mother's boyfriend coming at her with his hard-on at eye level as she slept in the daybed of the living room one grimy November morning. She was ten years old.

She had seen her friend Carly's baby brother's ding-a-ling ever since he'd been born and thought it was cute. She'd also seen Tina's family dog licking his balls with his ferociously red carrot-dick sticking straight up, a stupid look on his face. It was pretty much the most disgusting thing she had ever seen. But she hadn't been prepared for that morning with Ronald.

She hadn't always hated him. When he first met her mom, when her mother was waitressing, and he had day-shift at the cheese factory, he would bring over things for all of them, like Dunkin' Donuts, Chinese food, movies, and ice cream a few times. But that was when they were dating. It stopped after a few months. He moved in "just for a while," he said, because of the layoffs, and he was waiting to hear about a better job. That was when he started making comments about her friends and telling her mother that Claire was running wild and taking advantage of her "left and right." He slept until almost noon, but got up long enough to yell at Claire for taking too much time in the bathroom in the morning before her bus. He drank beer a lot (Genessee when they had money, no-name brands the other times) but told her mother that Claire's school was "full of potheads and gays." And he talked about respecting parents before, after, and during smacking her.

Initially Claire had protested and turned to her mother for support. But each time her mother said, "He's got a point.

You're not gonna amount to nothin' with a mouth like that. You'd better just as soon learn that here before you turn around and get in trouble." So Claire stopped talking to him entirely. This seemed to make him angrier. There was some satisfaction in that.

She'd never seem him hit her mother, but she always heard him call her "a tramp," "a whore," a "shitty cook," a "pussy," and "shit-for-brains." The one time her mom had gone off on him and started hitting him was when he called her a bad mom.

He'd drink harder and for longer times after each layoff, and it was after the second layoff of the year that he'd suddenly announced that—since his regular smackings didn't seem to work on Claire, that she still had "toilet mouth"— maybe spankings would work. The first time he did it her mother got so upset she had to go in the other room and wash the dishes. It didn't strike Claire that he was a perv, at first, because it was through her clothing and the hitting was kind of hard and she had taken off the day before to hang around Ninja Dave and Fat Mike without telling her mother where she was going, so she thought she had kind of deserved it. After that, though, spankings seemed to be for less and less reason, lasted longer, and were softer. She knew when she felt his hands linger on her ass and felt a bulge pressing into the front of her belly that this was not just about her doing wrong.

The November morning happened after the third slow spanking.

She learned how to go to places with her mind during terrible times. She imagined this island that she had seen from a video in school on the South Seas; only this time it was populated just by her and her friends. Fat Mike was there, standing ready to protect her. Ninja Dave was there playing music and cracking jokes. The social worker from school was there on the telephone—long-distance—getting Ronald arrested or arranging for him to get hurt. Ms. Deggio, her art teacher, was there doing an incredible mural-project with her, and the two of them were in grass skirts. The sun was warm, there was coconut smell everywhere, and you could sleep out on the sand at night.

There was usually a wet spot on the front of Ronald's military-fatigue pants when he finished the spankings. Sometimes, though, there was no bulge or wet spot afterward, just more anger than he started with. Those times her ass genuinely hurt, because he really started hitting hard. Taking a bath after helped, but then her mother would yell at her for spending so much time in the bathroom. There was a small hook-and-eye lock on the bathroom door that kept the door closed when you wanted it to and she would drift away in the tub staring at it and feeling okay after a couple of sobs. More and more it took lots of sobs. And it was harder to get the okay feeling, but she never gave up until she could find it.

Years later, there were times when her body felt like nothing. She would even pinch it to see if she were still alive. Danielle had told her about putting clothespins on your nipples and she tried it once, even though it made her feel like a major wacko to hide them in her bag and bring them into the bathroom. They didn't feel as bad as she thought they might, but she didn't repeat the experience.

Six years had gone by since the first spanking. She was different. Her body, she was told, was strong. (This from the gym teacher, not just from Richie or Carlos, whom she had both slammed to the ground and pinned successfully in the past.) She still cried a lot, but not around friends.

She still treasured her baths. Her hair would float freely in the water, spreading out like a fast-growing flower. She could breathe. Sometimes she would trace her fingers down the front of her body and cup her breasts in her hands. She would feel all of herself, the water kissing her. She would look at the door and the hook-and-eye and imagine Ronald smashing through it, only to be met by a .44 caliber bullet in the forehead. She could see him flying backward and parts of his head flying in different directions. She could hear her mother in the kitchen, washing dishes.

———

Ninja Dave raised his finger and moved it slowly. Wisps of coconut incense filled the room, a smoky curtain of sweetness mixed with the residue of the herb they had just shared.

He asked Richie, "One question: If girls don't want to get laid, then why do they dress like that?"

Ninja Dave had a reputation for asking the one question that cut through all the crap, or making the one statement that seemed to summarize wisdom in existence. They sometimes referred to this as "a Dave." Richie had to admit this was a good one.

"Maybe they just want to hang out?" guessed Richie.

"Then why the thigh-high leggings, those low-rise jeans, pants so tight you can see everything jiggle, and halters cut so short you can see their stomach muscles and tits pushed out toward your face?" asked Ninja Dave.

Richie meditated on this.

"One more question. Why do they make sure we are looking at them when they bend over slowly to get something or cross their legs or lift up their skirts to adjust their tights?"

Silence streamed through the room. Ninja Dave imagined he could hear the sound of Richie thinking.

"I don't know," Richie finally said.

"The answer is simple. The answer is within us. The answer is: Biology."

Richie had gotten a 42 in the second marking period in Biology. He still owed fourteen labs and was in danger of failing.

"I don't mean Biology like the textbooks. I'm talking about the biological imperative to fuck and continue the human race by creating other beings who need to fuck," lectured Ninja Dave.

He only talked this way around Richie. Richie was his disciple. "You see, the material we study in Health class is sanitized…sterilized. It's like the difference between real cheese that they make in big wooden vats in Switzerland versus Kraft Frigging American wrapped in plastic. That Health teacher is as lost as an anorexic girl in a kitchen. They tell you you're not supposed to want to fuck for five or six years yet, or to know that you want to but just to forget about it…play high school sports, write a poem, or some bulbous bullshit. Meanwhile everyone I know has been doing it since they're fourteen, fifteen, the latest… The truth is: knowing that you want to fuck is only good if you follow it up by fucking. Otherwise you are leading an unlead life. Which is what THEY do, once they turn nineteen. Leading an unlead life. You start doing that and you lose the ABILITY to fuck, the DESIRE to fuck. You don't even remember HOW to fuck. You become a bitch-boy. And you end up with, what? That's right: Viagra. Cialis. Levitra. Government-sponsored dick-relief at ten dollars a shot. I don't know about you, but to me that is the OPPOSITE of real fucking. Natural fucking makes us strong. They can't tax it. It is why they fear our generation. It makes us able to take over. This is their best-kept secret, what they fear us finding out: fucking does not deplete your energy. It GIVES you energy, and power, and mastery. You put your body in sync with the rhythms of the universe when you fuck. Jim Morrison said, 'The essential motion of the universe is a fucking-motion.' The entire development of the Church in western society was for the purpose of denying this reality in an attempt to control us. And that is why one of the most profound responses we can have to 'Health class' is to write—on the desks, on the walls, on the blackboard, and on every notebook we see—'Fuck You...Fuck Me.'"

Peter had spotted the woman at the first faculty meeting of the year. He acknowledged, to himself, a quiet, middle-aged lust for her. It was the most dangerous, slow-growing lust he could imagine. It was the kind he knew he would act on.

Of course there had been other temptations over the years, but they had been easily put aside. He and Patty had a sex life, at one point, and it had been good enough to ward off any thoughts of acting on a momentary flash of pleasure that would derail it. Such was not the case anymore.

There was something about her youth, the almost schoolgirlish way her shoulders and back tapered to her small waist, which excited him. She looked like a college freshman. This was a young woman, no doubt, and she had the trimness and tautness which he knew he must explore, feel, and taste. He imagined undoing her blouse, slipping her skirt down, caressing her youthful tummy before reaching upward and touching her breasts.

Peter had met her most briefly for the second interview meeting (perfunctory, in most cases) and didn't remember much. He didn't remember her looking this tempting at that meeting. He did remember that she was single.

She was the art teacher. He knew about the District's "non-fraternization" policy and frankly didn't give a damn anymore. He wouldn't come on to her publicly, or let it interfere with either of their jobs.

But he wouldn't stand in the way of their getting together, either.

THE WAY THESE PEOPLE LIVE

Alan tried to remind himself why he was at this meeting in the first place. It was one of those old-fashioned, classic wastes of time—not to be confused with one of those vaguely-purposeful events which somehow fall short of the mark, leaving you with a "Hello, My Name Is" sticker and a bellyful of institutionally-catered lunch. This was the first staff meeting of the state's outpatient mental health clinic in five and a half months. He still didn't get why he had to attend these things, because he didn't technically work here anymore. Alan had shown up for his regular monthly supervision—there were three interesting cases he had wanted to talk to the psychiatrist about—and had been invited/directed to attend this meeting instead.

His "supervising" psychiatrist, a nice Pakistani man, was supposed to whip some morale into a staff that had been burnt to toast for two years now.

Everyone smiled and took their seats. A new foreign psychiatric resident was present; Alan couldn't determine his nationality clearly. Before the meeting started the new doctor in training chatted with the older resident about housing prices and mortgage rates. They were both well dressed.

The couch looked out of place, given the overhead fluorescent lighting, and the stains on it did not bode well. The room had some kind of smell to it. Old school lunch smell.

Everybody looked down at blank pads of paper as the meeting began. His supervisor, the Clinic Director, spoke.

"Must have Treatment Plan."

A profound pause followed.

"We *need* Plan. Once we have Plan...in the book...the Plan Book" (and he paused for emphasis, looking around) "...all else will follow."

There was a lull. No one else spoke.

"For having the Plan: Plan must be *signed*. That day. If no sign, then no Plan. Awlsough...you responsible for sign, for Plan, in Book, from meeting with Dr. Mongee. He said other issue is Coverage. If you have Coverage, then you are okay. If not Coverage..." (he paused again) "...it is noted. *It will be noted.*"

There was a long pause.

"We make action. Action...Plan. Awlsough...*Document*. Must make document for Action. Action without Document is No Action. Something happen, they look..." (he held up his finger for ultimate emphasis) "...again...will be noted."

Alison tried to forget Elijah. It was because she liked him too much. She didn't quite understand how she could like him so much *in advance*.

Her math book and homework papers slumped off to the side of her bed. She just gave in, threw herself back on her pillows, and put her hands behind her head. She stared at her ceiling.

"You are so beautiful," she said out loud, not sure if she was Elijah saying it to her or herself saying it to him. She repeated it out loud four more times, with greater volume each time.

"What?" her mother called up from downstairs. "Are you calling me?"

"I'm all right," Alison shouted down to her mother. "Nothing. I'm good," she said, walking over to close her door.

She couldn't believe how much her mother snooped around in every area of her life lately.

———

For three mornings in a row Patty had been gone by the time Peter woke up. She would have had to have woken up by 4:45 at the latest, he figured. She was with a "Morning Meditation for Revelation" prayer group that met out near Laurent's Pass in the hills. She told Peter it was "too powerful to talk about."

Peter tried to comfort himself with food. He was going to cook his own breakfast. He stumbled out of bed five minutes before his alarm went off and picked up a box of pancake mix with tired eagerness. Just looking at the Aunt Jemima Original Style Rich Maple Pancake Syrup made him feel eight years old again. Like eating a stack of hotcakes while it snowed outside when he had the day off from school.

He mixed the powder from the box with an egg and a cup of milk. He greased the griddle according to directions. When it was hot enough he poured a fair-sized dollop of pancake batter, watched it harden and take shape. He put another one on and tried to guess what animal it looked like. A cloud. He heated up the syrup. After he had a stack of four pancakes he arranged them just like the way he did when he was little. Pancake, butter, syrup; pancake, butter, syrup. He poured himself his coffee and sat down.

The syrup tasted like sugary goo, with an aftertaste of movie-theater candy. He looked again at the bottle of syrup, with the warm picture of a robust Aunt Jemima greeting the day. "Original Flavor with Rich Maple Taste," it said. Underneath that, in smaller yellow letters, it added, "Made with 4% Real Maple Syrup."

He burst out in tears. He didn't want a 4% Maple Syrup life. He had never driven to work crying before. And he didn't know why he was doing it today. Not good.

When he got home, the pancakes were still there.

———

It was only a twenty-five minute ride to work for Alan, but it involved crossing a mountain. The mountain road could be interesting, boring, colorful, or dangerous. Winter was the worst—lots of dead animals everywhere. Maybe they were suicides. Spring varied, depending on the moods of his fellow drivers. He turned on the radio, to an obscure New Jersey station.

"Hello, Larry? Yeah, how ya doin'?" the voice crackled.

"Fine, Tom. What's on your mind today?"

"Well, I was listening to the previous caller? I think it's fascinating how these so-called black 'leaders' are the first ones, Lar...the first ones to complain about 'racism,' 'favoritism,' what-have-you, but how many people do you see up there on their podiums, in their ranks, in their organizations, who are white, or Italian, or Jewish, or what-have-you?"

"What is your point?"

"I just think it's fascinating. Apparently it's okay to have a double standard when they want to have a double standard."

"Um-hmmm."

"But they're the first ones out there crying 'foul,' asking for give-backs, what-have-you, if they feel their toes are being stepped on."

"Yeah. What is your point, Tom?" asked the radio host. "I don't understand it, y'know? Very interesting. I don't understand it."

"Well, of course you 'understand' it. The ordinary rules of civil society, of American society, are not supposed to apply to them because they are black. What's not to understand?"

"No, I don't understand..."

"Ahhh, you're full of it, Tom." There was a click. "People like Tom make me sick. They really annoy me. He 'understands.' He's just afraid to say what he feels. Many people are afraid. Because people are, by nature, basically serendipitous, overt, obvious liars. Next caller: Susan from Piscataway."

"Yeah, Larry. My husband works with the blacks, in Newark..."

"Mmmm-hmmmmmm."

"And what he tells me, about the way these people live, would turn your stomach."

"Thank you, Susan. Al, from Trenton."

"Yeah, Lar, how ya doin'? I was reading that Colin Powell..."

"Colin Powell doesn't seem to know exactly what he wants to be now, does he?"

"My point is..."

"Debra, from Short Hills..."

This was the Larry Burt show, beamed in to Alan's commute each morning from somewhere in Jersey via the services of a decaying upstate smaller station. He listened for those gem-like moments, usually once every three days, when Larry would completely go berserk on his callers or the state of world affairs and practically enact homicide and suicide on the air. Today he was merely wistful.

"Well, Debra...we haven't learned very much, have we? In all these centuries of so-called 'civilization,' so-called 'technology,' so-called 'progress,' the human brain remains our Achilles' heel, and now we just slide, slide, slide. Y'know one of New York's great senators wrote a book a few years ago, which didn't get very much attention. In it he had a phrase that we would all do well to commit to memory. It was: 'Defining Deviancy Downward.' Let me ask you, folks: how much further down can we go? We already have certified morons teaching in universities; a Ph.D. isn't worth the paper it is printed on anymore. We've had a sexual deviate in the White House, there are many of them in governors' mansions. We have lost it. It's gone, folks. This country, the United States of America...it's over, pal. Quit deluding yourselves. It's time to wake up and smell the poison."

An advertisement for Laser Hemorrhoid Surgery followed, then an ad for a winter cruise to Central America with Larry and his family on the "Queen of Luxury Cruise Ships" before more calls.

"Dominic, my paisan, from New Brunswick."

"Yeah, Lar...I found it very interesting that nowhere in the president's remarks last week about the black situation was there any reference to the tens of thousands of white people who have been ripped off, robbed, and mugged by these young felons."

"Well, of course not. They're his prospective constituency. He wants them for his people. He courts their votes. If he doesn't get them, the Democrats do."

"That we should continue to spend our precious resources on these scum-of-the-earth. They don't want to work, Larry. They don't want an education. They just want their designer-drugs, and their 'freedoms'...they're the first ones to carry on about 'freedom-this' and 'freedom-that,' but THEY DON'T WANT THE RE-SPON-SI-BIL-I-TY…"

"Yeah, Dominic…first of all, there are many black people who GO to work, come home, watch the news, and raise their families. These people are called 'Republicans.' And they are—beneath the skin color——just like you and I."

"Exactly."

"Thank you for your call. Kenneth, from Bayonne."

"Yeah, Larry, I listen to the show a lot."

"Thank you."

"Yeah. And I am African-American. I don't always agree with everything you say. Now when you talk about 'Black America'…"

"Let me ask you this, Kenneth: Do you have a family?"

"Well, I am…yes."

"You are what?"

"I live with my parents."

"How old are you?"

"Twenty-seven."

"What are you living with them for?"

"Where I live the rents are…"

"Forget 'rent.' Are you married?"

"No."

"Do you have any children?"

"Two."

"Where's the mother?"

"The kids live with her."

"Why aren't you living together?"

"Well, I'm trying to save…"

"No, Kenneth, you see…you're not married, you're not self-supporting, where exactly do you think your children are going to derive their values from? From government social workers?"

"I've got a job. And I see them every…"

"What's your point?"

"Well, the previous caller…"

"Kenneth, are you looking for 'sympathy'?"

"No, in fact, I voted for Bush twice and Republican in the election before that."

"Then?"

"I don't think it's fair to…"

"Oh, you don't think it is 'fair'? We're talking about a war, pal. How many 'fair' wars can you recall, Kenneth? Those individuals who would be your leaders have declared war in your name. You see, they mock you. You are like the White Man. Maybe you're a devil too, Kenneth. Because you work."

"All the black…"

"How many white people do you know?"

"My girl…"

"None. Right? Really, none."

"Where you start going wrong is…"

"Ahhh, get off my phone, you overt, obvious liar. You're a phony, pal. With a very transparent agenda. You know, they call in, they start with a compliment…he's a liar. It's a tactic. It's all tactics. Does he sound like someone who works for a living, like you and I? There is a nation of Kenneths out there. And they're going to be running things, folks. One day you'll turn on the radio and it'll be 'The Kenneth Show.' If I hung up on him, and you think that's bad, just wait until you see what awaits you in your future, folks."

———•———

Elijah was finding the school more cliquish than he had ever expected. Having come from a private school which encouraged seeing oneself—and others—in multidimensional terms, this was…more than a little disappointing.

He was standing right on the line between releasing into the general flow of things and continuing to hold himself back in cautious reserve. He could tell that other people— particularly a number of girls—were checking him out. He considered nodding to them when he saw them doing it, but—with the exception of Alison—that seemed like it would be hopelessly goofy.

There was definitely a vibe between Alison and him shaping up. He wasn't sure, but…he wasn't sure. It could be okay.

———

Angel's referral to the school psychologist went quickly.

"I want you to know that this evaluation is perfectly routine," Dolores offered. "All incoming students go through a screening process once their paperwork has been received from the referring district. In your case I have been asked to help the process along a little by seeing you in advance of your documentation."

Angel regarded her coolly.

"Now…it's not clear to me," she said, adjusting her bifocals, "with whom exactly you are residing."

He regarded her calmly. There was no need to volunteer anything.

"I said, I'm sorry, but we don't seem to have information on your legal guardian."

After a while, Angel said, "Mmmm-huh."

"Someone has to have signed you into the district," said Dolores in her "official" voice.

"Mmmm-huh," said Angel.

She stared at him over her glasses. *Oh, brother,* she thought. *This kid really thinks he can manipulate women.* "Well, who was it?" she asked.

"My aunt."

"Aunts are not legally able to sign children into school districts."

"Yeah, well she had a note from my mother."

"They accepted a note from your mother?"

"Yeah. She can't be living with us now. She has a condition."

"What condition might that be?"

"You have to ask her."

"How can we get in touch with her?"

"Through my aunt."

"Do we have an address, a phone number for your mother?" asked Dolores.

"She doesn't have a phone."

"Well, then, we're going to have to call your aunt and advise her that we are commencing psychological testing and ask to obtain consent."

"She works."

"Good. That's a good thing."

"She's not allowed to get calls at work."

"We'll be respectful."

"Is that all?"

"Yeah. That's all." Dolores wrote out a pass for him to return to class.

"So what is it you need?"

"Permission. A permission slip."

Dolores handed him the pass. Angel left. Dolores called Pacelli's class three minutes later to make sure he had gotten there.

He had.

APPETITES

Carlos waited for Richie in front of Pretzel Moment. They were supposed to have met in front of Shanghai Express in the Food Court, but Richie hadn't shown and Pretzel Moment was always the fallback location if plans got dicked-up.

It had been two weeks since the misunderstanding with Richie, Fat Mike, and Claire. Claire had been instrumental in setting up this first face-to-face. It wasn't like he and Richie had been friends since birth or anything, but life was too short to keep things messed up unless they had to be. It was sad to think of money separating people like this.

It was amazing how The Mall could be a really exciting place when you were walking around in groups of three or four and dead-boring when you were waiting around for somebody else. When you thought about it, it was nothing more than a bunch of sneaker stores with doofy-looking guards your own age walking around telling you you couldn't smoke. It was like you went from being told you couldn't smoke at school to being told you couldn't smoke after school. This was America in the New Millennium. What was the point of a war on terrorism if you couldn't smoke in your own town's mall?

A couple of wigger-wanna-be's from Stephens Manor walked by, giving him a nod and high-five, but no sign of Richie. Richie really was a piece of work.

A lot of the young moms who walked by with strollers looked fine to him. It was surprising to think that their bodies could be so firm and tight after whatever-the-hell childbirth was like, but some of them looked better than girls his age. He leaned back, put his hands in his pocket and gave one of them his "wassup?" smile. She looked away and tucked a blanket-corner in around the side of her little kid. He tried to double the intensity of his stare, ordering it to be sexually irresistible.

A scream from across the mall corridor broke the moment.

"Carlos, you dick!"

It had to be Danielle. The mother and her child quickly wheeled away. He turned to see her running, her boobs bouncing.

"Where were you fifth period? I can't believe it, you're at The Mall!"

"Wassup, Danielle?"

"Not much, wassup with you?" She brushed her slightly greenish-blonde hair out of her face.

"Nothing."

"So, like, what are you doing?"

"Waiting for Richie."

"Richie? I saw Richie over at Ground Round with Tina."

"Tina?"

"Yeah."

"Since when is Richie hanging around Tina?"

"I dunno."

"Anyone tell Tony?"

"Tony and Tina, y'know, they're through. It's like, 'Hello? Duh, they broke up? Like five billion years ago?' Do you want me to go over there and, like, give him a ride?"

"No, I want you to stay out of it."

"Like Richie is so…disorganized."

"Uhh-huh."

"So what happened that day with his car?"

"I don't want to talk about it, Danielle."

"What?"

"I said I don't want to talk about it with you. You're gonna get me aggravated." He looked at his watch. Richie was now fifty minutes late. The good will he had felt about getting together was long gone.

"Do you know anywhere I could score?"

"Like what, Danielle, grass?"

"No, I was thinking, like…Dust?"

"That shit's nasty," said Carlos.

"I know. It's not for me, it's for a friend. Hey."

"Whatever."

"So…do you know someone?"

"Yeah, I do. But he's a real sneaky bastard, so I'm not saying you can trust him or anything, y'know?"

"Well…it's for tonight and I don't have much time."

"Well, y'know where Hair & Beyond is?" asked Carlos.

"Yeah…"

"On the way to Red Lobster?"

"Yeah…"

"Well, not right there, but across from Best Buy? Right next to there is a bench. There'll be a guy on it. His name is Angel. He's from the city. He can fix you up," assured Carlos.

"Is that near that computer stuff store?"

"Yuh. Modem Madness or some shit."

"I know where that is. He'll be on a bench."

"Yeah."

Carlos hadn't sent Angel business before, and he was willing to use Danielle for an experiment because she annoyed him so much. If he heard she'd O.D.'d or something tomorrow he'd stick with the tried-and-true guy next time. If everything went okay, Angel would owe him one. Carlos had gotten used to being the only Latino in some of his classes and had gotten a fair amount of mileage from it over the years. A lot of kids were scared of him because of the combination of being Hispanic and being from the city originally. And he knew a lot of the girls dug it because they believed weird things about Hispanic guys. He wasn't going to argue.

The arrival of this new guy from the city meant, he supposed, that they'd have to fight at some point soon, just to let people know that...something. In the meantime he could still steer the kid a favor and have him owe him one.

"Thanks!" said Danielle, running off. "Oh, and do you want me to get any message through to Richie?"

"No, that's okay, Danielle. Just have a good time."

"Mmmmmmmmmm-maaa!" she said, giving him an unexpected kiss on the cheek and pressing her boobs against his chest. "Luv ya!"

Carlos wondered how Fat Mike fell into all of this. Maybe Fat Mike was whipping this all up—making Richie mad about the car-kick thing again. Because it was too much of a coincidence. Richie missing the face-to-face the day after Claire and Fat Mike skipped school together. He couldn't imagine what that was all about. He couldn't imagine anybody having sex with Fat Mike, least of all Claire, who was out to make some kind of national reputation for herself as Most Muscular Virgin. It was funny how they'd gotten to be friends, after she'd broken his nose and wouldn't let him slip his hand down her pants. Girls were weird.

Richie was a hypocrite. Here he was making this big thing out of what happened to his car, like it was World War III, but Richie himself had helped Ernie destroy Bobby's Monte Carlo and very few people knew it. ("You don't touch a guy's car," Richie had preached.") "Yeah, right," Carlos thought, "unless it's Bobby's car you're fucking up." "I said you don't touch a *guy's* car," Richie shot back. "Bobby is a freaking girl as far as I'm concerned. (Carlos hadn't had a clue why these guys hated each other. He just wondered if Bobby still wanted to get a piece of Ernie's or Richie's cars and wondered if he needed encouragement to get it.)

———————

Alison had heard the rumors that at least a couple of self-proclaimed sexy girls were out to snare Elijah. She didn't think he could care less. Unless...he was bored with her? Already? They hadn't even really done anything together yet, or spoken. He was the first guy in her life who she didn't really even want to speak with as much as hold and hug. It sounded so stupid. It wasn't about "making out."

Alison's friend Erica had been caught making out big-time with her boyfriend, Damien, upstairs during her twelfth birthday party. Erica's mother caught her and later gave her a lecture which concluded with "No one is going to buy the cow when they can get the milk for free." Erica and Alison had talked about this at length afterward. Neither of them thought of themselves as cows. They laughed trying to picture each other that way, with, maybe, bells around their necks. For the next week in school they both called each other "Elsie" every time they saw each other.

Plus they weren't looking for anyone to "buy" them.

Erica's older brother, now in med school, had given them free advice two summers ago:

1. Many men were nice, but most were pigs.

2. Most nice men could easily be lured into doing stupid things.

3. All not-nice men actively pursue stupid things.

4. All men valued sex over life itself. They would hump a gasoline pump if they were in the right mood. Men would jump in front of a speeding car to have sex.

He told them about the rat experiments in which the rats repeatedly pressed the lever to give themselves more cocaine, until they died. "And that's nothing compared to a sixteen-year-old raised on Carmen Electra, Jennifer Anniston, all the MTV babes, *Scream* movies, the WWF, Victoria's Secret catalogs, and their parents' *Hustler* magazines." So powerful was this force, Aaron had argued, that men would carry the association of Carmen Diaz's femaleness over to the girl sitting next to them in study hall because, after all, they were both females and had vaginas. He would fight for her attention as if it were Carmen's own.

Alison and Erica were transfixed, but couldn't avoid laughing. Vaginas? The thought of guys obsessing over them, meditating about them, planning their lives around trying to gain access to them seemed ridiculous, and pathetic at the same time. It made about as much sense as imagining someone pining away for, and writing romantic poetry about, the perfect nostrils.

Not that vaginas couldn't be fun, Alison thought. It was just that if what he were saying were true, it was a pretty weird way to look at the world: vaginas first, all else follows.

Alison hated the word, anyway. There was no alternative, she supposed. "Pussy" ended up sounding like some kind of stupid rodent name, as if you were supposed to talk about your pet gerbil down there, or something. "Cunt" was awful, because it sounded like a knife wound. But "vagina" wasn't much better. "Vagina" sounded like a bio class name for the interior lining of the lungs. Or something which might surround the spleen. It was about as sexy as the word "bacteria." Sometimes she would daydream in bio class as to what guys would be like if they had vaginas. It was hard to imagine.

"Dicks," on the other hand, seemed just about right. Maybe this was because so many of the boys in school really were dicks, and she'd gotten accustomed to it. It seemed like a perfect name for both the body part and the overall personality of most of the eighth-, ninth-, and tenth-grade males she knew. Elijah, of course, was excepted. What he had was, she imagined, beyond words.

She knew she wasn't the only girl to think this way about him. She hoped he would be strong. There were better female bodies around than hers. She imagined he went for the mind-body-unity thing, though. She just hoped that he would hold up under pressure, and that he wasn't too much of a guy after all.

———

Mona was never out sick.

Peter's secretary, Mona, had called in very early that morning saying there was "no way that I can come in today," without further elaboration. The gossip was that one of her sons was arrested for refusing to accept a speeding ticket (78 in a 35-mile-per-hour zone) from the same cop who had given him tickets for the same offense two other times, and that Mona was mounting an elaborate legal defense.

Sitting in her place this morning was a demure, smiling young woman in a pretty flowered dress. She smiled at Alan and then almost blushed for no particular reason. It drove him wild.

"I'm sorry…are you new here?" Alan asked.

"No. No, I'm just here for a while. I think just for today," she said.

"Oh. My name is Alan Mitchke."

"I'm Bonnie."

"Nice to meet you. So I shouldn't get to know you too well if you're only here for a day?" She laughed, beyond any amusement the lame remark offered. He smiled, beyond any pleasure the present held. He was already in the future. "I'm extension 357 if you're looking for me."

"Okay," she said, picking up a pencil with young awkwardness, writing "357" in the corner of the oversize daily calendar in front of her. He watched the pencil move. "ALAN"

Seeing her write his name was the biggest erotic excitement he had had in half a year. "Did they show you where the staff lunchroom is? And the ladies' room, and things like that?"

"No, no, not really," she said, giggling and leaning forward a little, as if those rooms might be passing by at that very moment in the hallway before her.

"Well, you go down there toward the windows, and the third room on your right..." Alan was aware that their heads were actually near each other as she leaned across the desk straining to see the direction of the hallway. Her breasts were not big, but enticing in their smooth lines. Even as he felt it, he knew he was back into this old thing of being attracted to young, carefree women, women who held the promise of having endless capacity for sexy fun. He had known for years now that this was likely a reaction to his earlier marriage to Evelyn, a woman of nonstop verbal and nonverbal gravity. Evelyn had been a Serious Woman with Women's Issues. He had been expected to damn well better relate to her on that level. Except for the times when she wanted to play like a

Girl, or a Flirty Teen, or a Moody Lover. At those times he was expected to become aware of her desires to be frivolous via extrasensory perception and to adjust accordingly. By and large, however, he was to relate to her as a Woman Who Needed Space.

About three times a year, for the six years since the divorce, Alan would try to figure out exactly what went wrong without simplifying it down to Evelyn being a spoiled bitch.

They had been one of the most improbable pairings of the century, according to most everyone: a well-meaning, if bumbling, rumpled social worker with a leggy, New York City model. Her body was, admittedly, outstanding. Few people knew, however, the grief, tantrums, and self-loathing that went into Evelyn's dieting and obsessive perfectionism. She hadn't been a successful model when he met her, but had been an earnest Village photographer who reluctantly, as she told her story, allowed a friend of hers to "turn the tables" one day and have her stand in front of the camera lens. In those days she looked good in ripped jeans, lots of layered primitive necklaces over t-shirts, men's leather bomber jackets, etc. Evelyn had a genuine toughness she projected well. It was not hard for her to become a successful, slightly androgynous, sex object.

The irony, of course, was that the more sophisticated and kinky the "shoot" she accepted (and the higher her fees), the more dead she had become in the bedroom. It was now absolutely out of the question to have children "for at least ten years." Additionally, she'd not told him of her general whereabouts more and more often. Whereas she used to encounter great-looking men once in a while, she now seemed to have several dozen men in her life on a near-daily basis. She told Alan that all of these were nonsexual connections and on some days he believed her. If she wasn't screwing some man, though, she'd either become a completely repressed lesbian or merely a very, very tense, shrill, disembodied nut. A few years of his own therapy had convinced him of the latter.

She had finally admitted that she had fallen in love with a straight male photo editor for *Elle* ("I think you'd like him. He's a lot like you, but artistic.") Alan withdrew with a minimum of harsh words, though he wouldn't hug Evelyn goodbye. A part of his soul had seemed to leave with him. It was the part that believed that miracles occurred naturally, gracefully, and lasted forever.

Alan looked at Bonnie. She was a woman, but she looked years away from middle age. Alan was thirty-six. He felt it and looked it. It felt like eighteen years of difference between them. How could that be? Bonnie's body seemed…fun. Wasn't that just awful of him? Her smile seemed like simple fun. Maybe even her thinking was fun.

What would it be like to be with someone who was just fun? What would it be like without the constant stories of chronic family dysfunction, past abuse, or previous marriages?

He went down to his office and wrote her name on a piece of paper, slowly. He wrote, "Bonnie & Alan" at several different angles and then drew a heart enclosing the two of them.

It didn't even feel silly.

DENSE

Ninja Dave had a feeling that Ernie was going to get jumped. Or something. Fat Mike and Carlos asked him in front of Grand Union to see their point: the kid had gone around hitting a thirty-five-year-old, Kenny, in the kneecap with a baseball bat just because he thought the guy was talking to his make-believe girlfriend, Debbie. ("Like he owns her.") The point was that Ernie was acting like he was freaking invincible and was too stupid to understand that the only reason people weren't fighting back was because they were likely to kill him if they hit him, he was such a measly, short, fifteen-year-old motherfucker. The kid was *dense.*

"More than that," Fat Mike explained, using his reasonable voice. "More than that. Forget the knees. Forget the hospital bill, which Kenny had to pay for out of his own pocket, since Super 8 doesn't have medical, forget everything. Except this: Ernie fucked up Bobby's Monte Carlo. He screwed with the brakelines and he put sugar in the gas tank. There is no way that is right. That is life-threatening and also spitting in his face."

"Just because Ernie thought Bobby talked to Debbie, too?" Carlos asked.

"Yeah."

"The kid is loco," said Carlos.

"Not that Debbie is any angel herself, now," Ninja Dave offered.

"Actually, she's a pig," Carlos laughed.

"Shut up. I live near the girl," Fat Mike said with authority. "My father and me plowed out their driveway in that mega-storm in February. She's got a fresh mouth, yeah, I'll be the first to admit."

"Did you see her at the Motley Crue concert at the Speedway? Oh, man, she was wasted," said Carlos. "This strange guy in a Megadeth t-shirt was almost humping her standing up and she was just stomping her feet all around, shaking her head all out of rhythm. It looked like an elephant on acid or somethin'."

Fat Mike cut the laughter short. "That's not the point. The point is nothing to do with her. Ernie is an asshole. Let me tell you something: the kid is going to end up dead, like soon, if he doesn't wake up. I mean, he's already had warnings and he doesn't friggin' blink. He also blew up this kid Tony's car in Good Hollow two months ago."

"He blew up his car?"

"Yeah."

"Before or after Bobby's Monte Carlo?"

"Before," said Fat Mike.

"Like practice?" asked Ninja Dave.

"We don't know."

"What kind of car was it?" inquired Carlos.

"Seventy-two Camaro."

"It was on the road?" asked Ninja Dave.

"It needed a new radiator," said Fat Mike.

"I know that car," Carlos said, excitedly. "I know that guy, Tony. I thought he had it on blocks. He had double-headers on that thing."

"I know," said Fat Mike.

"Those are bad. And he had holes, like, in the muffler, to be loud," Carlos said, excitedly.

"Yeah, well it got blown up."

"How'd they do that?" asked Ninja Dave.

"I dunno. It's something technical with stuffing something down something," said Fat Mike.

"M-80s?" asked Carlos.

"No, you don't need that stuff."

"Bobby's father knows they blew up his car?' asked Ninja Dave.

"Of course. They blew it up fifteen feet from the front door."

"When?"

"Two-and-a-half weeks ago."

"Oh, man, that musta been loud. Was it loud?" asked Carlos.

"I don't think so. I think it just fucked up the insides or something."

"Were there flames?" inquired Ninja Dave.

"I dunno. I wasn't there," said Fat Mike.

"What'd his father do?" asked Carlos.

"Call the cops."

"What'd the cops do?"

"Nothing. What are they gonna do? I mean, really, go over to Ernie's and ask him if he blew up Bobby's car?" asked Fat Mike.

"Yeah," said Ninja Dave.

"Well, they did that."

"And what'd he say?"

"He said, 'Naaaah, I didn't go near his fuckin' car!' And what are the cops gonna do? No eyewitnesses, right?"

"He had an alibi?" asked Carlos.

"The guy's clean as far as they know."

"So the cops..."

"You don't understand...the cops can't do nothin' against him," said Fat Mike with authority.

"Yeah?"

"Yeah. I mean they get some order telling him to stay away. He says he was staying away anyway. What's the fucking difference?"

"Man," said Carlos.

"Yeah, I know."

"Fletchersville police? Or state troopers?" asked Ninja Dave.

"Fletchersville."

"Those guys suck," volunteered Carlos.

"I know," said Fat Mike.

They snickered as a little old lady clutching her coupons, breathing harshly, pushed her cart into Grand Union, fast.

———◦———

This was the part of the job Dolores liked the least. Standardized psychological testing. WISC-Rs, I.Q. testing, recommendations for the Committee for Special Education re: modifications of the learning process. Even the projective testing and drawings left Dolores cold these days. The tremendous surge of excitement she had upon discovering that most emotional and learning problems were correlated with poor diet and nutritional imbalances was not supported by her district's hierarchy. Simply stated, they left her enough room to do workshops, try to raise the consciousness of the ever-stubborn faculty, and to reach out to the parents who so miserably poisoned their children with a steady diet of over-stimulating chocolates, refined sugars, processed foods, artificial colors, greasy fats, and toxic additives, but they did not want her assessment of this condition in the formal psychological write-ups. This left her in a double bind, wherein she had to work for hours putting together a summary impression of a child which, by definition, was woefully incomplete. She had clashed with building principals before over this and had been pleased to leave the junior high. That school was now being run by a "dese-dem-dose" ignoramus, and she was settled into the greener pastures of senior high. The principal might not agree with her, but Peter seemed willing to listen, even if he didn't want the nutritional evaluation written into the reports for the C.S.E. She had once pointed out to him that his attention span had visibly diminished by seventh period at a meeting not twenty minutes after he finished a KitKat bar with his lunch. He had tried to laugh, but she knew she had scored some points.

The psychological testing on Angel Rivera was, initially, unsurprising. She sometimes thought of this as the standard "Third World Just Moved From the City With My Dysfunctional Non-English Speaking Family Assessment Results." She knew this wasn't exactly fair, expecting specific results before testing the student, or learning about his eating habits, food allergies, etc., but she had been so right so many times that she was getting used to it. It was really a question of almost arbitrary whim as to whether she should recommend classification for special education for these students, as many of them weren't too likely to learn, anyway. The distinction between special ed kids who weren't interested in learning and regular ed kids who weren't interested in learning wasn't that huge.

Though his full-scale I.Q. was average, his performance I.Q. was considerably higher. On the WISC-R extremely sharp verbal abilities were noted, despite a poor general fund of information. The biggest surprise came with projective testing (which, she was surprised to find, he cooperated with in the first place, given his obvious problems with women). Angel had responded in a number of ways which indicated that he missed a father figure and a deep sense of order in his family and life. He seemed to have a strong sense of the importance of family, despite continually volunteering almost nothing about his own. Impulse control (usually quite damaged in these kids) seemed to be surprisingly strong and he did not match the typical profile of the inattentive youngster who could not maintain himself in the classroom. As she tried to explain later to Peter, "If this boy doesn't maintain himself in your school, it is because he chooses not to, not because he is unable to."

What she was not prepared to find, however, was the degree of rage that was broiling all through the projective testing. Quietly, and without affect, Angel was spilling over with it. There was no particular indication as to the source of it, and no information—or reassurances—as to its ultimate aim. She had expected a behavior-management problem in mid-development, sociopath in full bloom. She'd give him a chart to take home to monitor what he ate. It was better than nothing.

She called his aunt's home.

The Jiffy Mart answered.

Sometimes the coffee tasted like gravy, sometimes like charcoal. There were a few days where it tasted like chocolate-gray transmission fluid or some sort of essence of rusty furniture parts. Alan was supposed to have given up coffee, according to the nurse-nutritionist (or whatever she was) whom he had seen on the advice of one of his concerned clients four years ago. It was becoming common for some of the teenagers he saw to express concern over how he looked. There had always been the extra ten or fifteen pounds, but it was recent that he was no longer able to sleep.

On Saturday evenings was something that seemed better than unconsciousness: the Spanish-speaking variety show ("Sabado Gigante!!"—featuring Don Francisco, a small, shlubby guy who seamlessly moved from Goya bean endorsements and introductions of ever-new slender "model-spokeswomen" in tight evening gowns, to Spanish versions of Jeopardy and Hollywood Squares). The program was on for four hours straight on his cable network before they ran Spanish infomercials (largely beauty products or exercise machines), and—if you really persevered—at 3:00 a.m. they re-ran the Sabador Gigante show from the week before.

Alan didn't speak or understand Spanish. He was content to remain an alien observer, even as he liked to imagine himself part of the "family" of the show. Don Francisco would walk amongst the audience with his microphone so easily, so much one of them, one of us, and interview kindly old grandmother-types (who reminded Alan of his own thick-waisted, loving Jewish grandmother, dead in Miami Beach twelve years ago). Why was it that age alone can wipe out ethnic differences, finally? So that everyone eventually becomes a "nice, old grandperson"? He imagined there were surely some exceptions. He had a hard time imagining Scott Peterson this way.

In the rare event that he got bored with Spanish television (twenty minutes could go by between model-spokeswomen sometimes), there was the wild Japanese game show channel, the Discovery Channel, or—his favorite—the Exercise Channel. Where else could you watch tightly-muscled, fit, young women toning themselves through a series of repetitive exercises in leotards, short-shorts, swimwear, or an improvised assemblage of all three? This was not just getting lucky for him, it was rewound adolescent heaven. It was like the time his friends had discovered a hole in the back wall of the girls' locker room at the beach club when he was fourteen. The only difference was that he didn't go look through it, like Jimmy and Ross and Steven did, because he knew it wasn't right. If he was going to see Isabel LaBrecka strip it was going to be in his bedroom, candlelight flickering off The Doors poster, smooth incense wafting around their mutual nudity, not because he caught her unaware, in between undies and bikini. How very moral. How very nice. Becoming a nice guy had taken careful cultivation and years of practice. Fortunately for Alan there was now cable t.v. Maybe he could catch Isabel on the rebound.

He imagined there were friends of his who thought he went home and read novels until, say, eleven o'clock, thoughtfully encircling meaningful sections or quotes before turning out the light to dream of improved techniques and motivated approaches to his difficult cases to be seen tomorrow. Maybe Alan just wished there were people who thought of him this way. In his worst nightmare he thought that no one thought of him this way, that everyone thought of him as just another social worker collecting a check. Someone who went home, put his feet up, ate Breyer's Mint Chocolate Chip and watched twenty-one-year-olds exercise on t.v.

He needed sex, damn it. Even if he was a social worker. Even if he were empathic, even if he worked with young people, even if he worked with sexual abusers and their victims, even if he were nice, and even if he had a promising career as a voyeur. He wondered if he could measure on the fingers of one hand (one finger? One amputated hand?) the number of partners who awaited him for the rest of his life. At 3:00 in the morning watching t.v., it was a chilling thought.

Maybe what chilled him was the possibility that they might not look like the women on the Exercise Channel, but might look like the grandmothers on the Sabador Gigante Show. Because he would look like Don Francisco. Alan felt like somehow he shouldn't "get" one of those well-conditioned, lushly-maned beauties in her leotard. He felt like he somehow shouldn't be able to slowly touch them, encircle them with his arms, tracing the muscles in their backs, down, down, and down, peeling off the fuchsia nylon until only firm female muscle awaited his squeeze, his rub, his entry. It could not be. And it hadn't been.

He wondered what Bonnie looked like nude. He watched their leg-lifts. They were on hands and knees, shaking their wild manes of hair and extending one leg back, toes pointed toward the sky, sharing an exhilarated youthful "Whew!" Bonnie could be there. He put her there, dark blue leotard. Then no leotard, but an emerald green bikini. Then no bikini, but white silk panties only. Then naked. ("And UP, two, three, four, BREATHE, two, three, four...WHEW!!") The other women looked at the cameras, looked deeply into the cathode tubes of electronic digitalized transmission. All that she was wearing now—her smile—willingly, persistently and ever-more openly contacted him.

And this was how he found his way to sleep at 3:21 a.m., Wednesday.

The alarm went off at 5:35 a.m.

Coffee was really part of the car, he figured. He couldn't commute to work without it, any more than he could decide to drive on three wheels instead of four. The Dunkin' Donuts mug was festive and held at least six cups, he imagined. Too much coffee was a minor crime in the pantheon of crimes he was sure he would read about, hear about, or witness today.

A beat-up Chevy with a "Lawyers Are Leeches" bumper sticker passed him doing eighty in the left lane. A skeletally-skinny pale young man drove past in a 1991 Celica. The back window had a sticker on it that said "My Other Toy Has Tits." A mountain-man in a '93 Dodge Ram pickup passed him, a "Kiss My New York Ass, Hillary" sticker on its bumper. A "Fireman Do It Better—Find 'Em Hot, Leave 'Em Wet" bumper sticker was on the Ford Bronco in front of him. "Wife & Dog Missing–Reward for Return of Dog," read the back of a Nissan pickup going eighty. "East Galesville Football: Tradition Never Graduates" read the bumper of an '86 Cutlass sedan which cut him off doing seventy, then veered back into the left lane. An "If You Think Education Is Expensive, Try Ignorance" bumper sticker was on the Volvo turbo station wagon he just had to pass near Route 32. Had to be a teacher or an administrator. He'd never seen that sticker on the car of anyone who wasn't on a Board of Ed payroll.

He was tired. Alan would have giddy moments where he would imagine some sort of parallel universe of an honest nature, with the same people in the same vehicles commuting to work, only the bumper stickers read things like: "I Deserve a Raise & You Don't," "Gimmee More Money," "Raise My Credit Limit," "I Play With Guns." Sometimes in the stoned-like fog that commuting for a fourth or fifth day in a row like this could bring he'd imagine the cars being driven not by regular mortals but by mythic characters: The Prodigal Son in a Mercedes Benz, passing Mother Earth in a 1984 Saab. The Blonde Bombshell adjusting the rearview mirror of her Acura as Guido approaches in his Trans-Am, Peter Gabriel thumping out of eight speakers. The Serious Jewish Intellectual letting everyone pass as he putters by in his dark brown Mercury four-door with significant body-rust. A

JERRY SANDER

Female Victim In Her Twenties gripping the wheel of her Geo Prizm at ten and two-o'clock going fifty-four miles per hour in the right lane, hoping she was doing okay as her stomach begins acting up. A kindly-looking Wilford Brimley-type Senior Citizen drives past in a beige Olds. The left bumper has an A.A.R.P. sticker. The right bumper has one that said, "Give Me All You Got."

On this highway, on this day, there weren't any smashed squirrels, split-open skunks, or blown-apart raccoons. There were, he imagined, the bruised, bloody adolescent bodies of the kids Alan had worked with. Each of them in death, however mangled, clung to a deer. Dead and dead.

Alan sipped his coffee, but now he could taste it. He was almost to work. The sun was more or less up. He adjusted the rearview mirror to look into it. He didn't look too good. There was something about his color. Something was dull.

He hoped it would change before Bonnie saw him.

RETREATS

"So Crystal and I were trying on things, right?" said Claire, kicking off the session with a shot of energy.

"Trying on…?" asked Alan.

"Outfits. Duh. And Debbie has to yell upstairs, 'Dinner! Get down here for dinner!' Not like, 'Excuse me, I think we'll be having dinner soon…', but 'Dinner!' like we're dogs or something?"

Alan looked at Claire as she brushed her hair behind her ears. It did make them stick out more prominently.

"And I'm like, 'Oh my God! Where are my earrings!' And Isabel says, 'You weren't wearing any.' And I said, 'Yes I was. I was wearing those practically all week.' And this is the week that Shanequa—she's new in the house?—was found walking into my room when I wasn't there saying that she had to get back some mousse that she supposedly leant me? Only she hadn't leant me it? And you can ask Mrs. Johnson, who knows that Shanequa doesn't even use mousse, but uses that activating-gel-styling stuff? So right there she's a liar, and then my earrings are missing? And she's all like 'I-don't-know-what-you're-talking-about' but you could tell? That there's something just like…sly about her? And then Mandy comes running in? You don't know Mandy. She's gotta get her face in everything. And she looks around and disappears and the next thing I know she's saying that I said something to Isabel like 'you can't trust Shanequa because she's black,' which is like a major lie, because I've even had boyfriends—well, not boyfriends—but guys who wanted to go out with me who were black and I hung out with black people and if I don't like someone I'll tell them to their face, but it's not because they're black, right?"

"Mmmmm-huh."

"I mean it may be because they're black, but not BECAUSE they're black. I don't walk around calling kids 'niggers,' even though they call themselves, and each other, that—which, by the way, the teachers let them get away with, but if you say it, or even think it, they're all over you like flies on a shit sandwich. And I listen to black music, sometimes, anyway. Not all of it, but, a lot of it. And it's all they play at the school dances now, anyway, as if no one is white anymore. So, anyway, then suddenly Mandy's all in good with Shanequa, instead of like earlier in the week when Shanequa knew that Mandy took one of her tampons without asking and was going to get her back? And now it's all like 'Claire said this' and 'Claire said that' and all I want is my Oh Shit earrings back."

"What?" asked Alan.

"Those are my earrings. That's what my earrings say."

"Your earrings talk?"

"No…they…you're not even listening! The earrings have the words 'Oh Shit!' like in gold 14 karat, I dunno, something karat gold."

"Is it like on a design or something?"

"No. It's just the words…I don't believe this, what century do you live in? It's just the words 'Oh Shit!'. So Debbie's downstairs having a canary, now she's 'warning' me, to get down to dinner right away? And, number one, I'm not gonna eat because I'm dieting. Number two, it's Shanequa's turn to cook and—again, nothing against blacks—but she has to be the world's shittiest cook. I mean, she made these Pillsbury Chocolate Chip cookies once where you just cut it into slices and heat 'em up? Only she used Grand Union brand. And sometimes like the edges get burnt? But the whole thing she did was like you dropped a nuclear bomb on it or something? Like it was so wrecked you couldn't eat one? But when I said, 'Let's throw them away,' Donna, who was on duty that day, says, 'Stop starting with her!' like, again, singling me out? When every girl in the house was practically gagging and throwing up because of those cookies, which were supposed to be our 'snack,' so I finally screamed down to them to mind their business—or mind their f'ing business, I might have said—but I said the word 'f', not 'fuck' or 'frig' even, and I get grounded for a week, no calls, no t.v. for 'insubordination.' Like I care!"

Alan looked at her, face flushed, her knee bopping up and down in the air as her leg bounced against the ground, the rage barely contained.

"Like they're my mother? Well, they're not! And I'm getting out of that place if I have to run away. The only reason I'm staying there—and I swear to you, this is the only reason—because I could run away and I have several jobs waiting for me, and places I could live—is because there's this new guy at school who really likes me who knows I live in the Group Home, and I'm not gonna jeopardize that just so those squids can have a good laugh at my expense."

Tears were flowing now.

"Because, as God is my witness, when I get out of that home? I'm going to have a husband, I'm going to start a family, and those dykes and liars at the Group Home aren't gonna know what hit them." Claire sucked back some of the sobbing and held it in her chest. There was a silence. "One day they're going to run into me at The Mall. And I'm going to be there with my family, shopping in the linen department or something. And they're going to be all friendly-faced and expect me to be friendly back. And I'm just going to look through them, turn my head to the cashier, put my nose up in the air and say, 'Charge it.' And you know what?"

Alan shook his head.

"They wouldn't even let me put a sign up on the bulletin board that said, Lost: Claire's "Oh Shit!" Earrings. Please return to the Main Office when found.' You know why?"

Alan shook his head.

"Obscenity. That's not right. I'm sorry, but that misses the whole point of everything."

———•◦•———

Angel wasn't doing as well in his classes as he had first faked. They were getting to the part of the year where they expected you to remember stuff and write it down for them whenever they asked. So far all this town had been good for was making money. He didn't have his girl, he didn't have his baby. This was getting old. The psychologist lady was dogging him, asking him all sorts of stuff about his family, asking him for signatures, so he stopped going to school. He knew he had to go once every twenty-one days, minimum, to avoid being dropped by the district on attendance grounds. Once every few days he'd bring in a forged note, or get one of his drug customers to call in as his "aunt." Most of the times the secretaries just took the message and said, "All right." But the psychologist was getting seriously irritating. As he came to school less, she asked around more.

His girlfriend couldn't have disappeared into thin air. Somewhere out there was Angel, Jr., a tough-ass little motherfucker, dreaming about his Daddy.

They settled on a coffee house which modeled itself after a French bistro. Alan wasn't really sure what a "bistro" was, anyway. From the menu it was clear that you could get all sorts of things that were in between lunch and dinner, along with a selection from the wine list, twenty micro-breweries' beers, coffees, and teas. Neither Bonnie nor Alan seemed to have a feeling for what to order at four in the afternoon. They sat on either side of a small table and sank into deep curvy chairs with cushions which were too soft. The arrangement seemed designed to put you close together looking into each other's eyes, which Alan wanted, but also was afraid was a little too soon and a little too much.

Bonnie ordered raspberry-flavored Belgian beer and the fruit-and-cheese plate. Alan ordered a little-known Pilsner that he remembered from a party in New York City when he was still the husband of a lean, angular, semi-psychotic fashion model. If only people knew how bad it could be with a fashion model: the calorie counting, the tantrums, the expectation that he would understand, accept, and ride through any mood swings she invented any time of the week. He envied friends who told him that their girlfriends got predictably irritable and obnoxious once a month. Of it all he had liked the feeling that, in association with her, they belonged to a certain level of New York City activity. He never believed it was more than being privy to interesting invitations and events, but that was good enough. He guessed there were some who just wanted her tomboyish figure resting against their interior brick-walled living rooms for adornment as the joints were passed and the coke was snorted (this was, after all, the Reagan years), but he knew he was never a part of it. Social workers made poor adornments. And even back then he had been earnestly working to help truly insane-but-medicated adults who graduated from their month-long stays at Metropolitan Psychiatric Center to a confused, wandering existence on the Upper West Side of Manhattan as they shuffled to and from a loosely-structured "day-treatment program" in a building with puke-green walls and stairways that smelled like cigarettes, unwashed body odors, and yesterday's lunch (which, in fact, had been thrown against the wall—again—by a huge client named Darla.) Hey, maybe his wife's friends could set up a shoot in the day-treatment center, with her in one of those ripped halter-top t-shirt things, a boy's haircut, and hip-hugging panties, as they had done a few months before in what looked like a library somewhere in the city. The furor over this was calculated, of course, as it had actually been an abandoned library with a real-life card catalog file, with children used as background props. The free publicity which ensued (from the angriest letters, columns, etc.) had sold tens of thousands of "units" of the ripped t-shirts, not to mention affording tens of thousands of strange men the chance to view his wife in little panties. The arguments he had with her about this were notable for their brevity and lack of intensity. There was no sense arguing if you really were arguing about whether she "didn't mind" stimulating the sexual fantasies of thousands of men in one fell swoop. It was obvious to Alan that she not only desired that, but needed it the way humans needed food. Who would argue with a person not to eat food? She knew what she needed, she pursued it, and she got paid well for it. The only irony was that Alan had reached a point where he couldn't care less what she looked like in her panties and wished only that all the men who did care could spend an actual week living with her and appreciate the actual life of her body: the deprivation of food, the ingestion of mega-vitamins around the clock, the cramping, the stomach upsets, anxieties about impending bloating, water-weight gain, cellulite. When it had gotten to the point where he'd rather look at her in a magazine than sit and talk to her, they both knew it was all over, except for the lawyers' part. He had wished her well, and half-meant it.

It was funny, though, how he was now able to remember the earlier times. Undoing her dress, touching her small breasts, feeling them come alive, tasting her mouth with his tongue, feeling the fluttering beneath his hands, the teasing textures, the urgency, the whimpers of their love making, telling him that this was what she lived for, that this was a place of being together for all time, a place that they would guard and protect and retreat to, forever.

"It's so near, but I've never been here before," said Bonnie.

Alan focused on her face, which had a sweetness to it. He couldn't remember how he had succeeded in conjuring up Bonnie for his late-night Nude Exercise cable t.v. fantasy. She was just…a nice girl.

"My brother came here once with his fiancée."

"Oh. He's married?"

"No. Divorced."

"Oh. So…what do you think of the school, huh?"

"Well…," she said, giggling. "It can get a little bit much."

"The kids nowadays are like.."

"I know," she agreed.

"Not all of them."

"No."

"Even to…"

"I know. A lot of them don't have any respect. When I was a kid we'd fool around and we'd goof on teachers, but we wouldn't talk to them the way they talk to you guys," Bonnie offered.

There was a silence. Alan allowed himself to look at her eyes. They were very pretty. There was a blue that somehow leaned toward dark blue. It suggested a deep part of her which might welcome him like a pool, if only they would both stop talking.

Their beers and cheese plate arrived. They clinked glasses.

"Cheers," she said, giggling again.

"L'Chaim," Alan offered.

"What?"

"It means 'To Life.'"

"Oh, right. You're Jewish?"

"Mmm-hmmm," he said, downing the sharp, almost bitter-tasting brew.

"I had a friend back in school who was Jewish."

"Keep in touch?"

"No. She works for a book publisher in New York City now. She couldn't wait to leave Galesville."

Alan watched her lift a cracker and cheese to her mouth. There was a soft, sleepy sensuality to Bonnie's movements. The food and her mouth met. Alan was mesmerized. She chewed and he sat quietly, appreciating her.

"What?" she asked, giggling a little.

There was a cracker crumb on the lower left side of her upper lip.

"What?" she asked, giggling louder.

———•••———

During summers Father Mark had a reserved Sunday-night, 7:45 table at the Galesville Pizza Hut—something no night manager could later recall having been done for anyone else. Pizza Hut didn't take reservations.

It was for the select members of the group-within-the-Youth-Group. The elite of the Senior Youth Group.

Father Mark was also a familiar "regular" in the Rehoboth Beach, Delaware, Pizza Hut.

Employees of both stores would remember him later as always being with five boys or more, high-school age.

The Senior Youth Group made four retreats that summer.

Brian, Kevin, Erik, Richard, Devin, and Liam—the boys who were with him that summer—made seven trips, total. Their parents were happy that they had been identified as "Future Leaders of the Faith." Also—they had to admit—it gave them a breather to have the boys away.

ALWAYS GOTTA BE JEWS

Ninja Dave got probation for using numchucks in a fight that even the judge had to admit was confusing with a kid from North Bear Haven. Which was totally amazing, because usually only stupid people got probation. What you were always looking for was "Adjournment with Contemplation of Dismissal" pure and simple, which—while technically some kind of probation—meant if you didn't get busted within the next six months you were free with a clean slate. And you didn't have to report to nobody in the meantime. Not only did Ninja Dave get probation, he got community service.

Fat Mike and Carlos didn't know whether to laugh or cry.

"Can you see him serving candy mints and handing out magazines to old people in that rest home over on Wickham?"

Carlos snorted. "Nawwwwwww…he don't gotta do that. Does he?" He was high. "Naw. What I was saying…"

"Oh. Are you saying like…Aw, I get it."

"Naw. You don't gotta do shit like that."

"What do you gotta do?"

"You got to call this guy, right?, and like check in and act mad cheesy, like you're ready to go somewhere or do something and then in this real serious voice he says, 'All right, I'm gonna get back to you. Be ready to serve your hours.' And if you have like thirty hours that you have to do—which is usually what they give you—they'll assign you to, say, I dunno, rake up leaves in front of a church for about four hours on a Saturday and then you can ask the guy to count it as eight because you can say that you finished the whole job which was supposed to last the weekend in one day and the church guy says they don't need you anymore. So what are they gonna do?"

"Yeah, but they check, right?"

"Naw."

"They take your word for it?"

"Not only do they take your word for it, but the next time you do, like, three hours in something the guy automatically counts it as six if you've been not in trouble for other things. But you have to look really serious when they ask you about school and say, 'Naw, I been good!' You have to act very respectful, y'knowwhatI'msayin'?, and offer to do whatever the guy assigns you to. But the trick is that if you offer that, he won't assign you anything. I know kids who got thirty hours who got off doing twelve. What they tell you is to 'Be ready for my call.' Like they expect you to sit around after school and on weekends an inch away from the phone all dressed to go to work, but then they don't call. They just want you waiting for them. It's a power trip. It's a bunch of bullshit."

Carlos nodded. They were both very high now and the words seemed to carry more weight. Almost like an echo.

"What did Ninja Dave do, anyway?"

Fat Mike lit up another joint. With his body weight he could do most of a bag himself, probably, without getting wrecked. That long sucking sound of fresh air and aged herb followed. They looked at each other like old men. Fat Mike exhaled, blowing a sizable haze upward. "Something about assault. Just because he fought back. Some kid from Maplewood who'd been calling him a pussy-wimp at basketball games and at the mall."

Carlos pondered this. "That's an assault? Since when?"

"Well, he had some numchucks in his back pocket. So they were saying that the intent was to really fuck the kid up. Ninja Dave is fifteen and they couldn't prove what he was gonna do with the numchucks really so...he got probation." He passed the joint to Carlos.

"Who's his lawyer?" asked Carlos.

"Some Jew. Lady," said Fat Mike.

"Oh, is she....with straight brown hair and a voice like..." (Carlos pinched his voice and spoke through his nose.) "'Now it'd be in your INTEREST to show the court that you sought out COUNSELING...'" They laughed. After they were done coughing, Carlos said, "SHE'S the fucked-up one."

"Though her body ain't half-bad, y'knowwhatI'msayin'?" volunteered Fat Mike.

"Minus the..."

"Yeah, lose the voice, and..."

"...the attitude."

They tried to imagine this.

"How come it's always gotta be Jews?" asked Carlos.

Fat Mike took another drag. "See...where they came from, Jews, long ago they had laws saying that you had to be a doctor, dentist, or lawyer if you were a Jew."

"They were..."

"Restricted. Yes. To certain professions," Fat Mike said in his most understanding voice.

Carlos considered this.

"And...when they came to this country they built special colleges just for them with every spot in the college saved for Jews. Only after every Jew was accepted into medical, dental, or law school could they legally see if they had any spots left over for regular people. You know N.Y.U.?"

Carlos shook his head.

"New York University. It used to be called 'New York Jew.' NYJ. But when George Bush was elected...the FIRST George Bush...remember 'Desert Storm'?" asked Fat Mike.

It rang a bell but Carlos looked confused. "The game? PlayStation 2?"

"No...you were a little fucker still...anyway, remember when we bombed the shit out of Iraq?"

"Yeah. Kinda."

"Well, their request...I mean, the other guys...the other Arabs, the ones who weren't our fucking enemies then...who we helped....they had ONE request from that war. And that was that in exchange for letting us bomb Iraq the name of New York Jew be changed. You won't find any record of this. If you go look it up now they'll make it like it always had been 'N.Y.U.'"

"How come?"

"Well, who do you think controls these sort of things? Doctors, lawyers...and dentists. Who do you see riding those big Jew-boats on Route 67 on weekends going up to the mountains?" asked Fat Mike.

"Jew-boats?"

"Lincoln Continentals."

"How did you find this out?" asked Carlos.

"My uncle. He worked with this Jewish guy once who escaped from dental school, he said. He had to change his name and relocate just to be allowed to work in a warehouse. They were trying to force him to be an orthodontist," said Fat Mike.

"You're shitting me."

"No."

"He told him this stuff?"

Fat Mike nodded. "And more. He was a really nice guy. He had Giants' season tickets. He told my uncle stuff that would blow your mind."

"Like?"

"Like the men and the women when they go to bed have to have a sheet in between the two of them. Even when they do it."

"What?"

"It's true."

"Well…how can you even do it then?"

"Think about it. It's messy, but you can do it. You ever seen Jewish women shopping at Filene's?"

Carlos wasn't sure.

"Stocking up on the sheets while kind of looking both ways with their eyes and all? Well, what do you think that is all about?" He looked Carlos in the eye. "Eh?"

———

Peter considered the mound of memos on his desk. It was bad when he started to try to estimate its size in feet. He didn't even want to figure out what all the junk said. New mandates were coming down every day and were met with equally numerous complaints from teachers and support staff about everything they were supposed to document. He got tired of hearing himself say, "If it isn't documented, it never happened."

Peter thought back to the freer years, when he was Crisis Intervention Specialist (i.e., bouncer) and able to actually eat lunch. He tried to remember the feeling of lunch filling his belly in a satisfying way, rather than provoking the burn of his ulcer. It was a little like trying to remember the early, sexually frisky days with Patty. He was honestly happy, at first, that she had found a "born-again" belief. Then came the new local congregation to support it. He wouldn't be caught dead going into that church or being associated with those people. He and Patty weren't stupid, and they knew they'd have to talk about it a lot in order to preserve their marriage. But the arguments went badly. In the heat of one of them she actually implied that his ulcer was tied to his non-belief, as if Jesus were Maalox. He thought back to a fad that had caught on with teenagers in the high school about two years ago when a group of eight to ten of them became involved with a charismatic, born-again preacher who lived out in the sticks and who may, or may not, have been sexually involved with a few of them. He resented the simple smiles they radiated. Hell, you shouldn't be smiling at everybody you meet like that. It made it cheaper for when you shared the smile with someone you knew. He hated that look they got when they got their Jesus-nectar, "seeing everything so clearly." He much preferred them as the obnoxious pains-in-the-ass they were previously. At least that didn't resemble a George Sanders science-fiction movie.

Mona buzzed him to announce the arrival of Dolores, the school psychologist. He really dreaded conferences with Dolores, for she was never content to just make the damn recommendations and leave it at that. Though his own wife would annoy him with her sanctity sometimes, that was nothing compared to the fervor of this psychologist's nutty beliefs about food. He'd given up trying to talk to her about it and actually found the quickest way to end the meeting was to let her talk about it for a minute and then have Mona buzz him (by prior arrangement) with an imaginary parent phone call. Somehow the shrink had gotten wind of his ulcer and advised him, a year ago, of what foods to cut out of his diet to cure it. She thought nothing of making comments about other people's insides and bodily occurrences and he truly hated her for it. Knowing this, he had attempted (for the last three years, anyway) to go out of his way to be civil to her. Not only was Dolores on time today, she was never sick. Mona told him that she had approximately 278 sick days accrued and his guess was that she would never use them before her retirement. Not that she would ever retire.

"Come on in, Dolores," he bellowed in his "up" voice. "Whatchya got?"

"Hello, Peter. How are you feeling these days?"

"Fine, fine. So what do we have? Is this about the Rivera kid?"

"Peter, I'm very concerned."

"Um-huhh."

"This kid is going to blow."

"Ahhh-huhhh."

"He's sick. He could benefit from outside therapy, he thrives on power struggles, and he has intense rage toward women," said Dolores.

"Um-huhh, um-huhh. Well…what do you propose we do?"

"I'd like to see him tested for nutritional deficiencies, for a start."

"Yeah…"

"And then teamed up with someone who can provide some real limits and boundaries."

"Um-huhh….you got anyone in mind?"

"Well, no. That's your job."

He wanted to slap her across the face. "Let me see what I can do, Dolores. I appreciate the feedback. Uh, you gonna recommend we classify him?"

"Well, yes."

"Okay, put him on the calendar for next month. Notify the parents and the C.S.E."

"We're having problems contacting the parent."

"Well, if you have to make a home visit, make a home visit, Dolores. Just tell Mona when you're going."

Dolores' face reddened. "You know by contract we don't do that. That's what the social workers are supposed to be for."

"Fine. Set it up with Mitchke."

"How about if you set it up with Mitchke? I'm not sure he'd accept it coming from me."

"However it happens, as long as it happens. Just mention it to him, tell him I'll be talking to him about it. Oh, and Dolores," he said as she was leaving, "why don't you mention the nutritional testing to him, too."

"I intend to."

"Good. He's a good man. He'll understand what needs to be done."

———

Late. This would make him late. Alan had been dreaming, and this would make him late for his coffee, late for mailing the bills, late for the bagel, late when he ran his car over two dead squirrels (carefully positioning them between the wheels), late when he started crossing the mountain, late when the first bite of bagel hit his stomach, late to see the two people in the Stratus in front of him arguing (at 6:37 a.m.?) and looking like they were going to hit each other, late listening to the latest Al Qaeda threat on the radio ("an act of unrivaled spectacular devastation...rivers of tears" by this weekend), late listening to the disc jockey's promise to reveal "the secret on how to wipe correctly with three different toilet papers…after our 7 a.m. newsbreak…," and late pulling into the parking lot. Once you were late, there was no way to make it up.

The wild-eyed, disheveled mother and her slightly vicious-looking son were not late. They had been waiting for him for fifteen minutes in Peter's office. Peter was clearly annoyed. He didn't like parents waiting in his office for any member of his staff who was late without calling. Alan mumbled some half-expressed apology and they walked out of Peter's office together, into the main reception area.

Alan imagined there were a lot worse jobs than this, where he would have shown up fifteen minutes late and gotten called a "shithead," or given extra physical work to do, docked pay, etc.…

Alan had forgotten completely about Bonnie, but here she was, looking twice as cute as she had last week. (Where was Mona?) He didn't know how she could look twice as cute. Wasn't there a limit on cuteness? Bonnie was staring at him as the mother lit into him.

"I started thinking…you were supposed to be here at 7:15."

"Yes, well, I…"

"My son was supposed to have started school here last week."

"Well, Mrs.…"

"Don't 'Mrs.' me! It's already past 7:15. You're late. Everyone is late. I want him in school. The judge said he has to be in school. I don't want him on the streets!"

"We all want him to…"

"He should have been here at the beginning of the school year."

"Well, I did come in. In August, remember, for the interview with him, but you didn't bring him. Remember when you just showed up yourself?" Alan asked.

"Don't start with me," the woman threatened.

"Look, they said he was in need of counseling services. I had to interview him. And I told you that in advance. On the phone."

"I think YOU'RE the one 'in need of counseling services'! Why couldn't he start school without 'counseling services'?" asked the woman with the flushing red face.

"You have to ask your old district that. And his probation officer." Alan felt himself getting pretty tight and thought he heard himself starting to sound like a jerk. "Can we just go to my office…"

"No, I need to know if you're going to start him here today or not. Because, let me tell you something, if he gets shot on the streets of Galesville, or Deep Lake, I'm going to see to it that YOU get shot."

"What?"

"I said, I'm going to see to it that…that you…have…that you lose your job. We pay you people good money and all you do is not show up when you're supposed to," the woman said.

Alan was aware of Bonnie rustling papers. This was completely stupid and embarrassing. Kids were walking in the office now.

"Gepner, Alison," said the pretty girl to Bonnie. "You called me down?"

"Yes, your mom dropped off your lunch. You forgot it."

"Thank you," said the girl, smiling. She took her lunch bag and disappeared down the hallway.

Alan wanted to work with kids like that. Maybe his alarm clock would go off in a few minutes and he would awake from this startling dream to wander downstairs to find French toast with a slice of orange on it and an interesting article about spirituality and sex. Instead, the parent continued.

"The judge said he's going to lock him up and send him away in thirty days unless he's in school and today is twenty-eight days," said the mother.

"Look, I just got the re-referral last week," Alan said.

"I want him in school today!!"

Peter came out of his office and looked at Alan as if Alan were the delivery boy from a deli who had just brought botulism-and-cheese sandwiches.

"I'm going to my office now. I hope you'll follow me," Alan said, ducking around the corner.

He hoped they wouldn't.

PUNCTURED

Richie, Richie's cousin Jason, and the black kid called Sham-Guard were waiting in front of Burger King near the "No Loitering" sign. They were supposed to meet LeShaun, a six-foot-three friend of Sham-Guard's who was coming up from the city on Bus #89 with fifty-five vials of crack, twelve ounces of pot, and a hundred stamps of lickable acid. Richie looked in all the windows of the cars as they pulled up to the drive-thru, waving at kids he knew from school. Sham-Guard didn't think that was too slick.

"Yo...why you acting the fool?"

"Doin' what?"

"That's stupid, man."

"What?"

"That waving shit...we gotta job to do. You wanna do it?"

"Yeah, I wanna do it."

"Then stand here and do it. Look cool."

Richie thought he <u>had</u> been looking cool.

Jason spoke up. "You, why you doggin' him?"

"Naah, naah, naah, that ain't how it is. See, we're standing here...in Potatoville...every five minutes a cop car with Mayberry R.F.D. plates and Gomer Pyle-style crackers drives past, and Richie be waving to them, smilin' and shit. I want LeShaun, man."

"What if he don't got the stuff?" asked Jason.

"He got the stuff. He got the stuff."

"How you know him?"

"I know him from Kwami. Kwami is blood."

"How do you know LeShaun isn't a cop?"

"Haah." Sham-Guard busted out laughing. "How do I know you ain't a punk?"

"Fuck you," said Richie.

"Hey, hey, hey!" A cop car drove past. They looked down at their shoes, then looked up around the sky.

"Let me tell you somethin' about the cops in this town," Jason said. "You ain't gotta worry about nothin'…They don't want to catch nothing, they don't want to make no busts. They want to think we're here for the Have-It-Your-Way-Chicken-Special and leave it at that."

"Yo, well, they look like rednecks to me," Sham-Guard said.

"Well, they are rednecks, but they're lazy fat-fuck rednecks," declared Jason.

"They still racist, though."

"So? What's your point? You're with *us*, right?"

"Yeah. But you a cracker, too," said Sham-Guard, smiling broadly.

"I know five kids who got jumped, got fucked up the day before yesterday in Centertown because they were white," insisted Jason.

"I don't think so," said Sham-Guard. "Probably shootin' off their mouths. Flapping their lips, 'nigger' this, 'nigger' that…probably got what they had coming to them."

Richie saw a blue Taurus drive through with Alison and some other stuck-up kids from his grade in it. If the wrong people showed up now the whole deal could be blown. Even he knew that. Everyone was edgy.

"It's after five, man. He's not coming. The dude's not coming," said Jason.

Sham-Guard looked at Richie. "He's coming on a bus, stupid. The bus ain't here yet."

Jason jumped forward. "Who you callin' stupid?"

"Get the fuck outta my face!" said Sham-Guard.

"I'll stay right here and say it to your face. Whatchoo gonna do? You gonna take me down? Right here? Nigger."

Sham-Guard looked at Jason in a whole new way.

"The fuck's your problem?" Jason's words seemed frozen in space.

Sham-Guard pushed him away with both hands, as hard as he could. Jason fell, slamming onto his back. People were now watching. Richie threw himself forward, punching with both hands, missing more than he was hitting, before getting thrown off, too. Now on his feet Jason charged forward, screaming, "Why you fucking with me?"

Jason didn't see a knife, but felt two sharp punctures, like muffled explosions, in his chest. He fell forward and whimpered.

"Oh, shit!" said Richie, rolling his cousin over onto his side. "What'd you do? What'd you do, man?" He looked up at Sham-Guard's face. There was a mask. It wasn't the Sham-Guard he had known.

Jason was sputtering something. Blood pumped steadily onto the Burger King parking lot's black pavement. Jason's eyes fixed on Sham-Guard. "I thought we were friends."

Jason died before any of them could think of anything to say.

It took four minutes for the police to get the call from Burger King. Sham-Guard was three-quarters of a mile away, in a shed in someone's backyard, when they arrested him.

Bus #89 pulled up about twenty minutes late. LeShaun looked out the window, saw his man was gone and a pool of blood was where he ought to have been. He stayed on the bus.

There were other towns.

———•———

Hadleyville Falls was in an uproar.

The county's newspaper's lead headline the next morning was: "Midday Murder on Main Street." There was a page-three story, with a sidebar profile on "Kids Who Kill," and an accompanying article trying to describe the maze of programs, placements, foster homes, and probations which resulted in Sham-Guard living in town.

Ronald put the paper down in disgust and snorted. Maybe now that nice white children were getting murdered by niggers at Burger King people would take some action. He recalled the last mailing he had received from Gunther Haupt and The Invisible Empire: "Every crisis is an opportunity," it had advised. Ronald wasn't much of an organizer, or talker, really. But if this didn't mobilize people, nothing would. Hell, you weren't even safe from armed niggers while buying a Whopper anymore. He knew the only proper memorial to this white kid was revenge. Until then wooden crosses would have to do.

Claire had a friend named Zach. Ronald would ask him for some help. The kid knew how to walk the talk.

At sunrise the next morning, travelers on Route 27 saw— silhouetted against the rising sun heading towards the city— three sixteen-foot crosses, standing tall and proud on a glistening hill.

———•———

The eighth time Danielle and Angel "made love"—her words, not his—she wanted to talk.

Danielle wasn't doing too well in school. How had her grades actually fallen from a 23 in math to a 14 in the second quarter, when she had stayed after school once for extra help? They had given her a choice between seeing Mitchke—eeewwwwww, the pathetic guy who wore the same khakis over and over again, probably still from the eighties—or the school psychologist. At least SHE wore some colors and patterns. What a choice, though. Hanging or poison. She had HATED counseling, ever since she went when she was five and everyone tried to blame everything on her. The counselor, or therapist, or doctor, or whatever, took their side and said she was a "behavior problem," and her mother nodded her head up and down like she was an audience member in a Springer show where they bring out kids for "My Daughter Dresses Like a Boy Just to Upset Me" and the audience hoots and howls and would probably kill the kid if they could, except that Jerry, you can tell, understands both sides and that's why he is as popular as he is, which is more than she can say about those other bitches on t.v., or that old perv, Montel.

Angel gazed at her nude body as she talked. Her breasts swayed some as she gestured with her hands. He might just have to do her again.

"Do you know what I'm talking about?"

"Mmmm-huh."

"Cause I have a feeling you're just staring at my tits."

"No…"

"You pig!" She slapped him, laughing. He caught her hand before a second slap, grabbed her, kissed her mouth, then shoved her down toward his lap. She broke free, slapped him again and continued talking. "So…not only did I have to see her, I had to see her every week—which isn't bad because it gets me out of class, plus I can take as long as I want walking there and walking back—she never asks—BUT she put me in this group, too."

"What kind of group?"

"Self-Esteem Group. Like I have any problems with self-esteem! Like I'm a friggin' mouse or something. Me?! I mean, look at me!"

Angel lowered his head, came close to her chest, and took a long stare, three inches from her nipples.

"No! You hard-on! Not my tits, at ME?!! How do you say 'perverted pig' in Spanish?"

Angel started taking little licks with his tongue in the direction of her nipples.

"So, do you want to know what the group is about? Or do you want to leave? I'm serious: I'm getting pissed. Either you listen to me or you leave."

Angel calculated that being forced to leave would definitely lower his chances of getting laid again to zero percent. He sat up. "Okay, okay, I'm being serious. I want to hear. For real."

"Okay. The group isn't half-bad, except for Tina, who dominates it sometimes by not shutting up about all the bad things that SUPPOSEDLY happened to her when she was little which is, like, YAWN, OKAY, BORE ME SOME MORE after the first fifty times. Not that I'm not sympathetic or apologizing for what happened to her, because what's wrong is wrong, but what are we supposed to do about it anyway? When we're supposed to be talking about ways that guys give us shit and how we used to just take it and now we don't because we're changing."

"Mmmm-huh."

"You think this is all bullshit, don't you?"

"Me? No. But that lady been doggin' me, yo. No way I'm going into no group."

"Like you don't have any problems?"

"Not when you're giving up the booty!!"

They laughed and Danielle threw a pillow at his crotch.

"What's the 4-1-1 on her?"

"Like...?"

"I dunno. Stuff so I can mess with her head."

"No. She's cool after you get to know her. So you don't have to mess with her head. But she does go crazy about FOOD."

"Food?"

"Yeah. Ohmygod, 'Don't eat this, eat that, avoid food colorings, artificial flavors, etc.'..."

"What does that have to do with anything?"

"Right, I know. Thank you. Allergies...junk like that."

"But...?"

"Yuh. That's her thing. She thinks it's why we behave the way we do."

"You're kidding."

"No."

They both considered this.

"And they pay her for that?"

"I guess so. She's got a Volvo."

"Oh, well...look what I've got," Angel offered, pulling the pillow away and dropping his boxers.

"You ARE disgusting!" Danielle said, crawling toward him.

"And you love it," Angel said, his final word getting muffled by her mouth as she pinned him, hard, pressing every inch of the front of her body against his.

CURRICULA

Bobby and his cousin had chosen a night when the new moon left them under the cloak of darkness. They rode their bikes over four miles to get there. Their backpacks were full. Two paintbrushes, a half-gallon of bright-orange paint, a bunch of rags, and two berry-flavored Gatorades rounded out their supplies.

The two boys, hired by Zach, ditched their low-rider bikes at the house on the corner. It was 2:00 a.m. Creeping close to the hedges they inched forward, until they could see the sign on the small building across the street:

"TEMPLE BETH JACOB—President, Bernard Schein; Rabbi, Joseph Tennenbaum; Sabbath Eve. Services 8 p.m. Fridays—All welcome"

It was the only one in a three-town radius. It was the temple the Gepners, and Alison's friend, Robin, attended.

The boys looked both ways then skittered across the street. They ran to the side of the building under the cover of trees.

"Let's go...c'mon. Pop it open," one of them said, unloading the other boy's backpack.

"Yeah. Um, you got an opener or something?"

"What? Are you kidding me?"

"No. Don't you have a Swiss army knife?"

"Why the fuck would I have one of them?"

"For times like this."

"Fuck no. You have something?"

"Like what?"

"I dunno. A screwdriver?"

"No."

"How bout a quarter? You have one of them?"

"Wait…No. I have a dime."

"You're a fuckin' idiot, you know that? Do you how much time it takes to open that with a dime?"

"How about you, retard-boy? Did you think to bring anything?"

"Just open the can."

"I told you to buy spray paint."

"They'll be looking for someone who bought spray paint. That's why we bought this."

"Well maybe there is a fucking reason that people USE spray paint."

"If you want to get caught, be my guest. It's a little late now to question the plan."

"Is it opening?"

"A little."

Both boys got $45 from Zach, plus expenses, if they kept the receipt. Zach kept $55 additional of Ronald's money for himself. Ronald financed the enterprise by raiding the waist-high container of loose change that Claire's mother had been saving for a cross-country trip for all of them someday. He'd pay her back after he sold a few more of Gunther's books.

"You got the receipt from Home Depot, right?"

"Yuh."

"Make sure you give it to him on Monday."

"How about we get this done first?"

"Is it open?"

"Yuh. Dip in."

They finished quietly, then wrapped the brushes in their rags, careful to not get any on their clothes. They found their bikes and took off.

The next morning neighbors awoke to the two-foot-high messages on the front and sides of the Temple: "WE LIKE NIGERS," "JEWS GO HOME," and "WELCOME NIGERS."

The spelling error became a point of contention when Zach told them he shouldn't really reimburse for the paint because they'd spelled it wrong. "Stupidity has its price," he said. Bobby did truly resemble an acned, rat-faced weasel. After consulting with Ronald—who was exceptionally pleased—Zach gave in. It was an "investment," Ronald told him.

The crowd at the school board meeting was much larger than anyone had expected. The adults at the "Speaker's Dais" threw themselves into it, as if they weren't intimidated.

Nobody could believe that the skinny lady with the pointy noise and the cashmere sweater was talking about "cholesterol, blood sugar, and Syndrome X...insulin resistance" when a district kid had just been stabbed to death in broad daylight a few days before by another kid who, as best as they could tell, didn't have any feelings about it. It was beyond ridiculous.

From Dolores' point of view—as the new Committee Chairperson—the timing of the first open session of the Committee to Revise Health Curriculum was unfortunate. The school budget for next year had just been proposed and the crowd didn't look happy. She was trying to address their concerns. If they would only listen. Alan Mitchke leaned over to her and whispered, "I think you ought to let them speak."

"They're going to run away from the topic," Dolores whispered back. "The topic is the revision of the Health curriculum." Mitchke gave her arm a little squeeze and repeated, "I think you ought to let them speak. Lose the food lecture for now."

Dolores was embarrassed and enraged. Breathing deeply, removing her reading glasses, and setting her notes aside, Dolores spoke into the microphone, "Why don't we open it up to you for some comments from the floor at this point?"

Bill Kowalczik approached the microphone as purposefully as his recent hip-replacement surgery allowed him. He removed his John Deere cap as he began speaking and ran his right hand slowly over his balding head, patting down the few remaining strands of gray hairs. "Now let me get this straight. Not only do you want to raise the budget for the school upwards of one million four hundred and fifty thousand dollars for next year to do the same thing you all did this year, giving yourselves another round of big raises to boot, but now you're going to sit here and tell us we need to teach more of what fatty foods not to eat instead of teaching our kids how they're not supposed to kill each other? How 'bout the Ten Commandments? You ever consider them? For your 'curricula'?" (Applause broke out here.) "It's not very hard to understand. You don't need a Master's degree. All you've got to do is take out a piece of chalk—hell, I'll pay for the chalk myself, I'll BUY YOU THE CHALK!—and write the Ten Commandments on the board, maybe have the kids copy it over a few thousand times and discuss it. What do you think of that?"

Bill veered away from the microphone to return to his seat. Then he changed his mind and veered back. "Oh, and one more thing...you can forget about the raises. I don't know how much you're slated for in this next go-round, lady, but I'll vote 'No' and keep voting 'No' until my finger falls off before I give you people a raise for what you've been doing." (The applause was now thunderous and appeared to egg him on further.) "How much are you supposed to get for a raise in next year's budget, lady?" he asked again. He turned away and hobbled back to his seat.

Dolores opened her mouth and then closed it. She opened it again and started sputtering but was drowned out by the second person who started speaking.

"My name is Mary Dumont, and I've got three children who go here, ages twelve, fourteen, and sixteen, and I think it's time you stop teaching them about sex and how to make more babies. We've got babies having babies now. You should start teaching them some values."

Alan leaned toward the Committee microphone and said, "That's why we're interested in your thoughts about..." but no one heard him. A burly guy, Phil Zenrick, grabbed the mike.

Phil ticked off a list with his fingers. "Number one: You tell us you can't start off a school day with a simple prayer. Number two: You tell us that teachers who don't even know what they believe in are going to teach our kids about what they should believe. Number three: You let hoodlums and kids carrying weapons from the city into our schools and you don't do a damn thing about it until it is too late. I can tell you right here, right now, what I want you teaching in that 'values' class: *Nothing*. Got it? I'll teach my kids their values, and you teach the kids reading, writing, and arithmetic. Got it? If I want them having a condom, I'll give it to them. Just teach them what they need to do to get a job, please?! Is that too much to ask? In exchange for millions of our dollars? Oh, and another thing: I didn't get a raise last year. I'm a farmer, you see. No one comes around and says, 'Gee, Farmer Phil, you've been farming twenty-seven years now, that makes you a Step Twenty-Seven, so we'll give you more money than when you were a Step Twenty-Six Farmer, plus, let's see, how 'bout an across-the-board three or four percent just for still being here and, by the way, have you taken any courses on Theory of How Cows Make Milk so we can reimburse you with a raise for that, too? No, they don't say that. What they say is, 'Have you worked from five-o'clock in the morning to eight-thirty at night? And what do you have to show us for it?' And—you see—I have to work maybe fifty-one weeks a year instead of the thirty-one, thirty-two that teachers work. By the time you teachers are pulling into the high school building for your coffee and donuts in the morning, I've been up, working, for two, two-and-a-half hours. By the time you go home at the 'end of the day' I'm just having lunch before the second part of my day starts." (The audience was now applauding and cheering, even while Phil was speaking. He spoke louder to finish his thoughts.) "So if you take that seventy-five, eighty-thousand dollars a year that you all say isn't good enough for next year and you consider that it's for nine months work, part-time, because you're home by three, I'd say you're looking at a real equivalent of ninety, ninety-five, a hundred-thousand full-time dollars that's not good enough for you. And that's without an increase. My suggestion to you..." (The crowd was roaring now; Phil had to shout even louder.) "My suggestion to you is...if you can't get by on that, that you find yourself another bunch of kids to educate, because we are tapped out and we are just not going to give you any more. When it gets to the point where I can't even afford to shop in town for my clothes and have to outfit my whole family in leftovers at Sam's Club and watch all of you driving up to the high school in Volvos, Acuras, and Audis with little Nantucket flags on the bumpers from your summer vacations. I'm just not going to do it anymore. You can call me a farmer, you can laugh at me behind my back, or in front of me, you can call me whatever you want, but I work harder than you, and I'll be damned if I give you the last pennies out of my pocket."

———•———

Meeting in the Acropolis Diner felt strange. Nicole looked across the formica table to see the tired and sad-looking eyes of her building principal as he struggled to not talk about school. Or maybe he was struggling to talk about school. Either way, he was struggling.

Nicole looked at the design of the table-top, the deep swirls of chocolate color radiating outward in a Milky Way spiral, like syrup before it becomes part of chocolate milk.

Peter's tie was loosened, and he was leaning on his elbows. The light of the afternoon streamed in from the front window, hitting him at an angle that covered half of his face in a gray shadow, leaving the other half standing out more vibrantly than she was accustomed to seeing.

"...the mandates from Albany come down, and we barely have a chance to respond to them before they've changed again, let alone give us time to appeal the original ones. These are not the same kind of kids that we had ten years ago, or even five..."

Nicole looked at him, trying to figure out what he wanted. These after-hours-'work'-meetings-with-the-married-boss-whose-wife-didn't-understand-him, much to her regret, were not new to her.

"Sometimes I wonder..." His voice choked off as his throat muscles tightened. He didn't finish.

"You wonder?"

He sipped his vodka-tonic. Nicole had never gotten used to drinking alcohol in a diner. She played with her ginger ale.

"Yeah. Whether what we're doing makes any sense in the big picture of things."

A sizable silence followed.

"I mean we provide, give, share, instruct...and what's the difference? Things still fall apart, deteriorate, quickly become ineffective. Kids take everything they're given for granted. They turn around and degrade each other, for amusement's sake...'As flies to wanton boys are we to the gods. They kill us for their sport.'"

"I don't know, Peter. I have some pretty good days with the kids."

"Doing what?"

"Art."

"Well...yeah. That's fine. I mean, good thing. But, uh, there's more to life than art."

"Thanks a lot."

"No, I didn't mean...I mean, maybe if everybody had your approach, I dunno...I'm sorry that I didn't have the chance to observe you yet. The date came and went and...I know I was supposed to sit in last Thursday, but there was the whole thing with the school nurse and the kid on the playground who clubbed a bat to death, and the rabies question..."

"It's okay...."

"I will get around to it, though."

"It's okay."

"I saw the little exhibit up in the hallways of the, uh, African mask-things the kids did. Very nice."

"Yeah. We've got some really creative kids here."

"And a good teacher."

"Thanks. So...can I ask why you called?"

"Yeah. Names were just circulating in my head for Team Teacher Leaders, and I thought it'd be good to go with a couple of people whom everyone could get along with well."

"Uh-huh."

"And I thought of you."

"Thanks. Isn't that supposed to be a seniority thing, though?"

"No, the union backed away from any deal on the situation in the last contract, so I have discretion."

That was ridiculous. It would create havoc in her own department. Nicole sipped her ginger ale and looked at him. Peter was looking down. He looked even sadder than before. His eyes lifted up and made contact. Almost twenty years and a few worlds separated them.

"You don't have to give me an answer right now, today, if you want to think about it."

Nicole wondered what had ever happened to those little mini-jukebox things they used to have in the booths at diners in the past, where you punched in a letter and a number and music came up. She needed music but couldn't think what she would play that Peter and she could both listen to. Coldplay? The Carpenters?

"Will you think about it?"

"Is there anything else I should know? I don't remember the expectations for it."

"Well…it's a little bit more time, but there'll be a stipend. And a couple of update meetings to keep me informed."

"With all the Team Teacher Leaders together?"

"Well that would be ideal, but I don't know what people's schedules allow for, so it might be individual."

She took a big sip and let it wet the back of her throat before she talked. "I'll really have to think about it. I'm not sure how much time I have available, Peter. I'm very flattered, though. It's just that private time is one of the most important things. You know?"

"I understand."

"I'm not saying 'no.'"

"I understand."

———•◦•———

Father Mark's "Leaders of the Faith" outdoor midnight Mass had only eight elite members of the Senior Youth Group in it that May 5th. Because it was held at a private campground generously donated for the purpose in an arrangement with the diocese that ministered to Delaware, the local leadership had left Father Mark to his own devices.

Liam and Erik were standing tall, each holding an end of the table with the wine and wafers on it. They were nude, beneath their robes. They were well-oiled with the "Deep Woodlands Off" spray Father Mark had slowly spread over their legs, backs, and chests while saying a blessing to keep the mosquitoes away.

Kevin, clad only in the "initiation loincloth," stood quietly behind Father Mark, holding the cup at chest level. Brian, Kevin, Erik, Richard, Devin, and Liam—having already completed their contribution to the service—formed a semi-circle around Father Mark as he offered prayers in English and Latin. The purple robes they wore had obviously been designed for the occasion; once the top was delicately tied around their necks the robes fell completely open in the front, the material falling by their sides and cascading down behind them.

Kevin stepped forward and Father Mark took the cup from him. As Father Mark brought the cup down below Kevin's waist, touched his penis, and began massaging it firmly, three agents of the F.B.I., four Delaware State Policemen, three cameramen, and six members of the Mid-Atlantic Regional Sex-Abuse Task Force stepped out of the darkness, screaming. The area was flooded with intense light as Father Mark was shoved out of the way, twisted around, and handcuffed.

"No one move!! Your rights will be read to you shortly. Are you Father Mark O'Connell?"

Father Mark was speechless. Blankets were thrown over the boys.

State Police took the chalice into custody, immediately putting it into a tight jar. Wearing gloves, they immediately cordoned off the area and began a sweep for more physical evidence. A nearby garbage pail had eight semen-stained Kleenexes taken in for analysis.

"Are you Mark O'Connell?"

"Yes."

"You are under arrest. Resist us at your own risk, Father."

"Smile for the camera, Father!" said one of the cameramen. The video camera's red "record" light temporarily off, the cameraman continued. "This ain't no Fox Special, Father, and I don't think you'd survive the cut for American Idol, but your lawyer will sure want to see the last forty-five minutes of our program. Anything you want to say to the judge, you diseased reptile? Want to thank the Academy, that sort of thing, motherfucker? Want to say anything to their parents, you piece of mucous?" The red recording light went back on.

"I have permission slips in my car," Father Mark mumbled. "For the retreat."

He did.

When the team of officers searched the motel room where he was staying they also confiscated five empty bottles of Absolut vodka, six all-male pornographic videotapes, a pack of seventy-two unused condoms, a carton of Marlboros, twenty-eight empty Molson bottles, and eight Bibles.

LIGHTNING'S SON

Alison knew that this was THE moment. She had been absent for three days with the flu. Chills, fever, aches, delirium (she could have sworn the Springer show on Tuesday was "My Lesbian Slut Daughter Slept With My Husband's Bisexual Secretary"—wait; had she combined Tuesday and Wednesday's shows into one?)—and—best of all—she now needed three days worth of notes from math class. Elijah was in Math class. She already had his telephone number from three weeks ago. Robin had made some quiet inquiries on her behalf from one of the few guys who seemed to talk to Elijah after school. (She did let it slip, however, that it was for Alison, not her.)

Alison was about to dial his number. His number seemed so...centered. 277-2107. It was so...seven-y. Seven was a good number. It represented...something. Maybe there was something in the I-Ching about seven. The first four digits added up to 18, which in Judaism stood for "Chai," or Life. The 2, of course, standing for romantic partnership. The number really went with him well. She could see him as a 2107. The 277 part was like a grace note.

He walked with grace, but he was not, like, gay. There was no way he was a ninth grader, but he was.

He was the hottest guy in the school.

He wasn't from around this place. He was born in Paradise, probably. His mother was a Waterfall and his father was Lightning. He spent his early years in a loincloth.

She dialed.

Panthers were his friends.

"Hello?"

(Oh God, a girl.) "Umm…This is Alison Gepner, from Elijah's math class…is Elijah there please?"

"Just a second…ELIJAH! ELIJAH!! For you…"

"Hello?"

His voice stirred something in her belly.

"Umm, Elijah?"

"Yeah?"

"Umm, this is Alison Gepner, from your math class?"

"Oh…hi, Alison. You've been out, right?"

(Oh my God, my God, MY GOD HE NOTICED!) "Mmm, yeah."

"Are you okay?"

"Yeah, just home barfing. The usual." (That was REALLY STUPID; now he's going to picture me with puke coming out of my mouth. NICE JOB, Alison, REAL NICE!)

"Oh, I'm sorry."

(Oh my God, he's SORRY…..that is SO COOL!)

Alison forgot to say anything.

"So…ummm, you called?"

"Oh, yeah. Duh. I'm sorry."

"That's okay."

He is so UNDERSTANDING. She'd be able to talk to him for hours. They just seemed so much alike.

There was another silence. "So…is now not a good time to talk? Sounded like you had someone over…" (This was BOLD. And probably stupid. But…who WAS the girl?)

"No, it's fine. That was my sister."

(YES!) "Oh…because I am, like, REALLY behind in math now. I was doing okay up to polynomials and, three days out, I am going to need not just the notes, but sort of a

133

review of what I missed." She knew his grades were in the low nineties.

"No problem. You didn't miss much. Went over the quiz. Tuesday had a fire drill, wasted half the class. Wednesday was a little new…"

"I'm guessing you're really busy…"

"No, it's okay. When do you want to get together?"

This was excellent. The way he said "get together" sounded like he was talking about math, but WASN'T talking about math. Like he knew. They were speaking in some sort of code about stupid Math things while the whole time the Buddhist Wheel of Life was turning and they were on it and they were acknowledging it for the first time with words even though they had known it for a few lifetimes, a few karmas, several incarnations of passion and knowledge and wisdom. What was it that Carl Sagan said on that tape from science class? "We are made of star-stuff…"

Alison and Elijah. She wrote "A & E" on a piece of paper in front of her and drew a heart around it. It bothered her that it was also the name of a cable network.

"Hello? Are you still there?"

"Umm, yeah."

"Do you want to get together?"

"Yes."

"What about two-thirty tomorrow? Could you get permission to walk home? I could."

"We could walk to my house," Alison offered.

"Sounds good to me."

"Okay….good. And…thanks."

"No problem. See you tomorrow."

"See you, too."

"Bye."

"Bye."

134

God, why did she say, "See you, too"? She flipped over onto her back. Elijah was coming to her house. Tomorrow.

She looked at her closet. She prayed. Something in there must be right to wear, or she would scream.

———··———

Dolores had done as brilliant a job at shooting herself in the heart at the public meeting as Peter could've ever devised. It had enabled him to listen patiently to the concerns of the superintendent, who called him the next morning to express concern about how out-of-touch certain members of his staff seemed to the sensitivities of the community and to receive authorization from the superintendent to meet privately with any members of the staff whom Peter felt could use some improvement in the area of working cooperatively with parents in the community. A summary of their improvement, or non-improvement, in their demonstrated abilities to form alliances for the common educational good with parents should be put in their personnel record once it was completed. School psychologists weren't in the union, so Dolores was fair game.

The superintendent of the Hadleyville Falls Union Free School District, Elliot Greene, was six-foot-two, with weathered skin, ever-present crow's eyes, and hair that was still dark brown. He asked Peter where Dolores had come from, for how many years she had been on their payroll, and how much she earned.

Peter had, of course, the numbers handy, but it was more effective to promise to "get back" to Elliot on this (just to add to the gravity of the situation through the mechanics of a second call). When he did, he tried to use his best "shocked" voice. "I dunno, Elliot...with the courses she's evidently taken over the years she's been here and, um, cost-of-living, step-increases, what-have-you…it looks like she's pulling down ninety-six and change." (Peter knew that Elliot, himself, had been the subject of a lot of talk in the community for making upward of one-eighty-five and that he was looking to toss a few high-priced, high-visibility staff members overboard.)

"In other words, we could be getting at least two young staff workers for her position?" Elliot inquired.

"With a big hunk of change back in your pocket."

There was a rather long silence. "Well…let me know how it goes with her on this community-sensitivity stuff."

Peter thought that was a fine idea.

———

Alison had settled on an Indian-print blouse and hip-hugger pants. The pants were something of a gamble. It had taken her the better part of two months to believe that she looked good in them. But she did. She had prescreened her body from all angles.

It was one of those crisp late-spring days that you saw mostly in movies. Five variations of blue were in the sky, with nothing but yellow sun to complement them. It was warmer than she had remembered it since last summer.

Elijah was wearing some sort of madras shirt that was so uncool that it was cool. He had white chinos on, with no belt. She guessed he owned about five different belts. She had noticed each one of them. But this was what Elijah did: he put together "looks" for himself which had nothing in common with anything any of them had seen in *Teen People*, *Seventeen*, or *YM*. She had stopped reading those things anyway.

"Were you really sick?"

"Yuh. A bit. Kind of, actually. Not sick to get worried about, but definitely too pukey for school." Alison immediately regretted the use of the "puke" imagery. ("Again!") "You haven't been out all year, have you?" she asked.

"Not for sickness, no. I was out in December for my uncle's funeral," said Elijah.

"I didn't know that. Why didn't you tell me?"

"We weren't really…talking then, were we?"

"Oh, uh, probably not. But I knew who you were," admitted Alison.

He smiled. "And I was figuring out who you were. But…I didn't talk to anyone about it," said Elijah.

"Were you close to your uncle?"

"He was a good man. He smoked. He was three-packs-a-day for thirty years. Then he quit. Got cancer fifteen years after quitting. He suffered."

You could hear the sounds of their sneakers bending, crunching, and moving forward, carrying the weight of their bodies, the wings of their souls through the world. A dog barked, off in the distance.

"Did you talk to him much? Toward the end?" asked Alison.

"He started going to different places. Not hallucinating, just…leaving to be in different places. Places from his past, places halfway between this world and what comes next."

"What do you think comes next?" she asked swallowing. She knew what she wanted: to be grabbed, held, kissed with intensity.

"I have no idea. I think we are all given a glimpse of it when it is time, nu?"

"What did you say?"

"We are all given a glimpse of it when it is our time," said Elijah.

"Not that. After that."

Elijah looked puzzled.

"Did you say 'nu'?"

"Oh, sorry…it's just a little expression."

"It's a Hebrew expression though, right?" prompted Alison.

"Actually, Yiddish."

"Why did you say it?"

"It's left over from the way I used to speak."

Alison looked at him, not understanding.

"I'm Jewish. I used to go to a yeshiva in the city. I had to leave it. Intellectually I was beginning to go to places that made it too…weird to continue there. Even though we spoke English ninety-five percent of the time. I always liked 'nu.' It just sounds friendly," Elijah said.

"You're Jewish?"

"Yes. Is that okay?"

"Yes. It's very okay," said Alison.

"Why is that?"

"Because I'm Jewish."

They looked at each other in silence.

"Do you like sheds?" asked Alison.

"What do you mean?"

"I know the coolest shed in the world. Do you want to see it?"

"Absolutely," he said.

She offered him her hand. Elijah took it. They walked quietly.

"Do you think you could call your mother and stay for dinner? I'm terrible at math."

Alan was more than a little lonely. The "Sabador Gigante Show" on channel 43 was boring tonight, the handful of gummy bears tasted like petroleum derivative, and the three chocolate-chip cookies made him think about saturated fat. He couldn't remember if he'd had dinner.

The bi-monthly copy of *The Journal of Social Work* had arrived. The cover story was "Empowering Multiply-Handicapped-H.I.V.-Positive-Youth-at-Risk." The second story was a five-year longitudinal study about alcoholic women who beat their children. He turned to the section at the end titled, "Conclusions":

> *"...Though it would appear that the group which received professional Case Management services in conjunction with twice-weekly attendance at A.A. meetings had some impact on lowering the intensity and severity of the child abuse, a larger sample would have to be drawn over a longer period of time before a statistically significant conclusion could be drawn. Further research along these lines is strongly recommended. In the meantime clinicians and agencies are free to rely on individual anecdotal data, intuition, and further hypotheses to supplement the above findings."*

He threw it aside.

The half-light of his bedroom was comforting. He didn't want infomercials, the coy flirtations and innuendos of t.v. He wanted animal warmth. A connection. Someone to caress, lie down with and wake up with. If only Bonnie... Some rogue part of his brain considered calling her and just chatting, but he knew he would be even lonelier after that. He would either have to ask her to come over and sleep with him once and for all or not make the call. It couldn't be halfway anymore. Alan stretched out on his bed and it felt good. He wasn't in such bad shape. His body had manliness to it. If only Bonnie would notice.

Alan didn't make the call.

There were two cookies left.

He ate them.

JUST AWFUL

Patty was away at a New Millennial Conference ("Spreading Christ's Friendship Through Song, Story, Dreams, and Prayer!"), and Peter was blitzed. The Lean Cuisine dinner was about as satisfying as if he had eaten the cardboard and plastic it was wrapped in. The two gin-and-tonics made him feel slightly off-balance and, on top of it all, he was horny. Stupid, stupid, stupid. He wasn't looking to be horny. There wasn't any real room in his life to be horny. Four months without sex demanded that he either completely renounce the stuff altogether or have an actual encounter with a human being soon. He knew that Patty's new pursuits allowed for—and encouraged—"enjoyment of the marriage bed," but only between two true believers.

He was just horny.

He went downstairs into the rec room his son had long abandoned for college. Ross was probably getting it on right now with a great-looking college girl. Dad was stuck with his lonely middle-class, mid-level administrative after-hours hunger. After years and years of sacrificing and going in to work at 6:00 a.m and smiling through stupid meetings with parents whom he despised, taking shit from senior administrators who made all the wrong calls and spoke down to him and who had tried to keep his career stalled, evening after evening of attendance at bad concert-band recitals, awards ceremonies...no woman. No one who enjoyed his company. No one who laughed at his jokes.

He didn't know if he had any jokes. He tried to remember a joke. All he could remember was the "feminist joke" he told in the Faculty Room last year, which no one had laughed at. ("How many women with PMS does it take to change a light bulb?" Answer: "THAT'S NOT FUNNY, THAT'S SEXIST!" said in an outraged, screamy voice. No one had laughed, and he wondered if he had the punch line wrong because it was funnier when Steve Spisato told him it down at the Buick dealership a few weeks before. Maybe it was "How many feminists…") He realized immediately after telling it in the Faculty Room that it was a huge mistake.

Big f'ing deal. Let 'em sue me. It's not like they don't sue me anyway.

Peter uncovered his old Army footlocker and unlocked it. There was his "memorabilia." Clippings, his old canteen, the old uniform. There was a whole level of Army stuff. That was the top shelf. The bottom shelf contained his vintage porn collection.

It was stuff mainly from the late '80s and early '90s. There were some recent additions, quickly and slyly purchased when out of town for conventions. His trip to Memphis last month ("School Safety Brainstorming 101: Life After Columbine") replenished his supply. Each time he bought something new he parted with something old so they'd all fit in the one footlocker. If he hadn't done that he'd require twelve to fifteen footlockers by now, he thought. If his marriage didn't improve soon he'd require one-hundred-and-ninety-five footlockers with one big enough for him to stuff himself into.

He needed a fantasy goddess. Anyone who looked like Patty was out. O-U-T.

He needed another drink, too. He went upstairs and poured another G & T.

He came back and took out this month's copy of *Extreme*. On the cover was a raven-haired young woman with beautiful brown eyes, looking deeply into the camera, the curve of her long back subtly blossoming into one of the most alluring panty-clad bottoms Peter had ever seen or imagined. What was her look? Innocence? Or invitation? Both? He stirred strongly, trying to imagine even being in the same room with her. She would be the one for him tonight.

He turned to the Table of Contents. "Jeanie Goes to College." He allowed himself to slowly flip through the pages en route to page 42, his excitement building. "Veronica and Candy in Our Girls-Only Club House!" (a strawberry blonde in a dancer's leotards disrobing for the approval of a naked blonde with thin build and boyish hair); "Jasmine," page 28 (a beautiful young brunette, face resting on its side on her bed, as she arched her rear up toward the camera, nightgown pulled up over her hips); "Brittany," page 35 (young-looking...). He stopped. Peter couldn't believe his eyes. He flipped the page. A naked young woman, whose face had only partially shown in the previous photograph, squatting from behind, her bikini-panty-thong rising into the crack of her ass. In this picture she was seen lifting her white skirt up to her mid-belly, sporting girlish white panties and you could see her face clearly. She seemed to be giggling. He stopped breathing: this wasn't a "girlish"-looking woman; this was a girl.

A girl Peter knew.

She was one of the best-looking girls in Peter's school. It was Kendra—one of those quiet, loner girls. A tenth-grader? Eleventh? Peter's erection deflated as if he'd been kicked. He turned the page. She was on a chair, looking over her shoulder, the same skirt gathered up, the beautiful globes of her now-naked rear, almost pouting to the camera. He started getting aroused again. *How could I not be?* he thought. His mind raced and his blood pressure rose. How old was she? *How old is she?* She couldn't pose for this magazine—she was a minor. The oldest she could be was sixteen. She couldn't be posing here.

He looked at her smile. This was awful. He would have to report this. To whom? Child Protective Services? The police? How would he tell them he discovered it without losing all professional credibility? Without losing his job? It was awful. There were five more pictures in all. The last one was spread out over two pages. She was smiling—irresistibly—in each of the pictures, but she had been taken, seduced, exploited. He reminded himself that she had been abused. Hadn't she? Peter had to call and report this. He had to figure out a way to do it. Contact her parents? Anonymously? Have the school nurse do it?

He looked at the pictures again, slowly. "Photographs by Robert Whitlock and the Camera Obscura Studio." There was plenty of evidence. Maybe even more pictures. He looked at each of the pictures again. He tried to look at them the way a judge might. He couldn't. Maybe a female judge? He couldn't. Three of the pictures stuck with him. He would never be able to get them out of his mind. They were giving him a stronger rush of fear and excitement than he had known since first meeting Patty. His body knew this. His mind disapproved.

———

Looking at the pictures in the morning light was different. They didn't look as warm or inviting. The flesh-tones looked a little green.

Peter cut the pages out of the magazine, put them in a manila folder. He took one of the school "motivational" pens

("Let The Spirit SOAR!"), labeled the folder "TROUBLE," as if it were possible to forget that for a moment, or to forget what was inside. He stuffed it into his attaché case.

The phone rang. It was Patty.

"I've been praying for you, Peter. I miss you. I'm waiting for you."

"Um-huh."

"I had a strong revelation last night."

"I'm listening."

"It's a hard rain gonna fall."

"That's it?"

"Yes."

"That's not a revelation, that's a Bob Dylan song."

"What matters is whether it is true."

"Well, let's see if you're right."

"It's not a matter of me being right."

"Okay. Look, I have to go to work."

"I've been praying for you."

"Yeah, well, you already said that. Thanks. Me too. About the 'miss you' part. I'm, uh, here, though. Just like I've always been."

A few more words he didn't remember.

Peter began to get ready for school. He picked up the Kendra folder. Something had to be done.

"Can I ask you something really personal?" asked Alison.

"Yeah. Please do," said Elijah.

"Do you get high?"

Elijah looked at Alison with more than curiosity. "As in…?"

"Anything. Drugs."

145

"Two different things. Anything, yes," he said.

"Drugs, no?"

"Did someone tell you something about me?"

"No. In fact, no one seems to know anything about you," Alison volunteered.

"That's nice. I like that," Elijah admitted.

"I know. We can all tell."

"Do you like it?"

"I like you," Alison said.

Elijah reached over and messed with her hair. It was almost like a brother would, almost like a father, but it wasn't. It was like a future lover. She exhaled, sharply, almost against her will. She so much wanted to kiss him. "So…do you? Get high on drugs?"

"Would it change your opinion of me?"

Alison wanted to lie. She always wanted to try lying just a little, but it didn't come easily. She wasn't sure this was the stuff to mess around with, though.

"Yeah, it'd probably change things."

"Good. A point of view. Not average adolescent sheep behavior. It'd change my opinion of you, too…Isn't that so wrong? Aren't we supposed to be so totally accepting and above-it-all?" asked Elijah.

"You know what I hate?"

"What?"

"Them selling black t-shirts with the red 'A' for Anarchy fake-spray-painted on it at The Mall. I mean, how pathetic is that? Buying a well-made Anarchy shirt at The Rising Tide in The Mall, for God's sake?" Alison asked.

"With Daddy's credit card."

"And the place has a logo of a red fist. It should be a fist holding fifty-dollar bills."

"Anarchists are rolling in their graves," declared Elijah.

"I thought Anarchists didn't believe in graves," said Alison.

"So what did they do when they died?"

"I think they got cremated and they wore each other's ashes around their necks," she said.

They both thought about this.

"Would you wear my ashes?" Alison asked.

"Absolutely."

"Even if the color clashed?"

"Yeah. Promise," said Elijah.

"We didn't resolve the drug thing."

"Right."

"All right, I'll start. Hello, my name is Alison and I'm an alcoholic."

"Hello, Alison."

"Thank you, but you interrupted me. I do Ecstasy, have many affairs while I'm rolling, have tried crack, crystal meth, and regularly smoke pot to relax and think more clearly. I have snorted crushed-up Ritalin. I have done 'shrooms, but prefer old-fashioned New Mexican peyote. I drop acid because it makes chocolate-chip cookies taste better, and I love the way the sunsets look. I like the color aquamarine. I believe that heaven is probably aquamarine. I was disappointed to find that the aquamarine contact lenses you can buy—the ones that look aquamarine from the outside— don't change everything from the inside. They don't change anything at all. I smoke hash and then eat black licorice. I am currently looking to experiment with Special K. I do all this because my family doesn't understand me and school sucks. People think I don't feel school sucks because my grade point average is about 94, but you'd have to be a dead crustacean not to realize that school really, really sucks. I do drugs because I'm afraid college will suck, too. After everything in my life sucks completely, I will do heroin and be done. It doesn't have to be heroin. Actually I hope they will have some new drugs for me to move on to by then. I will wear black and listen to Coal Chamber. I will join the Cannibal Corpse website's chat room. I will get arrested, lie about everything to my probation officer, and become the most successful dealer in my school because I have a 94 average." Alison paused and took a breath. "O.K...your turn."

Elijah held his fake-concerned stare for two whole seconds then burst out laughing. "*And* you're an alcoholic."

"Oh, yuh...go on, your turn."

"I—"

"Wait a second," Alison interrupted. "I have an important question. Your heartfelt confession will have to wait."

"All right."

"If you were offered a free lap-dance by the most beautiful eighteen-year-old stripper in New York State— I mean strikingly, heart-attack-inducingly lovely/sexy girl you can imagine—a stripper—and it wasn't in front of anybody and only you and I knew...would you accept it?"

"You really want to know?"

"Yes."

"And this is all hypothetical?"

"Well, duh, what do you think, I really have the stripper here, waiting in the wings for you or something?"

"But you could get her?"

"Oh-ho, I think you just answered my question."

"Well, if she came so highly recommended..."

"Better than that girl in 'Grand Theft Auto.' Way better."

"And it's just a lap-dance? Well...YEAH! Why not?"

"Okay, good. No here's my second question: Would you feel guilty about it later?"

"Probably, yeah. I mean, it's not like she'd be carrying my baby or anything."

"Of course not. That would ruin her figure. You think she'd do that for you? I think not!"

"So you just want to know…"

"If you'd feel badly about the whole thing after you signed on."

"Probably. But not enormously so."

"Great. Now how secure am I supposed to feel about you, and me liking you, knowing that you have a gorgeous dancing stripper plotting to make you hers? To possess you?"

Elijah scooped her up in his arms. "Because you are the gorgeous stripper. It's your mind, your body…you'd be everything to me. I was thinking of you when you were describing her."

"Yeah, well thanks, but…I'm not eighteen yet."

"So you're my pre-eighteen, pre-gorgeous stripper," said Elijah warmly.

"I'm not saying I'm 'pre-gorgeous.'" Alison slammed Elijah with her arm. "And…I'm keeping my clothes on. For now."

"Yeah?"

"Well, what did you expect?"

"Don't ask follow-ups to hypothetical questions."

"All right. So: your turn to confess. You and drugs." Alison peered deeply into Elijah's eyes.

"I don't do them," he said firmly.

"Why not?"

"Too unimaginative."

"I don't either. My monologue was a well-crafted deception," Alison admitted.

"Good one. I'm not so sure it was well-crafted. It tended to drift," said Elijah.

"Where did it lose you?"

"Heaven being aquamarine."

"Well, all right. I accept criticism with equanimity. That's what Mrs. Ruppert wrote for a comment on my fourth grade report card," said Alison.

"So it must be true."

"Absolutely. Only I don't think my parents knew what it meant. All they said was that I should bring up my gym grade by being dressed for class more often."

"That hurts," said Elijah.

"I accepted it with equanimity."

"Mrs. Ruppert was a visionary."

"I know, and there is nothing in the school to even honor her yet," Alison said, wistfully.

"Well, she's still teaching."

"So you're saying you have to die first to get some recognition from the public education system?" asked Alison.

"No. You don't get it then either."

"But they might name something after her."

"A water fountain or something. They don't name schools after teachers; just administrators," observed Elijah.

"So…aquamarine…aren't you intrigued by what some of the effects would be like, from—say—tripping, or something?" asked Alison, her eyes sparkling.

"Acid?" inquired Elijah.

"Yeah."

"Sounds intriguing. But I don't want to lose my bearings and sacrifice a couple of billion connecting brain synapses for the purposes of a sensational light-show," declared Elijah.

"I'm told it's not that. It's like all your senses getting heightened at once. Doesn't that sound intense?"

"Yes."

"Want to try it?" asked Alison.

150

"Drop acid?"

"Yeah."

"Are you kidding me?" asked Elijah.

Alison took his hand. "No. Only we'd do it differently."

"How?"

"No drugs. We'll use Pez, or something."

"And?"

"And skip school and spend the day together," said Alison.

"Heightening our senses?"

"Yeah."

"With Pez?" asked Elijah.

"Yeah."

"We'll get into trouble."

"I know. We'll get a day of in-school suspension and our parents will freak. But it'll be worth it," declared Alison, with finality.

"Why?" asked Elijah.

"Because we are alive and we are young and some day we will be old. Because we have the day and the weather report for Thursday is sunny. Mucho oxygenation," said Alison.

"Heightened senses."

"Yes."

Elijah looked at Alison the way an exhausted wrestler looks at a quart of Gatorade under the shade of a palm tree. "You'll bring the Pez?" he asked.

"Absolutely."

"Can you get the orange kind?"

MISSING

Nothing in Claire's closet fit. Not the jeans, not the friggin' blue sundress, not the stupid orange tank-top, barely the hot-pink halter top. She was starting to look like a freaking clown, and no one was doing anything to help her.

"I am going to lose these pounds," Claire said to Carly as both gazed in the full-length mirror. "This used to make me look sexy. Now I look like a whale-on-steroids. No one's gonna want to sit next to me. No one's gonna talk to me. I'm just gonna be some fat lump-girl with friggin' monstrous ears. I don't care if I have to eat that Jell-O yogurt six times a day and nothing else, I am going to lose this blubber and become unrepulsive looking again if it kills me. If anyone offers me a cupcake, even, I'm gonna smack them in their face. If you see me even thinking about eating seconds, I want you to slap me onto my back before I can draw the stuff near my extremo fat-girl lips. I used to be muscular. Now look at me: I used to be like that girl-Marine in the first *Aliens* movie before she got blown up? Now I look like the Alien. And if Bobby and Ernie don't get off my case in Kehoe's class, I'm gonna rip out their vocal cords with my fingers and pee down their throat before they can say another smart-ass word. Because that new guy is gonna be mine. Because he's the first guy to come along in my life who is not a faggot, an asshole, or some dick who tries to hurt women. He's just...fine. And if anyone tries to stop me they're gonna answer to Jesus Christ himself, because I'll lay them out dead before I let this guy get away, as God is my witness."

She threw the last outfit on the bed in disgust, turned and eyed the rear view in the mirror carefully, assessing her butt. "Eight pounds will do it...no, twelve. You watch: Little Miss Priss Bagel-Girl doesn't have half the ass I do."

Carly burst out laughing. Claire glared at her before laughing, too. "Well, you know what I mean. She doesn't have half as good an ass as I'm going to have in about three weeks. Anyone wants that guy after then, they've got to come through me first."

They were known—not affectionately—as The Three Stooges. They were in Alan's office for the second time that morning.

Brendon, Nolan, and Jose (known as "Chico" to most of the students and some teachers) had been disrupting Ms. Handler's Home Ec/Domestic Sciences class earlier when they had been strongly "asked" to come down to Alan's office, sit outside his office and—one by one—talk to Alan. He had once seen the three of them together as a group and had regretted it. Nonetheless Alan decided to violate his own cardinal rule today and have them in his room at the same time.

Each of them had a compelling story. Each of them had been minding his own business when a paper cup, rubber band, fist, kick, or punch came flying out of nowhere, jarring him out of his reverie. In each instance it had been completely unprovoked.

The boys were big enough—and chronologically aged enough, Alan thought—to be fathering children, paying taxes, installing new roofs, fixing cars, and serving in the military in most parts of the world.

"Brendon was flicking boogers at me."

"Nolan said Jose had spit in my iced-tea when I wasn't looking. Jose told Nolan he was going to bitch-slap me in gym, in front of the class if I didn't pay him back five dollars which I didn't even owe him."

A little bit of this went a long way.

"Naaah, naaah, not even, don't even play that," said Brendon to Nolan upon hearing the accusations. "All this is because you broke up with Shaniqua Saturday when you heard she'd been doing it with Maurice. And I stood up for you. I said, 'Go ahead, go with Maurice, you friggin' ho. But I'm sticking with Nolan. And if he's looking to fight you,' I said, 'he's gonna have to go through me first. We two for one.' And then I turn around and you giving me crap, just because you got PMS or something. Naaah, naaah, naaah, naaah, I don't go for that."

Nolan lept in. "Nah, you see, the thing is Brendon is two-faceded. He wants to act like he's all everybody's protector but HE'S the one who's spreading stories and getting people to fight each other. All I did this morning was play with him (like I was gonna fight him), and I turned around he sucker-punched me. Serious! When the teacher wasn't looking. I mean, is it bleeding right now?"

Nolan held his nostrils specially, angling them closer for Alan and the others to consider.

"Let me see," Alan said, moving closer.

Brendon moved in with a technical interest.

"No, it's okay...Nolan."

"I didn't, y'know, you were playing, I was playing....I don't think any of this would have happened if it weren't for...Jose."

"Me?!?" Jose's eyebrows shot up to the ceiling.

"That's right. Sitting back there whispering, 'Yo, Nolan. Brendon said that Miranda called you Needle-Dick at that party on Friday, to another girl, because she said that you...don't have what it takes. You know what I'm saying?'"

"How do you expect someone to react to that?"

Brendon joined in. "Aside from the fact that it wasn't even true. Cuz I was there and she wasn't even AT the party, all right? So, word up, Number one: She wasn't at that party. Number two: Why you sayin' she at that party?"

Jose looked hurt. "I was talkin' about what I heard!"

"Were you at that party?"

"I was going to that party."

"Were you at that party?"

"I couldn't get a ride."

"All right then."

"I said, I talk to people who..."

"But you weren't there."

"No."

"I rest my case."

"You know, you got a friggin' attitude."

"Yeah? What cha gonna do about it?"

Suddenly both boys were standing, their chests puffed out toward each other, approaching.

"Gen-tle-men! Sit down!" Alan stood.

"Yeah, you just a pussy, you know that?"

"GENTLEMEN! Sit down and shut up!" They did, scowling. Jose's fists were still clenched. "Can anyone, ANYONE...take responsibility for what they did this morning?"

There was a long silence.

"I don't know how to say this without...insulting you. One-to-one, you're each okay. When we get you together it's like the deepest pit of hell. You come to school, you don't learn, you wreck it for other kids, you're not on track for finishing the school year successfully. What are you doing? You're wasting time. You are wasting everybody's time. There are about five kids waiting right now to talk to me about stuff other than boogers-being-flicked and who-called-them-a-pussy. I don't even know how to talk to you about these messes anymore. I think you're going to have to sink like stones and hit rock-bottom before you want to talk to me about the other stuff. So I'm taking you to the principal right now and we'll find out how he wants to handle this. I'm going to recommend that you spend some time in I.S.S. and write a personal narrative about your own role in what happened and how you could have made other choices."

"A what?"

"A narrative."

"Awww, that's STUPID!" said Nolan.

"That's messed up," muttered Brendon. "That's just a waste of time!"

"Come on."

They walked down the hall together. Unlike many other times, Peter was in his office. He seemed completely aggravated by Alan's arrival and even angrier to hear about the kids' waste of staff time. Peter leaned forward, his knuckles anchored to the folders on his desktop. His voice boomed.

"You want to behave like clowns or you want to behave like students?"

They shut up, despite a lot of funny things they wanted to say.

"Mr. Mitchke and I are going to get your disciplinary charts right now and see if there is any reason why you can't all be thrown out of school for the year right now. Wait here; if my secretary hears one word from any of you, I'll write up all three of you for insubordination. If you don't think that is fair, get a lawyer."

Peter and Alan walked out of the office past the secretaries.

"If you hear one word from those chuckleheads in there, start filling out three write-ups," Peter told Mona.

"For what?"

"Leave it blank. I don't know. Insubordination. I'll fill it out. Just get their names."

Alan hadn't seen Peter like this in a while.

"I'm sick of this crap, Alan. Can't you handle it?"

"Yeah, I can. I just wanted your approval for I.S.S. I don't want to get it into assigning it myself. I'm supposed to be a counselor here, not a cop."

"Fine. You want a Bad Guy, I'll be the Bad Guy. That way these little J.D.'s can still enjoy their time with you. Wouldn't want to upset that applecart, would we? God forbid."

Peter turned on his heels and started back to his office. He stopped and turned to face Alan again. "Did Dolores talk to you about that kid?"

"Which kid?"

"The Hispanic kid with the attitude."

"Can you narrow it down some?"

"No I can't, Alan. I can't. I don't need this today. I've already had three parent phone calls, unrelated to this crap. Some kid...lots of rage, blah-de-blah, might need a home visit, she says you do that kind of thing. Do you?"

"Possibly, but I'd have to know more."

"Well...connect with her when you get the chance."

"Is this a high priority?"

"What do you think, Alan? Would I have waited this long to bring it up if it were the highest priority? You know

Dolores. The kid needs vitamins, eats French fries, tacos…I
don't know. Talk to her and give her some direction on this."

Peter and Alan returned to the office. They stood
standing as Peter spoke to the three boys.

"You're all going into I.S.S. You take care of business and
write that assignment for Mr. Mitchke, you get out in one
day. You don't, you stay the next day. If it takes 365 days, you
do the assignment. Everyone understand?" The boys were
staring at their toes with their best "I've-been-bad" look. "Do
you UNDERSTAND??"

They all nodded, Jose first.

"Now go take care of business. I don't want to hear one
complaint from the I.S.S. teacher that you're giving her a hard
time. Now get out of here."

They shuffled out like good little boys. Outside in the
hallway, Alan could hear the sound of one boy being
slammed into the wall followed by "Ohhhhh!" and the sound
of giggling and muffled curses. They stomped off down the
hallway before either man could move after them.

"And I want to see those completed assignments," Peter
said, his voice still booming, to Alan.

Alan left quietly, like the fourth child.

It wasn't until midway through the next parent phone call
that Peter realized that the folder marked "TROUBLE" was
missing from his desk.

Alison was hoping for some sun. The Thursday morning
she and Elijah chose for tripping was as gray and damp as the
four days before it. Living in the Valley near the Hudson was
sometimes like living halfway up the nasal passages of a fat,
asthmatic secretary who worked for MobilExxon in an office

under a broken, flickering fluorescent light. Alison tried to be charitable in imagining why her grandparents had ever moved to this soggy, stupid part of the world in the first place. If she saw any more video on the Weather Channel of people in California or Arizona with the tropical shirts and sunblock on, she would kill the next person she saw.

Alison wanted real sun. She wanted to sweat. She wanted to have the trippy, Aldous Huxley kind of experience she had read about, where the sun exploded into a thousand smaller suns whirling you into tens of thousands of smaller solar systems, colors you never dreamed of, the taste of strawberries unlike anything your mother ever put on top of your Rice Krispies. She wanted her mind to melt as she listened to Joni Mitchell's "Hissing of Summer Lawns." She wanted it baked out of her, to see what was left. She wanted the horse without the rider.

She wanted Elijah the same way.

Alison had gathered up her books and assignments as usual. She put on a yellow L.L. Bean slicker—she loved how dorky it looked—and kissed her mother goodbye. She walked in the direction of the bus stop. Alison turned left instead of right, however, and walked directly to Louis' Luncheonette.

One hundred and five miles to the north, the State Police barracks, Troop K, received the forwarded Internet threat from the F.B.I. (forwarded by Kane county's Internet service provider). The F.B.I. had held it for a mere six minutes before the decision was made to share it with Albany and to release it to all school districts in New York State.

The message—posted in an AOL teen chatroom—said:

May 16th – 11 a.m. High school Jews will die.
Columbine will look like a walk in the park. Say No to
New York wetbacks, fags, nigers, spics, all their Jew-
friends. Yes to Palistine. Zarcarwi says hello. SAY
HEBE-PRAYERS, JEWS – YOU WILL NEED THEM
TODAY.

While each district was allowed to implement its own
safety plan, a lockdown with the assistance of local and state
police was recommended.

———

Principal Peter Epperschmidt swung into crisis mode.

"Mona, get out the crisis plan, please."

"What crisis?"

"It's not really a crisis, probably, but we have to follow
the plan."

"What's happening?"

"Right now, nothing. Later, probably nothing. But would
you please dig out the plan? Not, y'know, the whole
notebook thing, just the bulleted list."

"Dated?"

"'05. It should be under 'Crisis.'"

Mona came back in two minutes.

"There's nothing under 'Crisis.'"

"Check 'Disaster.' 'Disaster Preparedness.'"

Mona came back a minute later. "Nothing under
'Disaster.'"

"Well, where is it?"

"It's a folder?"

"It's a bulleted *list* of procedures."

"Well, it'd be under 'Procedures' then?"

"No. That would be the whole closing-the-building-at-the-end-of-the-year-stuff, opening-the-building…wait, check under 'Sudden Student/Faculty Death,' maybe."

She came back in a minute. "Nothing."

"Alright, let's think this through. Fast."

"What about 'Updates'?"

"That wouldn't make any sense. That could have an update for everything in it."

Mona walked back a minute later with the list.

"Where was it?"

"'05 Updates, Disaster.'"

Peter's face flushed. "How are we going to find anything that way?"

"I just did. You just have to remember when you update things."

Mona walked away and Peter summoned the assistant principals, as bulleted, and let them know that the superintendent okayed a lockdown. This meant all teachers were to lock their doors, take attendance, and no one was allowed in or out of the building. Including parents. Especially parents.

Peter looked up to see two State Police cruisers pull up in front of the schoolyard flagpole. He turned on CNN, just to check.

NEKOW ASCENDING

"Where were your born?" Alison stared intently at Elijah's profile, imagining her fingers on his sideburns. They were fuller than she first noted.

"For real, or…?"

"Trip-talking. We're high, right?"

"Stoned immaculate."

"I don't think you get 'stoned' on acid."

"Okay, then…wired. Wired alive."

"Groovy."

"So where were you born?"

"A nearby star. In a midnight sandstorm, which thrashed the surface of my planet with impenetrable swirls of red and purple moon dust."

"I thought it was a star."

"Oh, right. Red and purple star dust."

"Wow. Whoa…"

"How about you?"

"I was found floating on a raft in between the Polynesian islands of Nekow and Wawahookie in storm-whipped seas. My parents had——despite evident attempts to preserve our family——fallen off and drowned. All I was left with was a locket with their pictures in it and the word 'Hope' on the back. For a long time I took that as my name. In recent years I have used it as my middle name."

"And your first name?"

"Alison. It was the name of the hurricane that nearly killed me. It was the first storm of the season and the most ferocious. Alison Hope Gepner."

"Whoa."

"Never forget what almost kills you. Pay homage to it."

"We do the opposite in our society. We bury it fast and run."

"It never works."

"Alison Hope: you have much to teach me. Of your Polynesian ways."

"And you too, my friend. I want to hear the ways of your star-people."

"Let us continue the journey…at Friendly's in Garnerville. I want a Fribble."

"This is Principal Epperschmidt. All teachers should hold their period three classes and take attendance at this time. Code Blue, Code Blue. All students should be in their regular third period class at this time. CODE BLUE. Teachers: no hall passes should be issued at this time."

The calls to the Main Office began immediately. The first six teachers who called had never heard of "Code Blue."

"Tell them it's in their manual," Peter directed Mona.

"They say they never got a manual."

"If they were here the first day of school, if they got their first paychecks they got a manual."

Mona faithfully relayed the message. "They want to know if a kid died."

"Tell them no kid died, but that we're in a lockdown drill. Tell them there will be a brief meeting in the auditorium after school to explain. But first they have to do the drill."

Mona whispered into the phone.

"They don't know what to do."

"Tell them to lock the goddamn door and take attendance."

"The computer in Room 120 is down."

"Take attendance the old way then."

"What do you mean?"

"Tell them to take out a piece of paper and a pen and to write down the kids' names."

"What if..."

"I don't want to answer any more questions. I'm going to my office."

"Line three is Dave Appelfeld."

"Am I supposed to know who that is?"

"He's the Managing Editor of *The Hadleyville Falls Gazette*."

"How did he get this?"

"Scanner. Police scanner, I guess. Lots of kids have them. They tell their parents sometimes."

"Tell him we're having a normal day."

"He already knows we're not allowing parents to pick up their kids."

"How does he know that?"

"Because his son goes here. You gave him an award for the Business Leaders of America last month, remember?"

———

Elijah was wearing his almost-silky purple shirt with comets and sunbursts on it. It was as if he could read Alison's mind already. Everyone else in Friendly's was in Wal-Mart gray. A motorcyclist carrying a helmet shaped like a Nazi soldier's was at the cash register, paying and leaving. He stuck an unlit cigarette in his mouth. When he turned to leave Elijah and Alison could read the back of his t-shirt: "If You Can Read This The Bitch Fell Off." Alison nearly choked, laughing into her orange juice. Elijah waited for the guy to leave before he erupted.

"Did you see that?" Alison asked.

"Yeah."

"And we're not even high yet!"

"I can't get used to you saying that. It just sounds…"

"…so BAD, right? So, well, this is a day to explore BAD without, y'know, actually *being* bad, which you must admit is a huge improvement over the lives of most of our so-called friends and associates, eighty percent of whom are so fried-and-fricasseed that they can't remember what GOOD feels like anymore."

"I don't think it's a 'good/bad' thing."

"I know. It's more like 'totally impaired' versus only 'regularly impaired'—'regularly impaired' assuming you are a teenager who has to still live at home with your weird family and go to a school that is a Traveling Circus From Hell."

"It's enough to make someone want to…"

"…DROP ACID!!" Alison shouted, giggling too loudly, wrapping her hands around him, her face falling to the linoleum surface of the countertop. "Who needs brain cells anyway?"

"Be quiet! We're going to get arrested or something."

"For possession of Pez!! Yes!" Alison laughed more hysterically. "Ohmygod, that would be so outrageous! I so wonder if that has ever happened."

Outside, on the street, a Hadleyville Falls Police car did an abrupt 180-degree turn, flipping on its lights and sirens, racing quickly toward the high school.

Elijah's hand shot over his heart. "Jesus Christ! I thought they were coming to get us!" he laughed.

"Yeah, well, maybe," said Alison, laughing. "They just might. The day is still young. Close your eyes."

"Why?"

"Just close them."

"Okay, but how come?"

Alison took out the Pez dispenser and let Elijah blindly explore its contours.

"No way…is this?…who I think it is?"

"One guess."

"Hint?"

"It's not my first choice. I got it for you." Alison took advantage of the moment and gave Elijah a medium-deep kiss on the lips, lingering, then doing it again.

"Mmmmmm…."

"Okay. You guess?"

"Homer?"

"YESSSSSSS!!! You win!"

Elijah and Alison gazed at the Homer Simpson Pez dispenser with religious admiration.

"He's got three hairs. It's faithful."

"Original edition."

"Wow."

"And it's yours to keep."

"I'm speechless."

"We can trade him back and forth every six months. Like a friendship bear."

"Deal. What was your first choice?"

"Tweety."

"I can see it."

"So…I brought the, um, delivery device, did you bring the stuff?"

166

Elijah tried to look like all the drug dealers he had seen on t.v. and in the movies. He did it fairly well, Alison thought, looking both ways over his shoulder and in back of him before sliding a thin brown paper bag out of his pants' pocket. "Yo, yo, yo; check it out. It's sweet, yo." Alison lifted the top of the bag and peeked. "Orange?" she asked, raising an eyebrow.

"Mmmm-huh. It's the only kind I do."

"Here you go, hon." They both almost leapt out of their seats toward the ceiling as the waitress with the red hair and glasses slid two plates with muffins in front of them. "One corn, one blueberry. The Fribbles are on the way."

"I can't release her. I'm not authorized to release any students at this time."

"Of course you're 'authorized.' You're the Principal. And I'm the parent. I'm coming in to pick up Alison in five minutes. I'm on the way."

"I'm sorry, but I can't do that, Mrs. Gepner."

"Why not?" Alison's mother's voice tore through the phone like a dagger.

"Two reasons. One is because we're not letting any students in or out at this time. The other is because we don't know where she is."

"What?"

"She's missing. I'm sorry."

"Double check, please. She's never out. She had perfect attendance for three years in a row. I saw her leave for school this morning."

"She's out."

"She'd never cut. Alison Gepner. G-E-P-N-E-R."

"If it's any consolation, we have a number of students out each day and much of the time their parents are not aware of it."

"Not Alison."

"I'm not supposed to do this, but…do you recognize any of the following kids' names as friends of Alison's?" Peter asked, holding the attendance in his right hand, putting on his reading glasses and reading off fifty-three names, slowly.

Her mother didn't recognize a single one.

———◦———

"The mother is concerned about the Jewish angle," Peter told the superintendent. "She wants to rule out foul play. Though I've got to say, as far as I can tell, she's got to be just about the only Jewish kid out today. They're usually here plugging away at that G.P.A., y'know, trying to get a leg up on college. We'll talk to a few of her friends and we'll call if anything develops, but—as far as we know—this girl is cutting. When do we lift the lockdown?"

PURPLE GRACKLES

Alison squinted, trying to see a figure on the horizon. It was moving toward her but not walking. There was a thin line, a gray ribbon shimmering on the horizon. Maybe it just was the horizon. When it bent she heard the sound of a drum, deeper tones when it bent low, higher sounds when it barely flexed. But always the sound of a percussive surface resonating.

In between were the most delicious silences. Alison turned to Elijah—who sat quietly in an armchair four feet in front of her, eyes closed, arms resting peacefully on the padding—and said, "I've never appreciated silence before," which seemed kind of ironic, being that she had just destroyed it. But she hadn't. Because the next silence was being born even as the sound of her voice died away, the electrons scattering into the corners of the universe, their present incarnation expired. Like they said, "No hill goes up endlessly." Where had she heard that? It couldn't have been in high school.

Anyway, she hadn't wrecked the moment. Maybe the moment before, but that was over. She had a newfound respect for the past, but didn't need to say that.

The ribbon flexed up and down and the figure came closer, riding it. "Ohmygod," she may have said aloud. "Grandpa?"

He looked a little tired and a little confused as he rowed a beat-up dinghy toward her.

"Forgive me. They only gave me one oar, bubbaleh."

"You need to rest, grandpa."

"Never mind me, how are you doing? How are your grades?"

"You want to ask me about my grades? My school grades?"

His boat bobbed up and down wildly. Her grandpa quickly tried to balance the boat's direction by switching his oar to the other side, but it was of no use. He disappeared behind a swirling wave then reappeared. Alison had to catch his words when the front part of the boat bobbed down and he was still facing toward her.

"School is the stepping-stone, honey."

"That is all you have to say to me? Is that the only thing adults know how to say to teenagers? Even after you're dead?"

"You were hoping for…?"

"Something special. Direction. Wisdom."

Grandpa laughed and his boat dipped precipitously to the left, taking on water before being thrust up in the air and being pushed backward to the right.

"Direction? That's a good one. You always were the funny one. You want wisdom?"

"Yes."

"There is something better than wisdom you could maybe get."

"What, Grandpa?"

"A second oar."

And with that the scene was sucked away as quickly as the turning off of a t.v. set.

"I loved the shed, Grandpa," she said, crying. "I loved it. I still do."

Elijah held her as she sobbed.

The lockdown was lifted two hours after nothing had happened. Two hundred and ninety-five parents came in to pick up their kids anyway. Peter was sorry to have to report to Mr. and Mrs. Gepner that there was still no sign of Alison.

A description of her had been given to the State Police. They were on the lookout for a pretty, intelligent-looking girl with dark brown hair, wearing a yellow L.L. Bean rain slicker and wire-rimmed glasses. Alison's mother had cried when she gave these details to the police. She had become all too familiar with the details of the Polly Klaas case in California so many years ago and anything which reminded her of it, even the phrases "questioned by police" or "missing child," sent her into a panic and made her cry. Now she was somehow in this hell herself.

"We want to hear as soon as you hear anything," Mr. Gepner told the principal. "Anything at all."

"You have my assurance," Peter offered, sounding more like a funeral director than he had in all his years in education.

"I want to hear every song that ever meant anything to you. Or at least the top five thousand."

Elijah looked at her adorable, cute face. There was a rush of something into his heart. "That would take sixty-five years."

Her smile was devilish, young, and angelic at the same time. It felt like the opening line of a great letter. "Well maybe we could get the first five songs in today."

"Five a day, 365 days, that's…1,800-plus a year, that would only give us less than three years."

"True. What if we spread it out to five songs a year?"

"That'd give us…a thousand years. Together."

"Deal," Alison said.

"Deal."

"Do you think i-Pods will work 1,000 years from now?"

"They're designed pretty well. I don't know about the batteries."

"I think we should agree to reevaluate the relationship after the first five hundred years."

"Just to be safe?"

"Exactly. That way there'd be no hard feelings."

"True. Like if we wanted to fool around with other people after five hundred years, green light?"

"Yup. Good to allow for all contingencies."

"Build it into the plan."

"Is this us, do you think, or the acid talking?"

"I dunno. Kind of hard to tell, isn't it?" Alison said, giggling.

———

The two teenagers were found comfortably sitting on an old maroon bedspread, books in their laps, in Alison's own backyard shed. They were facing each other, reading aloud, mid-sentence, when the door burst open, a German Shepherd leading the way. (Alison's father knew someone in the State Senator's office who was able to get the local cops to wave the twenty-four-hour missing rule before dispatching the dog, who had been imprinted with the scent of Alison's black Good Charlotte t-shirt from her hamper.)

Alison looked up and burst out laughing at the sight of the dog, two uniformed cops (one of them holding her Good Charlotte t-shirt), and both of her parents bursting through the door in high-rescue mode. She was able to stifle it and transform it into giggles in time to hear her mother's shriek.

"Ally, Ally, Ally, darling, how did you get here? Are you hurt?"

"I'm fine, Ma."

Alison and Elijah put down their copies of Sam Shepherd's *True West*. They had been acting it out with each other. They were midway through the second read (having switched parts) when the dog burst in.

"Are you alright, honey? You look dazed. Al, doesn't she look dazed?" her mother asked, turning to her father.

"I guess."

"She looks dazed. Alison, I want to ask you this, and I want a completely honest answer."

"Shoot. Wait...is that my Good Charlotte shirt?"

"Never mind that. Honey," her mother asked, kneeling down to eye level, "...did you take anything? Did anyone give you anything that you took? Did you sip from a soda or something that was left sitting and was unsupervised?" (Her mother had seen a "Dateline" on this.)

Alison and Elijah both burst out laughing at this. Try as they might, it just seemed to evolve into deeper and deeper laughter.

"She looks dazed. I think we need to get her tested, Al. They can do a screening for everything. Soup to nuts. I want it done."

Alison let herself be led off to her parents' car, but not before she kissed Elijah on the cheek.

"What's that supposed to mean?" her mother asked, to the cops and no one in particular.

———◦•◦———

Claire had Carly approach Elijah between sixth and seventh periods, outside of Global. If things went wrong there was only an hour and a half left to the day, and if things went right there was just an hour and a half until she ran up the driveway to the Group Home, burst through the door to her room, jumped on her bed, and wrote in her diary. It made her nervous to look across the hallway and see Carly talking to him. She didn't think Carly would deliberately stab her in the back, but Carly was sort-of-in-between guys herself right now and wouldn't be so offended if Elijah fell for her instead of Claire. She had said she had "no interest" in him because he "isn't my type" but it had been said that Carly's "type" was any mammal larger than sixty-five pounds whose crotch swelled to bulbazoid proportions on demand and who possessed spending money. This was the largely-true observation of Layla, a very-smart-girl-with-an-attitude who had passed through the Group Home in two weeks flat before returning to her parents in Westchester.

Aside from Claire's sisterly affections for Carly, however, there was also the fact that Claire could kick her ass clear into next week in three seconds flat because Carly didn't know how to fight. At least Carly herself had never tested the theory, but seemed happy to let it go unchallenged.

Claire busied herself at her locker while looking out of the sides of her eyes. Carly's lips were moving now and Elijah was turning his head to the side when all of a sudden both of them looked over right at her. Claire finished her locker combination slowly, opened it grandly, knowing that he'd see the old Obsession photo (of the hot guy's naked chest and washboard stomach—god, she loved washboard stomachs)—

before she tossed her books. Then she slammed her locker and ran off to Global. There was no harm in letting him see that she appreciated fine things. (God, he was like a fine Arabian stallion or something...) The only problem was that if Carly didn't hurry up and finish whatever it was she was saying she wouldn't be able to let Claire know what happened until the end of next period because Carly had Chorus, had failed electives twice already, had five "lates" resulting in two in-school suspensions, and neither of them would be able to chat now because the "new rules"—"zero-tolerance" for lateness—sucked and were being enforced. Claire turned away from her locker, flicking her hair back (making sure her ears were covered nonetheless), letting him get a flash of her now-well-proportioned torso, ass, and legs in her best stonewashed jeans which hugged every molecule of her fourteen-pound-thinner, electrically-charged, happy-but-hungry body. (Thank you, Jell-O yogurt!) She was humming, with her voice and the rest of her body, as she walked past Elijah and Carly, turning her head just a fraction to offer a meek, girlish, "Hi!" before entering the classroom. She was pretty sure he had smelled the Obsession on her and would be thinking of her whether he wanted to or not.

It had gone perfectly. If only she now could find out from Carly where things stood. Instead, Mr. Congoli's voice bleated like a sheep: "Take out your books, people. Turn to 'Asia & The World Marketplace' on page 186, please. Claire, take your seat. CLAIRE: would you have a seat, please?"

She slid into the seat wordlessly. He wasn't just fine. He was awesome. State-of-the-art fine. Not an Arabian horse, but an Arabian STEED. Her boytoy, her stud-muffin. But with brains. And a heart. She could see, even in the way he tilted his head toward Carly, that the boy had a real heart. She breathed in and could feel connected from her hair to her crotch, her nipples, and her toes. This was really happening. She could die.

———

At lunchtime Alan wondered about purple grackles. When he was in third grade he discovered these regal birds walking on the grass in front of his house, reflecting purple in the blazing sun. He couldn't find, over the years, anyone who remembered them. Not by that name. "Ravens? Crows?" they asked him, looking at him skeptically. "No...purple grackles," he would answer.

The birds had moved very elegantly. Deliberately. Their coats changed to different grades of purple as the sun sparkled from one end of the solar system to the birds' wings to the color purple in their wings to his eyes. He knew he hadn't imagined it.

He wondered if Bonnie had ever seen them.

Maybe he'd call and ask.

He didn't.

SPAGHETTI STRAPS & FLAN

Bobby's mother was in no mood. The kitchen fuse had blown, the cat had peed on the kitchen table again, they were getting calls about the overdue payment on the Wal-Mart charge card, and the school had called about Bobby yesterday.

"Get up," she shouted to Bobby.

"Leave me alone."

"Get up."

"Get the fuck out of here."

Her face reddened. "You talk to me like that? You talk to your own mother like that?"

"Yeah. I guess so. Now get out."

"Get out of bed."

"No."

Before the word faded Bobby felt himself being flung upward and backward. His shock registered the same time he felt himself slam against the wall, his long, bony body crushed between the wall and the lumpy mattress.

"What the...?"

"You think I talk just to hear myself think?" his mother, the enraged whale, screamed, repeatedly pounding him against the wall.

"Alright, alright, I'm up. Let me out."

"Let me out? Let me out? Is that all you have to say to me? Is that the story of your life?"

"Alright, you're right. You're right. I'm going to school."

"I don't want them calling anymore! I can't take it! No more calls!"

"Who called?"

"The school."

"Who?"

"I dunno."

"Well, why didn't you ask?"

She slammed him against the wall again, just as he was starting to climb out.

"You're psycho. You know that?"

"Oh yeah? Oh yeah?" she said, throwing down the mattress quickly and running into the kitchen.

"Yeah. For a fact." Bobby quickly pulled on dirty jeans.

He didn't see it coming. The quart-sized can of Hawaiian Punch (Fruity Raspberry Burst) hit him in the head like a Scud missile. It slammed off his left temple and hit the ground of the bedroom a half second later, rolling in front of his dirty laundry.

"I don't want any calls!! Do you hear me? Do you hear me now? Is this what I have to do? To get you to go to school?"

"No, Ma. You just have to ask."

"Look. It's dented. You dented it. This is the last one."

They both looked at the can.

"It's not leaking."

"That's not the point. This is supposed to last until Thursday. For all of us. You see? It's always about you. 'Me, me, me.'"

Bobby held his head as it throbbed. He'd be okay.

"If I go to school they're gonna ask about this."

"You tell them and you're finished here. Go live with Social Services. You go live with the niggers. You want that?"

"No."

178

"Then go to school. And keep your mouth shut."
He did.

———•———

The first five photos of Kendra Iatsik's nude, or nearly-nude, body went up in the Language Arts wing—right next to Mr. Denardo's ninth and tenth grade French classes. They were excellent color-copies of the first part of the magazine spread. There was the squatting-in-the-white-thong picture, the panty-flashing skirt-lifting picture…Peter had so committed them to a deep part of his memory that when they reappeared on his desk—brought down to him by an embarrassed and outraged Home Ec teacher—he could tell which ones had been enlarged at a copier and which ones were reproduced at their regular size. The only change the young thieves had made was to scrawl "Lick Me!" right under the thong photo.

Peter took out a new manila folder, took the top off of a red marker and paused. Finally he wrote across the top of it: "PROBLEM"

The Home Ec teacher had reminded him that if this girl was the girl who everyone thought it was, whoever had put the photo up on the wall was not only in trouble administratively for displaying pornographic material on school walls, but was now in violation of a Section 9 Sexual Harassment statute as well. The rights of this individual girl had been violated, in addition to the fact that a hostile learning environment had been created for each of the approximately 550 females who were supposed to be taught in an atmosphere free of sexual harassment.

"Are you formally asking for a complaint to be brought up under Section 9, Diane? Or are you willing to let us do some digging, see what we can find, and handle it on a case-sensitive basis?"

"I've seen too many of those, Peter. Yeah, I'm bringing it to you formally."

"Doesn't the girl herself have to lodge the complaint?"

"Absolutely not. This event has made it impossible for all the girls in the building to learn today."

"O.K., well, then...It'll be taken up formally."

"Who is the Section 9 Investigator for our school?"

"It's me."

"You?"

"Yeah."

"Isn't that...kind of less-than-neutral?"

"No, not really, Diane. I have to wear many hats around here. Besides, it's just a fact-finding role, really. I make a recommendation and if anyone doesn't like it, it gets kicked up to the superintendent."

"So you'll be talking to everyone involved?"

"Looks that way. Do you know anything about this girl?"

"Nope. Just that her hair color is the same as in the pictures."

"Do you know anyone who'd have a grudge against her?"

"No. She's...got a lot of admirers, but she keeps to herself. Do you have any idea of how these pictures were taken? Or how they ended up here?"

"Nope. Not a clue. But I'm sure we'll have more to go on shortly."

"I expect this to be taken seriously, Peter. This is no joke. We have enough trouble with the male faculty."

"What do you mean?"

"In spring, early summer, when the girls start wearing the spaghetti-straps and short-shorts, low-rise jeans, and tank-tops. It seems that some of the men have a problem keeping their remarks to themselves."

"I'm not aware of…"

"Oh, c'mon, Peter, get real. Just because it's not in writing on your desk doesn't mean it doesn't happen about a hundred and forty times a day around here."

"If…"

"How are these girls supposed to protect themselves from uninvited comments by faculty who are grading them and helping determine their futures? By 'writing them up'?"

Peter remembered that Diane was thirty-eight years old and unmarried. He told himself to draw no conclusions about that.

After she left he took out another manila folder and wrote "Iatsik Section 9 Investigation" in his best handwriting.

———•———

Dominic Ippoliti (known as "The Duke" in legal circles) moved to suppress on thirteen different counts. Father Mark was nervous about the number thirteen, but The Duke persevered in his time-honored practice of ignoring his clients' fears and gut instincts and proceeded to mount the most professional defense possible, given the unfortunate circumstances.

Dominic's greatest successes had come within the past two years. The acquittal of an out-of-state father who was accused of abducting his own daughter in a nasty custody dispute was a major coup, as was his successful defense of two local policemen accused of sexually harassing a fellow cop who happened to be female. The Duke's cross-examination of the woman on the stand, following her tearful testimony, was now legendary within the county. Not only had the woman's case fallen apart in five minutes flat, the woman was lucky Dominic didn't sue her for making life difficult for his clients over the past year. (He had considered this, in fact, but it was further than the policemen were willing to go.) The woman quit her job a month after losing the case.

The Duke, it would seem, had a way with words.

Chief amongst The Duke's requested reasons for dismissal of charges against Father Mark were:

1. Inadequate supervision of crucial pieces of evidence (i.e., the chalice allegedly coated with five of the boys' semen);

2. The Deputy's initials on the paperwork-transfer were less than clear;

3. Failure to properly Mirandize his client before taking statements from Father Mark (The Duke always challenged on these grounds; even though there was a videotape of the Mirandizing this time, the sound quality was poor. "How do we know whose voice we are really listening to, Your Honor?" he asked.);

4. Failure of the prosecution to share all its evidence with the defense (the list of pornographic movies found in Father Mark's bedroom, forwarded to The Duke, was alleged to be incomplete and may have been tainted by the local police who viewed it for no other reason than to watch free porn); and—most important;

5. Press coverage and resultant widespread prejudice had made a fair trial for his client impossible.

The Duke was also prepared to argue that clergy-client confidentiality statutes made any statements made by the young men in question specious and inadmissible. ("From this moment on we only refer to them as 'young men,' kapish?" he advised Father Mark.)

In each instance, he pointed out to the judge, the case should be thrown out of court and closed. "There are thirteen different ways this unfortunate case is a waste of The People's precious time and energies, Your Honor," he said, gesturing with a heavy-looking stack of manila folders, before setting them down with a weary "thunk" on the desk before him. "In the interest of justice, we ask that this case be dismissed without further delay." The Duke turned briskly around and sat down.

What the heck. You gotta be in it to win it, he said to himself, flipping through his calendar.

Judge Reinhardt would take it under advisement and rule in two weeks.

———≫•≪———

Angel showed up on time for his appointment with Dolores. He was wearing a loose long-sleeved rayon shirt with a very sixties-looking paisley design on it. The shirt was, of course, open and loose over a t-shirt or something beneath it. God forbid he dress like a successful student, even for a moment, Dolores thought.

Angel sat down and looked directly into her eyes the way very controlling men often do. It bordered on a challenging look. He looked like he had been studying hard how to pull off looking like just a student, instead of appearing like a manipulative sociopath. Dolores immediately disliked him. More than before. For everything that he ever did to young women, for the things that he would do in the future to young women. For the things that he would never admit to anyone.

"Very sixties…"

"Excuse me?"

"The shirt. Very sixties," she said.

"Oh. Mmmm-hhhhh." He had no idea what she was talking about.

"So…I take it school hasn't been going as successfully as it could," she said, lobbing him a softball to open things up.

Angel looked at her. He didn't hear anything he had to respond to. School mattered to him less and less these days and it would be hard to make believe otherwise.

"Not going your way?"

"I don't get what you are really asking me," Angel said.

"I'm asking you if you are happy with your level of accomplishment in school thus far."

"Oh. No, I guess."

"Was school always this hard for you?"

"No."

"What was the last grade that was successful?"

"Fourth."

"And now you are stuck, spinning your wheels, in tenth."

"Well I was supposed to be in eleventh or twelfth, I think, but they lost my records when they sent them."

"Didn't anyone re-request them?"

"I think they did, but they weren't the same courses from the school I was in…"

Dolores scribbled a note to herself.

"Is anything particular going on right now, in your family, or with friends, for instance, which might explain some of the downturn in academic performance?"

"No. Nothing. Everything is the same."

"No recent deaths, divorces, money pressures?"

"No. Everything is good."

"Then…how do you explain it?"

"Explain what?"

"Your poor academic performance. And attendance."

"I dunno. I just don't feel like coming to school a lot."

"Physically, or mentally?"

Angel was genuinely confused by this. "I dunno. Like I said, I just don't feel like coming to school. Or studying."

"What has your diet been like?"

"I haven't been on a diet."

"No, I mean…what do you eat?"

Angel tried to keep a straight face. "What do I eat? The usual."

"Do you have breakfast?"

"Yes."

"Every day?"

"Yes."

"What do you eat for breakfast?"

"Frozen Reese's Peanut Butter Cups, sometimes Pop-Tarts, and Jolt."

Dolores scribbled quickly. "Jolt?"

"Yeah. It's a soda."

"Oh yes. With extra caffeine."

"Yeah. Wakes me up."

"Tell me about the peanut butter cups."

"What's to say? They are frozen. They're little."

"How many of them do you eat?"

"It's different each day."

"On average…"

"About seventeen. Eighteen."

"For breakfast?"

"Yes."

"With soda?"

"Jolt."

She scribbled some more.

"Do you take any multi-vitamins or supplements?"

"No."

"Tell me about lunch."

"What about it? Pizza and fries. School lunch."

"Every day?"

"That's what they give me. That's the only thing they make here that isn't bleeding or doesn't have a thumbnail stuck in it."

Dolores knew this was true. She had been embattled with the Director of Food Services over this for the past five years, writing memos, carbon-copying the superintendent, even writing letters-to-the-editor about the fact that the daily high school lunch was—almost without exception—bad pizza and greasy French fries. It was just barely assured that the soda machines—an exclusive contract with Pepsi that benefited the Varsity Club only—were closed during the regular school hours. The response to her entreaties was always the same: the Food Services Dept. was working within guidelines set down by the F.D.A. and strived to satisfy its customer base while assuring parents of a quality product. In other words, if the kids wanted crap, give them crap. Dolores fumed when she thought about the fat content of this. Angel was a perfect example of this whole "Failure to Learn Syndrome." She already knew what the answer would be to her next question.

"And what do you eat for dinner?"

"I don't eat dinner."

"Any snacks between lunch and the next morning?"

"Soda. Sometimes I have flan."

"Flan?"

"Yeah. It's a dessert."

"I've never heard of it."

"You've never heard of flan?! You don't get out much, huh?" Angel's eyes sparkled.

"Well what is it?"

"It's like, I don't know how to explain it, it's like a custard, with a lot of eggs and sugar, kind of a crusty top. It's very sweet."

"And it is…"

"Latino, yes."

Angel knew what she thought of him. He knew she had him stereotyped as some sort of bad-boy, tough-guy, probably running with a gang (he didn't) and that—additionally—she thought anyone with his color skin, his accent, and his ways (anyone who ate flan?) was exactly the same. She was a stone-cold gringo bigot. You could see it in her eyes.

"Angel, I'm concerned. I don't know specifically the fat and sugar content of the peanut butter cups you eat but, in general, your eating habits are very unhealthy. The protein content is minimal, and starting your day off with chocolate and caffeine sets you up for a glucose drop in very short order. Let me show you." She took out a piece of graph paper and started drawing.

Angel drifted, thinking of his missing girl, Rasheeda, and his missing mini-me, Angel, Jr. It was just wrong that they had fled. In a way they were acting on the same assumptions as this Honky Lady—that he'd be irresponsible, was stupid, violent, immature. O.K., he'd cut the dealer in the city, but almost anyone with a reputation to uphold would've after buying dummy crack (Ivory soap? C'mon, now…) He could've killed the guy, but didn't (as far as he knew). Besides that there was nothing else to label him violent except two prior arrests—aggravated harassment (of Rasheeda and her mother) and felony criminal mischief (for tagging commercial buildings with graffiti). Both had been bargained down to misdemeanors because they hadn't involved drugs. If he was going to be some sort of killer, people would've known it by now. He would have definitely killed by now. Probably.

He looked at this pathetic old lady in front of him, drawing hills and valleys on her chart. Total freak.

"...So after the sudden drop in blood-sugar, you are left with a craving for more, which you fill, at lunch, with a sugary, high-fat, high-carbohydrate lunch—oh, I forgot to ask you if you have dessert at lunch..."

"Yeah, I do. Ice cream. An ice cream sammich..."

"O.K., then...so...."

She drifted off into the graph again. Angel thought about himself. Feeling that the years were going too fast now. So he wasn't going to be a head-banger, and he wasn't going to be a stoner, and he wasn't going to be a prep...what was he going to be?

He kept coming back to what he was: a father. He would live as a father. He might even be a husband, with Rasheeda—if she let up on being a bitch so often. He could get a job, he could raise Angel, Jr. to stay out of trouble. He was always touched by that old Will Smith video where he holds his baby son and says, "I've got your back." That's what he wanted. To hold his son and tell him, "I've got your back."

"So I want you to keep a food diary for a week, alright?"

She was handing him something.

"Any questions about how to enter things?"

"No."

"I'll send a pass for you."

"O.K."

She wrote him a pass to return to class. He rose to leave. "See you next week," Dolores said.

"O.K...See you," Angel said.

Dolores thought that it had gone better than she thought it would have. She attributed it to her experience. It was because she was so ready for him, ready for his Prince Charming act. He seemed to be at least thinking about diet, about taking it somewhat seriously.

Most important, he seemed to have reached some sort of quiet place by the end of the session. There was a look on his face…She was familiar with the look.

It was the look of a good session.

Blown Away

Bobby and his cousin cut the last four periods of school to shoplift automotive supplies from United Liquidators' Bargain Barn. This was a touchy area for Bobby, as his Monte Carlo had been destroyed not three weeks before and his need to accessorize, at present, was limited. The shit was for his cousin, and it was payback for cooperating with what the two of them were about to do to Ernie's '73 Plymouth Duster.

They waited, and did some 'E.' Then they drank some Buds.

They rode through town, under a half-moon, on their two small Sting-Ray bicycles; it made them look half their age. In their backpacks were a big pack of sand, sixteen M-80's, four Gatorade glass containers full of gasoline, a package of the good kind of kitchen matches, a black grease-marker, bottle-rockets, and two packs of Redman chewing tobacco. Eight Banana-Coconut Auto Scent cutouts from Liquidators' (in the shape of a pot leaf, or something), two cigarette lighters, a funnel, two cans of WD-40 and a can of STP rounded out the inside of Bobby's knapsack. He had also left some homework handout from Health class in there. ("Knowing When to Say 'No'!" was the headline. "Hyuhhhh, right!!! How about 'Knowing When to Say Fuck You,'" he joked to his cousin before crumpling the assignment and throwing it in the Sunoco station's garbage.) The two of them on their bikes breezed past some old lady in a pink "Hugs Not Drugs" t-shirt, zipping through the car bays like a pair of flying squirrels on acid.

They ditched their bikes a half block away from Ernie's and walked as quietly as they could, choosing the grass on the inside of the sidewalk. His cousin farted and Bobby was about to say, "You nasty-assed motherfucker!" when he remembered they had agreed to keep their f'ing mouths closed until the job was done.

As they approached Ernie's house, they could see him in the downstairs family room, watching wrestling reruns ("Vintage Warfare") on t.v. The Rock was slamming some guy in a tutu to the ground. Ernie had a 48-inch projection t.v. in a house that was a micro-step above a trailer home. What were once flowers out front were now a ratty mess. The shingles on his house were coming off in pieces, the room was eroding, and the house hadn't been painted since Ernie's stepfather came back from the Vietnam War. (His stepfather had the best collection of *Hustler* magazines and videos in the whole county, including ones of girls peeing.) Still, Ernie had that fucking Mitsubishi/Japasuki projection t.v., or whatever it was, and if there had been a way to blow that up, instead of the car, Bobby would've done it.

Fortunately, the volume on the t.v. must have been deafening, because they had no trouble approaching the Duster without the two dogs, Junkyard and Lardass, waking. And, after all, it was 2:45 a.m.

They watched Ernie, the stupid, ass-kissing, underarm-sweating, garbage-eating, breath-stinking, pimp-for-Richie shove his sixth Ring Ding into his mouth. With an upward nod of Bobby's nose they swung into action.

Bobby stuffed three M-80s into the tail pipe as his cousin quietly opened the back doors. He could smell the gasoline slowly leaking out over the upholstery of the back seat. His cousin laid out five M-80s on the seat.

Bobby took out the funnel, opened the pack of sand, and quietly poured it into the gas tank.

They weren't too sure what to do with the front seat, so they settled for just dousing it all in gasoline and laying some more M-80s at odd angles. The M-80s in the tailpipe had a long fuse, so they figured they'd be able to light it, light at least one in both the front and back seats and get the fuck out of there to watch the whole thing blow from the corner.

Finally Bobby took out the grease marker and wrote on the front windshield: "I Suck Richie's Cock Every Day and Like It." He used his best "anonymous" handwriting to fool the cops. This was more work than he had figured, and more work than he had done in school since whenever. They both looked nervously inside as Bobby labored over this. No problem: Ernie was watching some black MTV sluts dancing around in those low-rider bell-bottoms. Fag.

Wondering if they had enough time, Bobby's cousin whispered, asking if he could write some shit on the rearview mirrors. Bobby said yeah, and he scrawled, "I Like Boys" on the left one and "Do My But" on the right.

"Two t's," Bobby whispered.

"What?"

"Two t's in 'butt.'"

"No way."

"Just add it, you friggin' moron."

"Don't talk to me like that. I don't even think you're right. What'd you get in English last quarter. A thirteen, right?"

"Just do it and let's blow the fucker up."

"It was a thirteen, right?"

"How the fuck do I know? I don't remember that shit."

"So you're the expert now, on spelling? I got a fifty-five. 'Butt' has two t's only when you are adding on to it."

"Adding on to 'butt'? Like, how?"

"I don't gotta justify this to you."

"You're strange, y'know that? You're like…a poster child for retards-with-hope."

"Oh, fuck you, like you're not."

"I don't go around 'adding on to butts.' Faggot. Rump-Ranger."

"Butt-chunk."

"You're too stupid to know what I even mean. I'm leaving it."

"'Butt' with one 't'?"

"Yeah."

"Hey, it's your funeral."

"Yeah, like who didn't spell 'nigger' wrong the last time?"

"Shut the fuck up."

Lardass stirred; he could hear something in between the commercials for Stridex and stuff for jock itch.

"Wooooooof!" A low, half-hearted rumbling gave forth from the old dog.

"Oh shit. Shut up. Shut up. Did Ernie hear?"

They looked over…ohmygod…Ernie was rubbing the front of his pants to a Mariah Carey video. Mariah Carey??? That old divorced hag? Holy shit—she *did* look good, they had to admit, in the "classic" video. You kept waiting for her to make the wrong move and show her pussy. Bobby and his cousin froze, mesmerized, staring at Mariah's longed-for pubes. Ernie continued to rub himself, absent-mindedly. Bobby and his cousin would puke—and laugh—if Ernie whipped it out, in earnest.

"WOOOOOOFFF!!" Lardass offered again.

"Oh shit, let's light up. FUCK Mariah Carey."

"Duhhhh."

"C'mon, like she'd ever look at your dick, you homo. Let's go, go, go. I do the pipe, you get the front, I do the back seat…and FAST."

"Oh fuck…we should've had two matches."

"We got about a hundred and twenty-eight."

"I mean two boxes, to strike 'em."

Bobby had to admit his cousin was right.

"Alright, no problem. We do…Plan 'B.' I light the back, we quickly come over and light the front, use one of the lit front ones to do the back. And we have to jet, double-time."

Lardass lumbered to his feet, stumbling forward, knocking Junkyard out of his slumber as he bumped into him. "WOOOOOOOOFFFF!!!" A much different, angrier bark. Junkyard was awake.

"Oh shit…that's Junkyard." They checked Ernie; he had stopped rubbing himself.

"Let's do it."

Bobby ran around behind the car with the matches and struck a match. It flamed and fizzled out. He struck another one. It flamed and fizzled out.

"Don't leave the empty matches!"

"What the fuck are you talking about?"

"I mean, the ones that didn't burn. They can trace them."

Bobby ignored his pinhead cousin and quickly—professionally, he thought—lit a match that stayed lit. He brought it to the long fuse and held it a fraction of an inch away. It caught.

"Let's go!! Open the front door! Open the door, doofus!"

His cousin did. The match quickly burned down to Bobby's finger and stung him. He blew it out.

"Great." He lit another one. They both were aware of the seconds passing as the fuse in the tailpipe burned.

He brought the lit match to one of the front M-80s. He chose one with a long fuse. It caught. "Beautiful...Hand me one of the back ones."

"What?"

"Hand me one of the fuckin' back ones, FAST!"

Junkyard started barking ferociously. Not to be outdone, Lardass joined in, in his best remembrance of years past.

"Why can't it just be on the front ones that we throw in back?"

"No time. Gimmee it. Get ready to run. GIMMEE it!"

Lighting the new M-80 with the already lit one, Bobby dropped the match. It was almost out anyway. The entire carpet of the front quickly lit up. Bobby's shins began to roast and his cousin's sneakers burst out into flames.

"Holy shit!" Bobby dropped the unlit M-80 and the lit one. He slammed his shoulder against the front door in an attempt to do an emergency rescue of himself, like he had seen once on a show where a car went underwater, only the door was already open and he spilled out onto the cement, shattering his shoulder as he hit.

His cousin was already fifteen yards away from the car, flames shooting from his feet and—somehow—his ass. Or— at least—the ass of his pants.

For some reason Bobby reached over to the front door and tried to close it, thinking it would cause more damage to the car that way. That is when the front seat blew. Forgetting that the fuses in front were shorter than the ones in the tailpipe, he was caught with his right hand on the door when the entire thing exploded outward, taking his thumb, most of his index finger, and the top third of his middle finger with it, skyward, in an arc of orange and yellow explosive flame. The sound was deafening, as heat roasted the insides of his eardrums and flames caught onto his face. He rubbed out the flames in his face and he could see the lights in the neighborhood going on, as the sound of enraged dogs grew closer. He ran, ran, ran, not knowing if he was on fire. He couldn't breathe, but he ran anyway. He collapsed a few moments later, rolled over a few times ("Stop! Drop! And Roll!"—from kindergarten) and sat up. Ernie was out on the front yard, screaming. The Duster's top was burning and another explosion—the tail pipe, finally!—took out the entire rear of the trunk, sending it skyward, hitting the tree near it, with shrapnel flying past Ernie at a couple of hundred miles an hour.

Good M-80s! Bobby thought, before looking down to realize that his thumb was missing and that a hunk of gore was there in its place. A fraction of a second later the pain hit. It was excruciating. It was worse than your nuts in a vise. It was like having a tractor run over your head slowly, then back up over it, then keep doing it.

Bobby was swept up by his cousin, who was on his Sting-Ray. He threw Bobby onto the handlebars and started riding, FAST. They did a block when Bobby's ass slumped through the handlebars, causing him to fall off the bike, vaguely in front of the bike, just at the same time his cousin decided they needed to accelerate. His cousin basically ran him over, in a sideways direction, before careening off the bike, himself. Bobby's bleeding hand braced his fall, getting gravel, dirt, squirrel shit, and miscellaneous pebbles in his thumb-stump as he felt the wheels go over him. He screamed, as did his cousin.

Then they laughed.

"What happened to your thumb, buddy?"

"I don't know. It's back there."

"You wanna go back and get it?"

"I don't think so. Fuck."

"You gotta go to a hospital. I've seen this shit in movies. They can reattach it."

"Not if it was blown up, you moron. You ever see that?"

"They reattached that guy's dick."

"That was cut off, not blown up."

"Can you ride your bike?"

"I don't know."

"Well, you got to, because it's here and they'll trace it."

Bobby sat on his Sting-Ray. There was no way he could ride it. He wanted to pass out, puke, shit, sleep, and be dead all at the same time. He could hear Junkyard in the background.

He put one foot in front of the other and began to peddle.

———

Bonnie walked into the gym with some trepidation. It had been three weeks. During this time she had eaten: cheese cake (once); Sara Lee crumb cake (three times), brownies (also three times), and lasagna made with whole-milk cheese for the past three days (the original day she cooked it, and two left-over days). Additionally she had gone off her balsamic vinegar-and-oil dressing to return to the gloppy ranch dressing she had loved as a kid. But she wasn't welcoming a return to the pudginess associated with most of her teen years.

She flashed her I.D. card at the effortlessly-thin eighteen-year-old blonde who sat at the desk ("Hi," the girl droned, her voice dripping with condescending sweetness) and headed for the locker room. Was it her imagination or was there something in the way the girl greeted her that was saying it was so wonderful that even someone as chubby as

Bonnie would make the EFFORT to try to exercise, even though it was probably a hopeless endeavor? She wanted to deliver a Sara Lee cheesecake to the girl and...better yet, tie her arms behind her in the chair and spoon-feed it to her, in between helpings of lasagna. She calmed down and tried to check out her figure in the full-length mirror without appearing to do so too obviously. She took a deep breath and sighed.

When had her body begun to betray her? Just the added little padding on the hips, the added little padding on her butt, the added little chub to her belly, the added little padding to her cheeks when she smiled, the added little padding on her calves...Little plus little plus little plus little plus little plus little equaled...FAT. No, all right, not fat. Chubby? Yeah.

Age twelve. It wasn't fair. She had been lean, long-legged, muscular, and the best in her class at soccer. She was the second fastest girl in her class. She was described as "foxy" by most of the boys in her class, right up until ninth grade. After then the adjective began softening up, until "really cute" replaced it. There was some power in being considered "a fox." There was nothing but "niceness" associated with being "cute." A cute girl was expected to wait around for a guy to notice her. A fox was expected to have a long waiting list of guys waiting to die to be with her, to become electrified in her presence.

The fox years had come and gone quickly. She wasn't destined to be one. She knew it was even stupid to want to be one anymore. She was mature, she was reasonable, she was in her right mind. She wasn't going to be a movie star, so why did she keep reading about them all the time? Why the subscriptions to *People*, *In-Style*, *Elle*, *Us*, and—worst of all—*Cosmo*? I mean, did she even need to read about "Secret Hot

Spots to Drive Men Crazy," or "Touch Him Here for Torrid Summer Sex" when she didn't even have a boyfriend? Was there something about the idea of becoming a total slut that was so compelling that she couldn't cancel her subscription to this monthly parade of bimbos-without-a-clue? Was she addicted to the confessions of these tall, blonde exhibitionists who didn't have to work for a living, except to let people take pictures of them from different angles? ("Here's my ass! Here are my breasts! What do you think? Wouldn't you want me? Aren't I okay, really?") It was pathetic. It was far sadder than porn.

So were the photo features of the worst fashions worn to the Oscars, the Grammys, the MTV Awards. She guessed it was fun to catch celebrities looking like slobs. As if that made her less chubbed-out. In a way, she thought, it did.

Two girls in their underwear caught her looking at herself and looked away fast. "Nice," she thought. "Like I really need to compare myself some more in my life." She quickly put on her baggy athletic shorts and hit the treadmill.

It felt good to walk. It felt good to walk long and fast. It felt good to tell her mind to shut up. She was o.k. when she shut up. Her breathing deepened. The clutter of the diet-magazine/comparison world was swept away.

She was thinking about Alan. Why? He hadn't called again since the day after the café. She must have made a total idiot of herself.

And what, even, if she hadn't? Would she even want him?

Well, yeah. He was pretty good for a divorced man. He didn't seem to be a lech, sadistic, or cheating on anyone else. This already defied the odds for any guy over twenty-five.

199

Unless he was gay. He was in social work, after all. Helping people? Through talking all day? Not exactly the most masculine profession.

The jury was out. Maybe he was just making believe he was sensitive and wanting to help people. Maybe he had a whole other secret past life in another state. Maybe this was the only career he could find. And it was kind of sickening the levels of attention he got just because he was a male social worker. Like he was a *Weekly World News* story about a great white shark who became a household pet and babysat for toddlers in a little round pool on the side of the house while the parents were away at the movies. Shut up, Bonnie, just shut up and admit that you have no idea about men. He could be a killer, he could be a rapist, he could be the father of your children.

He could, even, call.

———

Bobby's mother—called by the hospital at 3:52 a.m.—arrived wearing a ketchup-stained t-shirt and pink stretch-pants. She didn't seem to notice his heavily-bandaged hand. Bobby was embarrassed to see her fat heifer-like body waddling around the emergency room complaining to the nurses.

"Do you know what it's like getting called like that? Do you know what it does to me? I need my sleep. They nearly gave me a heart attack. I can't be running around for you in the middle of the night. I've got the sugar diabetes. I could lose my foot. I've got to deal with Bianca, Billy, and Barbie at home, crawling all over me, you think I don't need my sleep? And what did you do to your hand?" she said, directing her gaze at him.

"It got messed up."

"Got messed up? Got messed up? At three o'clock in the morning it gets messed up?"

"Yuh."

"How do you think we're supposed to pay for that? Huh? We don't have insurance. You think emergency rooms grow on trees? Do you?"

"No."

"And tomorrow is bowling. Tomorrow is my bowling league. We're in the semi-finals. You knew that when you did this. You wrecked my sleep because tomorrow is the semi-finals. It doesn't mean anything to you, does it?"

"Ma..."

"No. I know you did this to inconvenience me. Just you wait. Just you wait and see how I'll inconvenience you. The day before bowling when we're in the semi-finals. Unbelievable, this kid," she said to the nurse as she signed him out and got the after-care sheet of instructions. "Drive me here, drive me there, come get me in the middle of the night, well what about me? When am I supposed to sleep? WHEN?"

JERRY SANDER

BEYOND THE DRESS CODE

Peter hated these Section 9 things, even before they centered around pornographic pictures of students that he, himself, had brought in. The parties involved were rarely completely satisfied and everyone walked out of his office looking at him like he was a complete schmuck—a sellout. They'd leave, grumbling, threatening, implicitly or explicitly, further appeal. Usually there was no further follow-through, but the prospect of Elliot's review or—worse yet—a legal challenge to his decisions made the whole thing fraught with tension.

Additionally there was the "right-and-wrong" thing about setting down some moral standards for the kids and providing a decent atmosphere.

Peter hadn't gone into school administration to become a Sunday-school teacher. He was personally uncomfortable with the latest wave of politically correct redress to all the various ways people alleged to have been "hurt" by good old-fashioned jokes. The stuff he had heard the secretaries telling each other, on their breaks, made his ears curl. Most of it centered around dick size. Should he write them up? Say they made it a "hostile environment" for him? Say that he couldn't function because he now knew they might be sizing him up when he talked to them about memo-circulation and the special-events calendar? The truth was that the only "hostile environment" he knew of was trying to wake up at 5:00 a.m. on a dark February morning when freezing rain and wind-chills below ten were howling around his Buick Century.

Peter didn't buy this whole "victimhood" trend. Everybody was a victim nowadays. Everyone had a list of excuses as to why they couldn't do his or her job. And they all centered around "prejudice," "sexism," "racism," "homophobia." Now everyone needed Oprah to hold his or her hand just to get through an eight-hour work day.

None of this changed the fact that he had to interview everyone, appear to be neutral, help all parties come to a resolution, and write the damn thing up so that further review would uphold his wisdom.

Peter had to hope that the Three Stooges would somehow turn on each other and allege that the photos came from one of their homes. Or that one of them had given them to him earlier in the day, only to have the others take it. Something like that.

The fact that that might not be technically true was different from the fact that it was absolutely necessary to know that this problem didn't emanate from anyone who was employed by the school district.

Such as himself.

Mona buzzed.

"Yes?"

"Kendra Iatsik is here."

Peter could tell from just the slightest molecular twinge in Mona's voice that she disapproved—of Kendra, of all the males in the building who found Kendra attractive, of thongs, of the prospect of Peter questioning Kendra alone without a woman present, of Peter's whole approach to this (which she knew nothing of)...of everything. Mona's ability to communicate disapproval in four little words while announcing someone's arrival was a miracle. The woman was skilled in a million annoying directions. Peter knew for years that she thought she could do the principal job better than he in a heartbeat.

She also knew exactly what she was doing and that she held the school together. When Peter was out of the building for meetings, hearings, etc., he trusted her more than he trusted his A.P.'s. He'd just have to put up with her.

"Send her in."

"Okay."

"Oh, Mona?"

"Yeah?"

"Are her parents, or an attorney, here with her?"

"No. She's by herself."

"Okay. You know she was entitled to that."

"Yes, I know. We all know."

Peter felt the muscles in his arm tighten and he found himself wanting to punch something. Why was he trying to justify anything to Mona? It was like trying to push water uphill.

"Just send her in."

"I already did."

Peter looked up; the ravishing girl/woman he had seen so very, very naked a few nights before was sitting in his office, staring at him. Probably sizing him up. Peter blushed—goddamn it!—and hung up the phone in a reasonable rhythm.

She was wearing a short white skirt (what was that? vinyl?), a trim light-blue tank-top and white boots. She looked far better than her pictures. And her pictures—although terribly inappropriate, illegal, immoral, wrong, and corrupted—were, Peter had to admit, memorable.

Peter sensed his fear rising from his toes. He grew cold, slow and deliberate. He dare not feel. He was the Section 9 Arbitrator and he was the building principal. He had business to do.

"You called for me?" And she smiled.

How the hell could this girl smile on a day like this, he wondered. "Yes, I did, Kendra. I'm Peter Epperschmidt, your building principal. I don't believe we've met before."

"Yuh, uh, hi." She went to extend her hand, but gave a little wave instead. He watched the tips of her waving fingers, touching electric particles of air in his direction, then sinking back to rest on her upper thighs.

Either Peter was reading into it too much or the girl was already mocking him. The little wave probably communicated a type of contempt, as if she were saying, "Ummm, like, I could be in math class learning something right now instead of wasting time with you." Peter thirsted for a G&T so badly he could practically taste the lime on his lips.

"Please. Have a seat."

She did. He studiously avoided noticing anything about how she crossed her legs, or whatever the vinyl skirt looked like as it clung to the luscious outline of her body.

"You know you have the right to have your parents here for this meeting, as well as the right to be represented by legal counsel."

"Yeah, we know. We got the letter."

"And?"

"They didn't want to come. And I don't want a lawyer at the moment."

"I see. Do your parents...understand the essence of the situation?"

"What do you mean?"

"Do they understand what happened the other day?"

Kendra shifted in her seat. "I don't know what they understand." She stared directly at Peter. Her eyes were crystal-clear blue and gave him the most direct gaze he'd had from a female in many years.

"Well…it seems kind of important that they'd understand. I'm not exactly comfortable proceeding without hearing from them about this."

Kendra rose, smoothing down her skirt and walking slowly toward Peter's desk. "Here," she said, laying a folded-up piece of paper onto his desk. Peter studiously avoided looking at her perfect rear when she returned to her seat. He flashed on having stared at the unclothed version of it before this was all wrong. He focused on the note:

> Please excuse us from attending the Section 9 meeting with yourself and Kendra. We wish for the meeting to proceed without us. We are respecting Kendra's wishes and are not seeking an attorney at this time. Kendra can speak for herself regarding this matter.
>
> Sincerely,
>
> Paul and Joanie Iatsik

Paul and Joanie had each signed his or her first names, with Joanie signing "Iatsik."

"All due respect, but I need to verify that these are their signatures."

"No problem."

Peter buzzed Mona.

"Yeah?"

"Could you come in here for a moment, Mona, please?"

"Yup." She appeared in the doorway almost instantly.

"Would you do us a favor and please call Mr. and Mrs. Iatsik to verify that they sent this letter in with Kendra today? It's important. You might also ask guidance to compare signatures."

"On what?"

"Whatever they've got."

"What would they have?"

"I don't know, permission slips?"

"They don't keep them."

"Something about class selection."

"They don't get a say in that."

Peter was getting really steamed. It felt like both these women were laughing at him.

"Never mind. Just get the parents on the phone."

"Will do." Mona turned on her heels and left.

Kendra smiled. "Is she always such a bitch to you?"

Peter was stunned. "That's not appropriate."

"Oh, well...excuse ME. I forgot, we're in 'High School.' I'm sorry. But...you have to admit, she is a little frosty to you."

Peter mulled it over. This was not good. He could really take a liking to this girl. He focused on the form in front of him. "Preliminary Investigation/Section 9: Iatsik Incident Report."

"We have some work to do, Kendra, and I want to get to it. We owe you nothing less."

"Thank you."

"No problem." He couldn't believe he used the same phrase she did. He needed a drink. "Let's see...we can fill out the top part later, just specifics, age/date/address/year in school...you're a sophomore?"

"Junior, with some sophomore classes."

"How'd that happen?"

"I spent some time goofing off, got mixed up with stuff...finally got it together, started coming to school. Have a lot of catching up to do."

"Ummmm-huh. And what do you see yourself doing after school?" (This wasn't on the form.)

"A model. I'm going to continue being a model." She brushed a strand of falling hair away from her face.

Against everything that was right in the Universe Peter felt a most delicious rush of warm energy through his body. The pictures flashed into his head again, against his will. Or, against part of his will. The thong…

He started saying something, then stopped. The words didn't come out—only the first couple of sounds.

"W…w…wwww…I'm sorry. I was going to say thhhh, thhhhat is very much related to this whole incident this week. I want to extend my personal apologies, and that of the entire school to you, Kendra, for what you had to endure. I can't imagine what it must have been like and I only hope your friendships with other students and adults are sustaining you through this difficult time." Peter was flying by the seat of his pants here, weaving in some auto-pilot remarks he often used when kids had relatives die.

"Yeah, well…"

"I have to be honest with you, though, and tell you that we have to gather the facts of the situation wherever they may lead and that any information you provide us with may be used at a later date in a criminal prosecution—should that be indicated. That is the reason you were invited to bring in a lawyer."

"You mean, like prosecuting whomever brought those pictures in to school?"

Peter stared at her, breathlessly. "No…not so much whomever brought them in to school, but…whomever is responsible for corrupting the morals of a minor."

"Oh…corrupting the morals of a minor?"

"Yes…This might involve the photographer."

Peter thought he could detect just the slightest of smiles at the corner of her lips.

"So the kids who put those pictures up are off the hook?"

"No, absolutely not. In fact, we are waiting to talk to them and they will be dealt with. Make no mistake about that."

"You are going to deal with them? Severely?" There seemed to be a twinkle in Kendra's eyes now.

"I will go wherever the investigation leads, and whomever needs to be dealt with will be dealt with."

"And...that is supposed to make me feel 'protected'?"

"I realize that nothing can make up for what happened."

"Uncorrupted, maybe?"

Peter was lost.

"You've seen the pictures, right?"

He couldn't say it. It was like she knew when and how he saw the pictures.

"You've seen the pictures. I bet you stared at them. I bet you really liked the pictures." Kendra stood. "You know it always amuses me when men try to get inside of women's minds. Maybe it's a substitute for trying to get into our pants, or something, but you pursue it with some...misplaced vengeance. Look, I think you have a good idea of who put the pictures up, you have the name of the photography studio, I guess, and you've met with me. Are there any other questions you want to ask me?"

Peter had at least twenty questions, all of them prurient and unrelated to the investigation. It "amused" her; men "amused" her?

"O.K., then, I'll be going now. Thanks for your interest in this. It's kind of cute."

"Wait a minute."

"You probably think that things like this don't go on all the time with kids, right?"

"What happened this past week with you and your pictures is unprecedented here."

Kendra giggled. "Well, um, maybe you should be checking out the Internet, too. Perhaps? Profile pictures, chatrooms, downloaded videos, IM's, weblogs, NetMeetings, spycameras, duh!!?? I don't know how to say this, but there are thousands of us out there who don't feel awful about our bodies or our souls. I mean, weren't you a teenager once, too?"

Peter stared at her. He got the image of himself in an ROTC uniform, rifle pointing straight up.

"I don't like what happened at school here last week; a bunch of pervy horndogs, huh? But...unless it was pervo teachers doing it, I mean, we're all teenagers, right? I don't expect us to be perfect."

"Ummm-huh. So you are saying you don't want this investigation to continue?"

"No, I'm not saying that. I think it might be interesting, actually. It might amuse me. And I don't like the thought of people seeing the pictures without paying for them."

"You mean..."

"I mean they were from a magazine that makes its money through sales, not through free distribution of pirated copies."

"I see. Well, Kendra, I have to tell you that I have an obligation to the other kids, each and every one...children whose good mothers and fathers put them on the buses in the morning, expecting that they come here and learn and leave at the end of the day slightly better, more informed. These are the ones who might be harmed by the establishment of a hostile environment, one which might impede their learning."

"You mean when they're not on crack, E, crank, rock, weed, schnapps, beer, K, or 'shrooms? When they're not hammered on Jack Daniels, blotter acid, Ketel One,

Hypnotique, and whippets? O.K. Yeah, my pictures might do it, I suppose. I've been told that by a few guys, actually." She started breezing out of the room. Her white skirt swung in the breeze, as much as vinyl could swing.

Was she actually laughing?

"Let me know how it all turns out. I want to know what crackhead brought them in to school, instead of just whacking off to them at home quietly. If you think I'm asking for home schooling or any nonsense like that, you're totally wrong. I'm going to come to school every day and I'm going to look my best, because I'm going to be a model. I will not be run out of this school by skanks, losers, and druggies. So...get used to me, because I'll be here. I like my body, and I feel bad for anyone who doesn't like theirs."

She was gone. Had he imagined it, or was she looking up and down his body as she made her last remarks?

"Mona, please give Ms. Iatsik a pass."

"She's already gone."

Peter closed his report folder.

"Oh, and I got machines. At all the numbers."

"What?"

"For the parents. Home and work."

"I'm going out. Use my pager if you need me."

"I've got the art teacher on your Palm for a 12:15."

"Reschedule. I'm out."

And he was.

The first G&T got him ready for the second one, which was smooth.

IN IT TO WIN IT

The report from Carly about Elijah was highly annoying. Claire eyed Carly carefully. Carly was popping her gum and adjusting her bangs back in a rhythm that suggested honesty, but it could be a very good imitation of the same, Claire thought.

It had been impossible for her to get the straight story in the three minutes between classes, so they had cut the bus and were walking home. As usual Claire had no books to bring home. Carly had a few, which Claire offered to carry, hoping that she'd feel like she owed Claire something. The trouble with spies was that you never knew when they were a double-agent or in business for themselves. You had to treat them carefully.

Carly reported that she had said hi and introduced herself and asked him if he was Elijah. He said yes, and who-wants-to-know, and she said she blushed and said that she wasn't asking for herself, but for her best friend, Claire, who was wondering. Elijah said something like well-whataya-want-to-know, or what-does-SHE-want-to-know and she asked if he was new. He said yes and she asked if he needed friends because she and Claire knew kids could be mean in a new school.

Claire was irked to hear the "she and Claire" remark. It was supposed to be about her, not Carly-and-her.

Carly then said she had asked if he was in any extra-curricular activities or anything. He said, according to Carly, that he had extra-curricular activities but that they didn't involve school, or school clubs. And here is where Carly was afraid she really screwed up.

"So you're saying you get high?" she had asked him.

"Oh my God, you said that?"

"Yeah."

"That was totally stupid, you know."

"Well...the way he answered the question was like, 'oh yeah, I have ACTIVITIES, heh-heh, but they're not like LEGAL activities."

"That's not what he said."

"But you had to be there."

"Well that's why I sent you there."

They looked at each other. Carly shifted her weight from one foot to the other. Carly had been quietly mirroring Claire's diet and, in fact, had lost two pounds more than her.

"So what did he say?"

"He said, 'I don't do drugs.'"

"Just like that? Like, 'I don't do drugs'?"

"Yuh."

"And that was it?"

"No...he said something else."

"Well???"

"The bell was about to ring. He was gathering up his books real fast and—this is when you saw us both looking at you—he said, 'Drugs are for the unimaginative. I take my own adventures.'"

Silence.

"No way."

"Yeah."

"Where'd he get that? Sergeant Phil from some third-grade D.A.R.E. class? Some MTV commercial?"

"I dunno."

"I can't believe that. This is so friggin' obnoxious."

"Yeah."

"And HE said it?"

"Yuh."

"So, like, he and Miss Priss don't get high, he's saying, and he thinks you and I do because we have, like, no imagination?"

"I guess."

"Or, that he's saying he's boning her all the time so they have no time to get high?"

"He didn't say."

"But he implied it."

"He didn't mention her."

"Did you?"

"No."

"Did he say he had a girlfriend?"

"I didn't ask."

"And then the bell rang?"

"Yeah. I was late to class. I got detention. It was my fourth time."

Claire was oblivious to the self-sacrifice involved on Carly's part.

"Did he ask for my number?"

"No."

"Did it feel like he was curious though?"

"No."

"Y'know, I don't appreciate the attitude, Carly. Just give me a report straight, okay, minus the editorial comments."

"Okay."

"Cause...assuming you are telling the truth and not holding back any key pieces of information, Carly, he's either incredibly stuck up or he's getting laid 24/7."

"Yeah. And I'm not holding anything back."

Silence.

"So how do you get through to a guy who is getting laid 24/7?"

Claire thought. "Hmmmm. I guess if he learns that the girl he is screwing is laughing about him behind his back. That might cause him to rethink things."

"Yuh," said Carly, brushing the bangs out of her face.

———

Patty Epperschmidt and three other women from the Church had taken on an "initiative" offered as a challenge by Minister Terry to bring The Word to the most troubled-of-troubled young people. She, Margaret Bellingham and Cindy Hannaford had all been present for the New Millennial Conference Weekend ("Spreading Christ's Fellowship Through Song, Story, Journaling, and Prayer!") The three women had several things in common (which they concluded, during the final fried-chicken dinner of the weekend, was no "coincidence"):

1. They all originally had dirty-blonde hair which was now colored, or tinted, something with more "zip";

2. They had all had some modest success with low-carb diets, only to watch in horror as the pounds came flying back after one or two modest binges on summer vacation;

3. All of them had come to Jesus later in life, having been raised in a secular culture that valued garbage, promiscuity, and alcohol abuse;

4. They had all cried nonstop through the Mel Gibson movie; and

215

5. They were determined to translate the messages of the weekend into practical action, rather than leaving it as "mere feel-good inspiration."

Though none of them had been raised with anything beyond Santa Claus/Easter Bunny pleasantries, they now regarded themselves as anything but weak-willed, penny-social church-ladies. In fact they had no problem being considered Crusaders for the Faith.

And certainly the belly-of-the-beast nowadays was public high school. A place where even mentioning Creation, itself, was against the law! A place where kids could go to get drugs, condoms, and pornography, trade girlfriends, spread diseases, invite each other to all sorts of debauched parties on weekends while their parents weren't around, a place where even a moment of silence during the morning announcements had to be fought for and defended in court. (God forbid you even mention Jesus' name, you'd have Alan Dershowitz on "Nightline" mocking you, just like his people had originally mocked the Lord when he came to the Israelites offering them a New Covenant. Didn't these people ever learn?) If the kids in public schools didn't need the word of God, who did? And Patty was already in possession of knowledge about how bad things had sunk in the school, by virtue of her marriage to Peter.

Not that she exploited the connection. In fact, Peter had made it clear that he wanted nothing to do with her efforts to identify and support students who have come to Christ in the face of a teen culture which, she said, "degrades, humiliates, and antagonizes those of the Christian faith." Patty asked, and Peter answered, but each time Peter made it clear that adults who were "outsiders" were not welcome to "proselytize" within the school.

Yes, it was legal for the kids to start a Bible club.

No, the club couldn't meet during school hours.

No, he wouldn't schedule a meeting between the three women and the Guidance Department.

Yes, having a monthly "prayer circle" in front of the building—before school hours—was probably legal, even if it might not be a good idea.

"Why not?"

"It is too divisive. Not everyone is like you, Patty."

"Do you think Jesus was afraid of being 'too divisive'?"

"I thought he reached out to all sorts of people, actually, Patty, and didn't make people feel excluded. He didn't make them feel weird because they weren't in his little club that met before school."

"That's the Hallmark-Card version of Jesus, Peter. He reached out to sinners, yes, but he made it clear that a Judgment was coming and that people would, in fact, be divided into two groups."

"Yeah, well we have about twenty-nine little groups within the high school—not two—and we have enough problems with them hating each other as it is."

"The twenty-nine are an illusion, Peter. Two."

"Bullshit, Patty."

"Two groups." She looked into his eyes with an intensity he hadn't seen before. It reminded him a little of Kendra.

"Two groups, Peter. Those who are awake to God's love, and those who aren't." She bore into him.

Peter took a deep breath. "Are you talking about me, Patty?"

"Am I, Peter?"

"I'm going to guess that you are suggesting I consider which of your magical two groups I'm in. And I'm going to suggest that you have become a very simple-minded person,

Patty, who has lost her appreciation for the subtleties and nuances of personality that make people unique."

"You think you are 'unique,' Peter?"

"Actually, yeah, I do."

She shook her head with sadness. "Do you think when The Judgment comes you will be asked to walk off to a separate area to be considered as utterly 'unique' when everyone else will be judged either as a sinner or saved?"

"Actually, yes, I do. I expect there will be a special holding area there, with a 'Do Not Trespass—Hold for Peter' sign and that special considerations will be given."

"And what will those special considerations be? That you are an alcoholic? That you have administrative tenure in a school district? That your collection of pornography is one of the more complete ones in our county?"

"Actually, Patty, I expect to be given special compensation because I was married to you. I think it just might be possible that I be considered for sainthood. Saint Peter. Well, Saint Peter Epperschmidt."

Her look turned to stone.

"Because I don't act like a mindless sex-kitten for you, Peter? Because that's the only way you can imagine being a man?"

"You know, Patty, a mindless little sex-kitten sounds kind of okay to me right now after what I've been through with you."

"And what have you been through with me?"

"The Judgment. The Apocalypse. The Big Freeze. No sex. No love. No food. No warmth. Just Jesus."

"You would find those things in Jesus if you would open your mind just a tiny crack and consider that the universe may just happen to be larger than Peter's stomach, balls, and need for constant attention."

"Really, Patty? The universe may be bigger than my balls? How would you know?"

She ignored him.

"I mean, I know you've seen the universe a lot lately, floating around in the clouds, chatting with the prophets, archangels, cherubim, having iced tea with the Holy Ghost, trading recipes with Mary Magdeleine—I believe that, I really do—but I know for a fact that you haven't seen my balls lately."

"Do you think anyone would want to, Peter? Do you?"

A stony silence.

"Get a grip on yourself, Peter."

"Go on, say it—Before it is 'TOO LATE.'"

"O.K. Get a grip on yourself before it is too late."

"Go get your head examined, Patty. And fast."

"The day after you go into rehab for your alcoholism, Peter."

"I'm not an alcoholic, Patty. Though if a person ever needed an excuse to become one, you'd be it."

"And keep telling yourself you are not a sinner, Peter, and are in no need of God's love."

He was flustered, for the first time. "I never said that. It is your strange definition of love that is in question. As well as your plans to screw things up in the high school."

"I think you've done a pretty good job of that yourself."

"Stay out. I'm not kidding."

"The kids will have a Bible Club. We have a teacher who will sponsor it. It will happen. This month."

"Who was it who said, 'Beware the man whose God is in the heavens…'?"

"I dunno, Peter, who was it? Did you get that as graffiti on some kid's locker? Written on a bathroom wall?"

"No, it was George Bernard Shaw, actually."

"First of all I'm not a man. Second of all, my God is not in the heavens. He'll be in your High School."

"Oh yeah? What will he be matriculating as? A transfer tenth-grader? You know what is most galling about you, Patty?"

"Tell me, Peter. I want to experience the full extent of your twistedness."

"What is most galling about you is that you actually believe that YOUR presence and YOUR invitation and YOUR IMPORTANT POINTS OF VIEW are essential to the presence or non-presence of God in our High School."

"It doesn't have to be me. It just has to be, obviously, someone other than you. But it could be you, if you'd open your heart and mind to Him."

"I'm going to open my heart and mind to about fourteen hundred students, a few of whom have two parents, some of whom have two parents who are actually married, hundreds of whom are in various stages of intoxication before, during or after school, a lot of whom have been passed on to ninth grade because they failed eighth grade twice and now are convinced that the way to pass is to fail, about eighty-nine angry faculty members—one-half of whom should have retired when Gerald Ford left office, the other half who were born and raised listening to gangster-rap—a cadre of resentful secretaries, a dozen hand-holding social worker/psychologist types who continue to mandate more expensive social services than our building has budgeted…that's where my heart and mind will be tomorrow, and every day after that, Patty. If I want Sunday school on top of that, I'll go to Sunday school, okay?"

"It's not about you, Peter. The idea was to bring God's presence into the building for the kids. You seem to have this consistent problem, thinking that it's all about you."

"And you don't, Patty? You don't think this is all about YOU? You can't just let kids discover their own beliefs for themselves? Maybe from reading different philosophies? From hearing other points of view? Maybe they don't want to believe anything about God at all. They have to have Patty's Personal Recipe for Salvation rammed down their throats, like so much government-surplus cafeteria cheese?"

"I struggle to continue to feel sorry for you, Peter."

"Better read more parables or something."

"I pray for you every day."

He didn't have a ready comeback for this.

"You can have your Bible Club. After school hours. You can't proselytize during school hours and you can't put up any posters without my signature. And I don't want any crosses larger than two inches high on your posters." He looked at the sadness in her face. It seemed genuine. "Look...I don't want to come on like some Communist Chinese guy persecuting Christians for their faith, Patty, but I'm bound by certain rules."

"You are bound, Peter."

"I have to answer to the students who don't happen to share any of your beliefs, the parents who are offended, the teachers as well as to the superintendent."

"I know, Peter. Your Higher Authority. I am sorry for you, Peter. I don't think you ever wanted to end up this small, did you? This fearful."

"I want you to stop making believe you know me at all, Patty. Just don't try. Spend your time with Jesus. It's a better match. Maybe the two of you understand each other. Maybe he's not disappointed and sick to his stomach by the idea of being with you for an extended period of time."

"'No servant can serve two masters. Either he will hate the one and love the other, or he will be devoted to the one and despise the other.' Luke:16"

"Have you even heard anything I've said, Patty?"

"'The Lord will judge his people and have compassion on his servants when he sees their strength is gone and no one is left, slave or free. Deuteronomy 32:36"

"Are you talking to me, or to yourself?"

"If you get rid of the poison maybe you can learn to love yourself, Peter. Maybe you'll even find a way to like the kids you are supposed to be helping."

MORE THAN ART

Zach had stayed after school twice a week for two months in a row now, but not for the usual reasons. He could regularly be seen carrying armfuls of art supplies, recycling and "found objects" for his art teacher, Ms. Nicole Deggio, filling the Dumpsters out back, stacking things in the class closets, and walking the hallways exchanging casual conversation with her after the other kids left. Zach had found art, it would seem.

And that is how he wanted it to seem.

Ninja Dave had asked him a week earlier if he had "turned into a fruit" and Zach punched him hard in the face.

"Why do you think I'm hanging around her, dumb-fuck?"

"I don't know, you fairy. You want to win a poster contest? How the fuck should I know?"

"What's my nickname?"

"What?"

"No, what's my nickname?"

"Rump Ranger?"

"C'mon, what's my real nickname? The one Richie and you gave me in sixth grade?"

"Pussy Hound?"

"Exactly."

"Ahhhhh...soooo...you're getting into her pants?"

"She hardly ever wears pants."

"Up her skirt?"

"Duhhhhhh! What, you thought I liked art?"

"You've seen her pussy?"

"Would I tell you if I did? Knowing your reputation for shooting your f'ing mouth off all over school?"

"You know what her underpants look like? The color? The style?"

"What makes you think she wears underpants all the time?"

"You've touched her pussy?"

"Look at me. Look at me."

He did.

"Would I tell you if I touched her pussy?"

"I don't know."

"Would I? Consider it."

"No?"

"Would I tell you if we did it doggy-style in her apartment on a Sunday morning when I came by to bring a box full of junk that the auction house threw out?"

"You did it doggy with her? Ohmygod, that is HOT! What did it look like?"

"Dave, you can't be trusted, my friend. If I told you I was boning her it'd be like telling the whole school. And it might get her in trouble."

"But it's true, right?"

"I can neither confirm nor deny."

"When you did it from behind, was she in pants or a skirt?"

"I told you. I'm not going to repeat myself."

"Oh man, I don't know which drives me crazier: her skirt UP while you did it, or her pants DOWN..."

"That's *if* she was wearing anything at all."

"But wearing something is totally hotter than wearing nothing," offered Ninja Dave.

"I agree."

"So which?"

"Look: this conversation never happened. I'm just explaining that...I'm not going to be applying to the Art Institute of Freaking Chicago or something," Zach said.

"I wish you hadn't told me the details."

"I didn't."

"You could get a pair of her undies probably, right?" asked Ninja Dave.

Zach just looked at him.

"Yeah, well, thanks. I think I've got to get my rocks off soon."

"Call Danielle," suggested Zach.

"I can't. She's got some disease."

"You're kidding, right?"

"No, for real. Something. Plasma...sores, something. She's fucked up. That's it for her. She's gonna get these huge disgusting things that ooze, I think, and if you come near her or touch her, even her underwear, you can get them too," said Ninja Dave.

"AIDS?"

"No. Some...phantaplasma thing, I dunno. 'Psycho-plasma'? Once a month or something. In addition to the regular once-a-month stuff. You could ask her. She knows that people know, but they're not supposed to."

"Who told?" asked Zach.

"One of her girlfriends."

"She could still blow you though, right?"

"I don't think so. Well, I mean, yuh, but at your own risk," said Ninja Dave.

"Well, gee, that's really a lovely thought. Big oozy things."

"And they get crusty too, later."

"Hey, shut up, okay? I think I'm gonna puke," said Zach.

"Can I ask you one more question?"

"Yeah."

"Did you and Deggio use a rubber?"

"I'm sorry: those kind of details are off-limits."

"How come?"

"It's just very intimate."

"Got it." Ninja Dave looked sort of defeated, but admiring of Zach.

In reality Zach had gotten as far as sitting at a desk doing some sketches on a Thursday afternoon while Nicole breezed past, the soft folds of her flower-print skirt touching molecules of air which touched other molecules of air which touched Zach's lips, nose, and fingers...the most delicious transport of fragranced energy he could ever recall. There was a scent, some herbal thing. But even it had to be subtly blended with the natural scent of her body. Some molecule of her sexual essence combined with some element of that herbal stuff. Some intimate part of her was now in him. He had taken a deep breath, stood up, and stretched. His "System-of-a-Down" t-shirt rode up over his taut belly, his arms went to the side. His muscles flexed. He knew his jeans fit him snugly and he knew he was half-hard.

Nicole had stood motionlessly, her arms full of poster-board and construction paper. He was just about her height. He was well-built. She allowed her eyes to take in his whole frame.

She's looking at it. She wants me, Zach thought.

Ohmygodthiskidhasanerection, she thought. *And no underwear.*

"Thanks, Zach. For everything. I have to go now. So do you. It was good, though. The help. It was helpful. I have to go."

"Can I walk you out to your car?"

"No. I have to...no. Ladies room. Then...nope. It's o.k., I can get to my car fine."

"See you on Tuesday?"

"Yup. Yup, Tuesday."

Nicole went home and almost forgot about him.

Alan called Dolores, hoping to get her message machine. She picked up.

"Hey, it's Mitchke. Were we supposed to talk about Angel Rivera, or something? Peter said something."

"Oh. No, it's under control. I just need you to make a home visit, make sure he's enrolled in the district legally."

"That's not something I do. There's someone up in the Business Office who handles that stuff. Deb Randolph. She sends out certified letters and if they don't respond she goes out there."

"I think Peter wanted you to go."

"I'm happy to let Deb handle it first."

"Okay."

"Anything else?"

"Nope."

"Is he doing okay? The kid?"

"No, but I think I'm reeling him in."

"Good enough. Bye."

Zach had finished smoking a blunt no more than a minute before his phone rang. He answered it.

It was her.

She wanted to know if he could come in after school tomorrow, instead of waiting until Tuesday.

"Yeah, I could do that," he told her, clearing his throat and taking a sip of Dr. Pepper. He hadn't known that she had his phone number.

Zach leaned back and cranked the stereo. AC/DC filled the room. It was "Balls to the Wall." He smiled. There was a word for that, for when you were thinking something and something just like it came on the radio without you even knowing it first. He just couldn't remember the name for that.

From where he was sitting he looked through his CDs. Someday he'd get one of Danielle's friends to alphabetize them for him. His eyes passed his Stained, his old Eminems, his Korn, his Slipknot...they rested on The Doors.

He got up and pulled "Strange Days" off the shelf. You could never go wrong with The Doors. It was easy-listening.

He walked over to the night table next to the bed and opened the drawer. He pulled out a connected sheet of three Intense Sensation Durex condoms. He put the condoms and The Doors disc in his backpack and smiled.

Judge Reinhold convened the court at 9:30 on a Wednesday morning. It was the first thing on the docket for the day. The judge's milky blue eyes looked bleary beneath glasses which slipped low on his nose. His voice sounded bedraggled and bored already.

The Duke wore his light brown suit. It had brought him good luck in his big kidnapping dismissal two years ago. Father Mark wore a light yellow button-down Lands' End shirt. He shook The Duke's hand vigorously, smiling. The Duke brought him close and whispered in his ear, "Wipe the smile off your face. Look concerned. Look like you're taking this seriously." Father Mark made the adjustment quickly.

The judge cleared some residual phlegm from the back of his throat.

"In the case of The People of the State of New York versus Father Mark O'Connell the court has thirteen motions to dismiss before it, which it has taken under advisement. After careful consideration the Court finds all thirteen motions to be without merit and dismisses them without comment. A trial date is set for July 15. That is all."

His gavel slammed, hard.

The Duke didn't blink. He flipped through the pages of his daily planner and inked something in for the 15th of July.

Father Mark lost two shades of coloring in his face and neck. The Duke pulled him close, his hand on his shoulder.

"This means nothing. Preliminaries. Setting the tone. Doubt is the appetizer. Their case is garbage and we tell them that. We tell them we're not going to back down. Unless you want to." He looked deep into the cleric's eyes. "You wanna plea-bargain? Because it can easily come down to that."

"I don't know."

"Well you think about it."

"What are we talking about? I mean, what would they want?"

"Hard to tell. These are just the preliminaries. Warning shots. You want me to contact them? Or wait till they come to us? That's always better. Either way, they know we say they've got squat."

"The judge didn't think so."

"He did what he was supposed to do. It has nothing to do with the way it's gonna finally go, you'll see."

Father Mark looked at him the way a scared child looks to a parent.

The Duke squeezed him on the shoulder and left.

———•◦•———

The sunshine was abundant and delicious as Alan pulled out toward work. The road was clear, the traffic sparse, the coffee strong.

Five minutes later he gained on a truck in front of him.

"Keep Honkin', I'm Reloading," read the bumper-sticker.

Alan passed Zach on the way into the parking lot. He was walking away from school with Bobby and Bobby's cousin just as most students were walking toward the school. Zach wore his "D.A.R.E. to Keep Cops Off Donuts" t-shirt.

The "priest-abuse" case was big now. Cover stories in *Newsweek* and *Time* about other abusers ("Criminal Clergy?"— with a grainy picture of a nondescript-looking guy being led off in handcuffs; "Organized Crime?," with a picture of a gathering of Cardinals in a cathedral) had made Father Mark's case bigger than it would have been (which was still huge, Alan thought). Alan had been there, actually, when The Duke had argued (unsuccessfully) in his last appearance that "…recent publicity has been so PERVASIVE, REPETITIVE, and PREJUDICIAL, Your Honor, as to render the possibility of a fair trial for my client MOOT. I, therefore, ask for dismissal."

"Denied."

"Then, in the interest of justice, Your Honor—at the very least—I request that this trial be moved to a different venue, where the possibility of finding an untainted jury is increased."

"Denied."

The 15th of July, apparently, meant the 15th of July.

Alan's summer might be glorious. No kids. No parents. No helping anyone. He had his summer reading list all ready. Nothing in it was about helping anyone. There were three monster movies he was looking forward to renting on DVD. He still hadn't seen that one about fire-breathing dragons that attack England.

Alan took his time walking into the building. It was so beautiful out that even the parking lot looked good. He passed three "I'm N.R.A. & I Vote!" cars and—whoa!—one "Magic Is Everywhere" Nissan. A Dodge truck had a "U.S. Marines" decal with an eagle opening a can of "Whoop-Ass." It had been nearly four years since the World Trade Center.

Alan walked in the building and stopped. Bonnie was sitting there, as a building "greeter" (a post-Columbine school job title).

"Uhhh, hi!" he fumbled, thrilled to the sight of her, but feeling enough guilt about not having called to sound screwed up.

"Hi." She had a way of smiling and talking at the same time that melted him.

"You're in today?"

"I guess so. But not for Mona."

"Well, yeah, duh." He hated it when he sounded like one of the kids. He couldn't tell if it were him trying to sound like a kid, him thinking he'd be cooler if he sounded like a kid, or just him being insecure and sounding stupid.

"How've you been?"

She didn't seem furious. "Good."

"Is there any chance we could talk later today? I could take my lunch the same period as yours?"

"I'd like that."

"Eleven-fifteen, then? I'll come by?"

"I brought a salad." (She had kicked ranch dressing again; it was a fat-free Walden's Thousand Island day.)

"I can grab one of those government-cheese sandwiches from downstairs, and we can sit under one of those trees out there."

"I'd like that."

Nicole was clearing up scraps from the desks before her, looking amazing in a clay-colored blouse, Indian vest, and Southwestern-style skirt when Zach entered. He had worn his Jim Morrison shirt. It was black and Morrison looked as horny as Zach felt. The back of it said, "No one here gets out alive." True shit. Morrison had a way with words. Zach also wore it because it might bring them—as representatives of two different generations—together. He had his I.S.D.s (Intense Sensation Durex) and Doors CD in his backpack. His nose searched for her fragrance.

"Zach, would you sit down?"

What if she sat on his lap right here? In school. That'd be so friggin' hot.

Nicole sat at a student's desk, then pulled it closer to him. *YESSS....*

"Can we talk?"

This was going to be, like, birth-control kind of talk. He would be mature.

"Zach...I think...I really value your coming in to do extra art. I think you have some really interesting ways of looking at things. I hope you've enjoyed it, too. But I can't stay after any more."

"Why not?"

"It's...I don't think it's fair. To either of us."

232

"Why not?"

"We have very different roles. We are at very different places in life right now."

"Not so much. You're just a few years older than me."

"That's true. But they are a big few years."

"Age is just a state of mind."

"Maybe so. But the state of mind that is different in being a teacher and in being a student is huge."

"What's that mean?"

"It means that whatever vibe is developing here has to be understood, and stopped."

"You mean 'killed'?"

"Yeah. I mean 'killed.'"

Zach swallowed hard. "Why? Because you get paid to care? Because for you it's all an act?"

Zach quietly did the math. She was 24 (he knew someone whose older brother graduated with her), so she was born about 8 years after Morrison died. She didn't have any more connection with Morrison than she did with Frank Sinatra he realized, too late.

Nicole looked into his eyes directly. "Because I'm starting to feel things that will end badly for us."

"So…you want me, but you don't have the balls to come get me?"

"I want you…to grow up and to find someone good for you."

"What if it's you?"

"It's not me."

"What if it is?"

He took her hand. She looked at it—at him holding her hand, at her hand being held, at her hand wanting to be held, by him, by anyone, by a male, by someone her own age, by someone older—and she considered using the phone to call Security.

"Can I ask you something?" Zach asked. "What is that herbal smelling stuff you were wearing the other day?"

"Amber and heliotrope."

"You didn't answer my other question: What if it's really you for me?"

"If it is…we'll talk about that after you graduate."

Zach's face turned to stone and he threw Nicole's hand to the side. "Don't bother waiting, bitch. One thing is for sure though: I know you'll be alone, and needing to get laid. Bad. But I won't be the one. Because you'll be old by then, and I won't. You'll need an old guy. There are a lot of them around but most of them will be married. And they won't want their wives anymore. Because their wives look like you will start looking, right around then." He stood up and walked for the door. "You might get lucky and snag somebody. But you'll always think about me. I know you will."

Nicole sat and rocked, her right hand holding her stomach for a long time. A million miles away would do. A million.

WHITE GYM SOCKS

Claire set to work as soon as she saw someone at the bus stop. She was disappointed to see that it was Meredith. Meredith was like one of those odor-absorbing sponges they had for sale at the hardware store for ten dollars—she just absorbed information and never spread it around. Though Claire was looking for maximum P.R. firepower, Meredith would be a good dry-run.

Meredith was looking exceptionally mousy today. You could transplant her to, like, Oklahoma in the 1880s, or 1920s, or something and she'd fit in. What a waste being so naturally slim in so boring a personality. Her medium-brown hair was medium length and sort of brushed back on her medium-tall body. "I'd rather drink Drano and eat rat poison than go to school being her," Claire said to herself before greeting mouse-girl warmly.

"Hi! Nice outfit!"

"Thanks." Meredith was suspicious.

"Ohmygod...did you hear about, what's-her-name, that girl in English who always wears that funky stuff?"

Meredith's eyes narrowed. "Who do you mean?"

"What's-her-name? Miss Priss...never wears anything tight? 'Earth-colors,'—quote-unquote—barf-on-a-burrito. Boring stuff. YOU KNOW!! The Jewish one."

"Alison?"

"I guess so! Right! Alison..."

"What about her?"

"Ohmygod…were you at DeShawn's party Saturday night?" (There hadn't been one, but there was no way Meredith would ever know that.)

"No. Why?"

"First of all—and I've got to say that I wasn't there, but someone I know who never has lied to me WAS—the girl was drinking AND doing 'E' and then throwing herself into the laps of different guys? And then went upstairs and—I swear to God, I'm not making this up—they say she came downstairs at about 12 midnight *totally nude*, except for white gym socks, kissed what's-his-name, the Hispanic kid from the cheap condos, on the lips…"

"Angel?"

"Yeah, Angel."

"Wasn't he with Danielle? Who's got that…disease?"

"I don't know. Was he? Wait…that's not all!"

"There's more?"

"Well, yeah…then she takes him by the hand and walks him upstairs, him STARING AT HER NAKED BUTT as she walks up the stairs right in front of him (!) and they go to the bedroom and THEY DO IT, with no birth control or anything…"

Meredith was staring at her.

"Three times."

"What?"

"They did it three times."

"How do you know?"

"She told my friend. She was bragging."

Meredith pondered this. "Whoah…"

"Right?"

The bus came. Claire gave herself some credit. The walking-up-the-stairs-in-front-of-him-naked image seemed particularly artful. And tonight would be the Internet. I.M.s

236

would spread this to about 287 people in half an hour. She guessed the real test would come around fifth period, by the time Alison heard it back to her, ten times over. But she cared less about that than Elijah's reaction the first time he would hear.

The Duke had never gotten quite used to calls at 3:00 a.m., though they were occasionally an occupational necessity. The voice at the other end tonight was thicker than anything he could quickly place as one of his clients.

"Have you heard anything?"

It was the priest.

"Like what?"

"An offer?"

"For what? A plea bargain?"

"Yeah."

"No. Why would they do that? Plus we've got more than four weeks to go."

"That doesn't seem like much time."

Father Mark picked up the vintage .357 magnum in his right hand and explored its textures as he talked, holding the phone with his left hand.

"It's an eternity to the courts. Sometimes you don't start talking until three minutes before the trial."

"Do you think they will call?"

"What are you, nuts? Of course not! If you want me to call them, I will—but I don't advise it."

There was a pause. "Why did you call me 'nuts'?"

"Look—Father—you are what we call a 'high-profile' case. Alright? You are the equivalent, as far as the media is concerned, to an Al-Qaeda-Serial-Killer-Who-Might-Have-

AIDS-Running-A-Day-Care-Center. *After* killing a puppy on the Internet. Kapeesh? So—no—*no* district attorney who ever has to run for re-election again in this century will be calling you to see what your NEEDS might be at this time. If you want ME to call HIM, fine. But don't be surprised if they won't talk. They are going to try to bluff. And so am I."

"I want this to go away."

"Well, so do I, pal…there are a lot of other places I'd rather be than in a courtroom with this case. I'd rather be in Maui with a surfboard."

"You surf?"

The Duke was pissed enough to put on his glasses.

"Why did you call me at 3:00 in the morning?"

"Because I'm looking at all my contingencies. Just like you said to do."

Father Mark stared into the barrel of the revolver, looking to see if he could see the bullet, hidden in its chamber, sleeping, waiting embryonically, to be propelled outward at lightspeed where it would meet his flesh and blow his head apart. He tried looking further…into the dark space that would be on the other side before the angels would come to transport him from this world of pain, semen, and despair. Beyond the angels there might be peace.

If the angels came. Maybe there would be nothing more than gore.

"Can you make it go away?"

"Yeah. With a letter from the Pope, the Dali Lama, the head guy from Hamas, and Ariel Sharon. This ain't going away, my friend."

"I need it to go away."

"Well…isn't that what prayer is supposed to be for, Father?"

Father Mark considered that the stupidest thing he'd heard in years. He stroked the gun, hung up the phone. Then he realized that the gun—if you half-closed your eyes and squinted, and just felt it—had something of the quality of a very erect penis to it.

"How'd I 'FEEL'? How did I 'FEEL' to not be called by you, to not know if you gave a damn or were too selfish to bother to speak to me for three minutes, or to have to wonder if you just thought you were so much better than me that you were out of my league, or to have to guess if I'd done something to offend you, or if you just decided that I wasn't as hot as any number of thousands of babes whom you regularly cross paths with every day of your life (and don't deny it), or to have to guess if you're, like, actually GAY or something or just another guy who says he's straight but acts like he hates women? How'd I 'FEEL'? Well, gee now, let me see, hmmmm…I might have to get back to you on that."

Bonnie's eyes were fire and steel. Gone were the warm, rounded, youngish tones that had so hypnotized Alan when they first met.

"I felt like I wanted to slap you five times fast and then run you over in my Toyota, you selfish jerk!"

"You have just a Corolla, right?"

"I'm not joking! This isn't funny. I know you want sweet-and-charming girl back, but you're not going to get her if you don't listen to me, you twerp!"

"You're serious, right?"

"What did I just say? Yeah, I'm serious, I'm DAMN serious."

For a half second Alan felt like he was with Claire.

"And don't be thinking I'm one of your 'clients,' because I'm not. I'm the one who was with you in the bistro, remember?"

"I called…"

"Yeah, you called the next day and then, nothing, like you'd gone off to Serbia or something."

"You could have called ME."

"And, by the way: do they teach you people ANYTHING else to say in Counselor School, or wherever they gave you your degree, OTHER than to say, 'How do you feel?' It is SO retarded sounding."

"All right, so…I'm a retard."

"Yeah, you are. We can agree."

"Okay, good."

"Yeah good. You retard."

Bonnie was the first to laugh, her mouth half-full of a forkful of salad. "You ARE…seriously retarded."

"I think the term is 'profoundly.'"

"Well, whatever it is, you're it."

"I know," Alan said.

"I think helping weird people all day long takes over your life and I have no idea how, or if, your brain works anymore. What *do* you think about?"

"Bumper stickers."

"Bumper stickers?"

"Yeah. Funny ones."

"Yeah, that's exactly what I mean. I'm passing by right in front of you and you can't see me because you're seeing funny bumper stickers."

"You're passing by?"

"Yuh."

"Any chance you'll stay?"

"Where? In the retard class with you?"

"No. In whatever class they put you in after you get extra help."

"Well, don't count on me bailing you out all the time. It's boring. I need some zip in my life, not some...project or something. You'll be waiting for that 'extra help' a long, long time, Alan, and I'll be off with some boy-band singer or something."

"Boy band?"

"Yuh."

"Aren't they so over?"

"Yeah...about eight years ago. That means there will be a lot of unemployed boy-band guys in their young twenties out looking to recapture their glory days, cruising girls like me."

"Did you ever like any of those bands in the first place?"

"Hey, it might be good for a fling."

"You're feeling you're needing a fling?"

"Hey, I need something after whatever-you-call-it I've just been through with you."

"You've been through something with me? I thought I was going through something with YOU."

"What are you talking about?"

"I've been thinking about you. A lot."

"Well, gee. Half-credit. Maybe if I waited another ten years you'd say something about it to me?"

"I said something today."

"Yeah, you said 'hi.' Let me ask you something, seriously. Is this as good as it gets with you?"

"I...I never knew you had this side of you."

"What 'side of me'? Is that the OTHER thing they teach you to say in Counselor School? Are you just going down the list of things to say to me?"

Alan looked at her face, alive with anger and laughter.

"Does this matter to you? Does it really? I need to know," Alan asked.

"What do you think? You know what? You are a SUPER-Retard! What am I doing out here with you, under a tree, when I could be inside reading *Cosmo* about eight-ways-to-lose-weight-while-having-orgasms-while-improving-my-life-spiritually-at-the-same-time-as-clearing-up-my-credit-card-debt-before-Christmas! I mean, which one of us is the social worker here, huh?"

"So it does?"

"I have to say it?"

"Yeah. You do. Long story. But I need to hear it."

"Do I have to sound it out, write it down, and draw it in your hand at the same time, too, like Helen Keller?"

"No. You just have to say it."

She stopped. "Okay. It matters to me. You matter. That's why I consider you such a retard."

"Super-Retard, you said."

"Yes."

"There's a difference."

"O.K. But now that you've gotten into the category, just know that—unlike you—I don't get paid to work with Super Retards who piss me off. So consider the patience all...expended, okay?"

Alan leaned forward and kissed her, catching her completely off guard. Her mouth tasted a little like salad dressing. He couldn't believe he'd done it. He pulled back.

She straightened her hair and smiled the most amazing smile he'd seen in a long time. "Oh...you know...you are so weird. I probably tasted like salad dressing, right?"

"You know what else I think about? When I'm not thinking about bumper stickers? I think about grackles. Purple grackles. The way they looked in the sun. The way they walked around like they knew everything and belonged right where they were."

"Do you have any gum?" Bonnie asked, her tongue slowly journeying across her teeth.

JUVEY

Peter called for Nolan first. He was the biggest, and the stupidest. His Intro Spanish class (repeated after failing it in both ninth grade and in summer school) was close enough to Denardo's French class to make him the lead suspect. Peter made sure Nolan had to wait for fifteen minutes first, nervously shuffling around on "the bench" in the Main Office, trying to wonder which infraction had finally caught up with him. Today would be different, however.

Peter had Nolan searched and patted-down by Santo, the Security Guy. He was asked to put his cigarette lighter on the table, empty his pockets of change and notes ("Susan Pogue gave head to Ninja Dave three times on Saturday AFTER taking it doggy-style from Fat Mike Friday night when they were both rolling on E…"). Unfortunately, no drugs were found.

"What am I in here for?" he asked Santo.

"I'm not at liberty to say," Santo offered, half-apologetically. The truth was Santo had no idea. It was a free ticket to try to scare a kid though—something never to be passed up.

"Cutting?"

"I just told you—I'm not at liberty to say."

Nolan bit his lower lip. He could think of four cuts in the last two days. This would be too fast to act on them, though, unless someone had tipped them off.

"How come you searched me?"

"We share that information on a 'need-to-know' basis."

"Well I need to know."

"I guess they decided you DON'T."

Nolan pondered this. Santo disappeared into the principal's office, with the contents of the search.

Peter's door opened. He didn't usually get involved in the cut follow-ups. A.P.'s handled the write-ups.

"Mr. Belardi...in here now, please."

Santo gave him his best "screw-you-you-loser" scowl and returned to the hallway patrol. Nolan sat quickly, but spoke up.

"How come you had me searched?" The door quickly closed behind him. Peter walked in front of Nolan and sat behind the desk.

"I'm not going to answer that. You don't call the shots here. I do."

"So what'd I do?"

"What'd you do? What'd you DO? Probably a lot of things, Nolan. To start with you've wasted about the last nine years of school. You've gotten slowly more inept and pathetic just when you're expected to develop some social skills. You lie and you make lots of trouble for kids who do what they are supposed to at this school. In addition, you've shown yourself to be a horrible role model to your younger sister. She enters high school next year, I believe, and at this rate she'll probably be a grade AHEAD of you within two years. And you make life a living hell for our teachers. Aside from that...I can't think of much more that you 'DO.' If the question is 'why am I here in this office today,' the answer has to do with Kendra Iatsik's picture being put up on the wall near Denardo's French class the other week."

Nolan said nothing.

"To begin with: It was entirely inappropriate for you to bring those pictures into school in the first place, even if you had kept them to yourself."

Nolan looked like he had been slapped. "But I didn't!"

"Didn't what?"

"Bring them in."

"I believe you did."

"Well, you can believe anything you want, but I didn't."

"Where did you get them, then?"

Nolan looked at the ground.

"Let me tell you about a place, Nolan, located in a beautiful area of suburban Troy, New York. It has about two hundred and fifty boys—I'm sorry, but there aren't any girls there, and certainly none who look like Kendra—two hundred and fifty boys who the courts have decided can no longer successfully be educated or contained within their home communities. The difference between them and other boys is primarily that these boys have committed crimes. But they aren't old enough for adult jail."

"Juvey?"

"Yes. Only not all of them are there for violation of probation, like you would be."

Nolan shut up and suddenly got very meek. The friggin' principal had done his homework.

"There are boys there who have set people on fire after spraying lighter fluid on them for a joke, boys who have stabbed their mothers, boys who have done some very bad things. Boys who hide razors on them and evade detection so they are there for them when they need them at night. When these boys are placed there, Nolan, their cases are reviewed once every eighteen months. Mr. Belardi, I want you to know that not only do I know that your probation was due to expire last week, but that I have been in contact with your

Probation Officer, who has agreed to extend it another four months. This would run until the end of summer. Possession of stolen property, felony-reduced-to-a-misdemeanor-if-you-stay-out-of-trouble, pot-possession, vandalism, trespassing… it's clear where you've been investing your energies. One incident—just *one*—will set in motion a judicial review, with the school able to make its recommendation to the Judge. I know, technically, that it isn't the school's petition that brings you to the court, but the court always wants to hear from us. You'll have your lawyer, sure, but the Judge is a friend of mine—we were in R.O.T.C. together, actually—and I have a feeling he will see the school's point of view pretty clearly, despite the efforts of any paid mouthpieces your parents can come up with."

"So what are you saying I did?"

"One call—which I could make right this moment—would set this all in motion."

"What do you want from me?"

"Simply to acknowledge that you brought in those pictures, that it was a mistake, and that you apologize to the girl."

"That's not true."

Peter picked up the phone.

"Wait."

"I'll also see to it that your sister doesn't meet with any unnecessary unpleasantness when she gets her classes assigned for ninth grade and isn't called down to the office for any small offenses she might not be aware of committing. That her gym classes aren't with any bullies, that her locker isn't next to any morons or sex offenders. I would want her to have a better experience in this school than you have prepared her for. I would want her to have a clean slate."

"That's all you want me to say?"

"Everyone makes mistakes. I want you to acknowledge yours, in writing."

Nolan stared at him, hard.

"You can be 'right,' or you can be 'smart.' For once." Peter threw him a pad and a pen. "Take your time. We have to be able to read it."

———·◆·———

Claire signed on at 8:35 p.m., using Ninja Dave's screen-name. (*Thanks, Danielle!*) Richie was on I.M.

<u>DarkNinja</u>: Hey.

<u>MajorMojo</u>: Hey.

<u>DarkNinja</u>: 'Tsup?

<u>MajorMojo</u>: Nothing. 'Tsup there?

<u>DarkNinja</u>: Nothing. Boring

<u>MajorMojo</u>: F***in' A.

<u>DarkNinja</u>: Right?

<u>MajorMojo</u>: Yuh. Tell me about it.

<u>DarkNinja</u>: Your parents home?

<u>MajorMojo</u>: Yuh.

<u>DarkNinja</u>: Can't even play music.

<u>MajorMojo</u>: My mother took away my Slipknot CDs. She said the covers were Satanic. Can you believe it?

<u>DarkNinja</u>: The masks and everything?

<u>MajorMojo</u>: Yeah. Said it looked like "serial killer" outfits and that one of the guy's NOSES look like a dick.

<u>DarkNinja</u>: You're kidding. Your mom said "dick"?

<u>MajorMojo</u>: No. She didn't say the word, but that's what she was saying.

<u>DarkNinja</u>: Your mom's hot. In an old sort of way.

<u>MajorMojo</u>: You're a sick f**k.

DarkNinja: She didn't even listen to it?

MajorMojo: No. Said she couldn't hear any of the words anyway because the music sounded like someone was being killed. Said if I didn't like it I could go live in a group home with other mass murderers.

DarkNinja: OMG!

MajorMojo: Dave...is this really you? Or is this Danielle?

DarkNinja: It's me. Why would it be that little ho Danielle?

MajorMojo: She has everyone's screen-names and passwords. It kind of f**ks everything up.

DarkNinja: How come she does?

MajorMojo: Because she's blown most everyone in our class and they're stupid enough to give it to her.

DarkNinja: She do you?

MajorMojo: She wanted to, but I said no. I don't want whatever crusty disease-of-the-week she's got. Hepatitis 'G' or something you don't find out about until you're in college.

DarkNinja: Then you don't know WHICH bitch gave it to you.

MajorMojo: Are you really Dave? Is this Danielle trying to fool me? If it is...

DarkNinja: Calm down, boy! I am who I am—Ninja Dave speaking. How do I know you are who YOU say you are.

MajorMojo: Hey, don't start f***ing with me. YOU said "hey" to me first.

DarkNinja: How do I know you're not some skanky thirteen-year-old bitch trying to meet older guys?

MajorMojo: How do I know you're not some old queer?

DarkNinja: If I were why would I be chasing some ugly, greasy loser with pimples like you?

MajorMojo: Hah-hah-hah. Lick me.

DarkNinja: You wish.

MajorMojo: You are so gay. You know you'd love to take a trip up the Hershey Highway.

DarkNinja: I would have humped your mother but the dogs beat me to her.

MajorMojo: Your mother got fired from her job as a crack-whore because she was too slutty.

DarkNinja: Guess what I heard? This is for real now— no kidding around, aiiiight?

MajorMojo: Aiiight.

DarkNinja: You know that little prissy Jewish girl in Global Studies, Alison? Dark hair?

MajorMojo: Good body?

DarkNinja: Her tits aren't bad.

MajorMojo: If it's who I'm thinking of, she's got a nice ass.

DarkNinja: What difference does it make? You're interrupting me.

MajorMojo: I'd do her, but I wouldn't go out of my way for it.

DarkNinja: Wait till you hear…

MajorMojo: You're saying you WOULDN'T do her?

DarkNinja: I don't know. I guess so.

MajorMojo: That's right, I forgot: you're a Gaylord.

DarkNinja: Would you shut the f**k up?

MajorMojo: What's your problem?

DarkNinja: I'm trying to tell you about this little bitch.

MajorMojo: So tell me.

DarkNinja: Last Saturday night, at DeShawn's house, she did Angel upstairs in the bedroom after walking downstairs totally nude (except for white gym socks) and was sitting down in his lap in front of everyone. Nude. And then walked him upstairs—walking naked upstairs in front of him—and did him three times.

MajorMojo: Not possible. DeShawn was in Pittsfield last Saturday. With his aunt. He was thrown out of his house. There wasn't any party.

DarkNinja: Maybe it was Friday.

MajorMojo: Not possible. He was out-of-friggin' state as of Wednesday. Missed three days of school, duh. Remember?

DarkNinja: Yuh. Maybe it was the week before.

MajorMojo: Someone has been feeding you some bull***t, my friend.

DarkNinja: How do you know? You know everything?

MajorMojo: I know when someone is bull***tting me. I can't believe you believed this. Unless you aren't Dave.

DarkNinja: I don't know exactly where or when it happened, but it DID with this Alison girl. She's a slut.

MajorMojo: Yeah, and I don't give a f**k one way or another.

DarkNinja: Didn't you say you wanted to do her?

MajorMojo: Don't you understand, you dumb f**k? She's one of those "good-girls," she's not strutting-her-butt in front of Angel or any other Chico at DeShawn's or anyone else's house, you stupid motherf***er? And she doesn't even interest me, o.k.?

DarkNinja: You don't care about what Miss Priss does when the lights go out?

MajorMojo: What's with this "Miss Priss" s**t? You sound like a f***in' faggot!

DarkNinja: YOU'RE the one who doesn't want to hear about naked girls, now WHO'S THE FAGGOT!?!*? You're like "Eeeeeewwww! Girls!!"

MajorMojo: I'm plenty into bitches. Just the slutty kind, though.

DarkNinja: Name one.

MajorMojo: One that I'd want to do?

DarkNinja: Yuh.

MajorMojo: You know that girl, Claire? The loser from the Group Home? With the big friggin' ears?

DarkNinja: Yeah.

MajorMojo: The one with no fashion sense who thinks she's so hot? Who's every move and word tells the world, "I'm a slut and I need a stud to do me NOW."

DarkNinja: Yeah.

MajorMojo: Even though she is a little goofy looking and majorly stupid, I'd do her in a heartbeat. She used to be on the fat side, but she's looking good lately. I'd do her at a party. Hell, I'd do her on the loading dock at Meatland.

DarkNinja: Even though you said she's a "loser"?

MajorMojo: Well, uh, YEAH!! What's your point?

DarkNinja: You're saying you don't like her, but you'd do her.

MajorMojo: Of course. What does one thing have to do with the other?

DarkNinja: You'd do her before you'd do Alison?

MajorMojo: Alison is like...you'd do her in a hotel room after you married her, or something. Claire is like...you'd do her in the bathroom at Wal-Mart and then brag about it later at the Sunoco station and the word would get around and STILL she'd love it. Plus I've heard she does anal.

DarkNinja: You f***ing pathetic s**t-for-brains loser. You should be dead.

MajorMojo: Excuse me?

DarkNinja: You should be run over in a car ten times then have your nuts squeezed in a vise then your heart cut out before having each of your limbs cut off slowly with your little dick saved for last.

MajorMojo: You're not Dave, are you?

DarkNinja: I'm going to kill you. I know where your locker is, I know what classes you take, I know where you live. I'm going to kill you.

MajorMojo: F**k you. I'm not scared, you pussy.

DarkNinja: I have a gun.

MajorMojo: So does everybody.

DarkNinja: You are dead. Tell your mother to pick out a gravesite.

MajorMojo: Pussy. Pussy, pussy, pussy. Bring it on, you…WOMAN.

DarkNinja: My face will be the last one you ever see. And I'll be laughing.

The next morning Richie did what he had been trained to do in fifth grade D.A.R.E. class. He went to his parents. They went to the police. His deposition read, in part, "…I'm being stalked by a psycho bitch."

THE TRUTH

"Your friend, Nolan, has already confessed to bringing those pictures in. He's also given us a heartfelt apology to Kendra and any other students hurt by his thoughtlessness."

Brendon had nowhere to go with this. He squirmed.

"I know you helped him post them on the wall. You'd be doing yourself a huge favor by simply admitting it in writing."

This was the easiest interview for Peter. What he was accusing Brendon of doing was, in fact, true. That helped get the confession. The investigation was going well.

Claire's English teacher—less than ten years older than Claire, herself—sat at her kitchen table, Claire's essay in hand. The last day of regular school for the year was tomorrow. It was 10:00 at night, the news was on ("Hidden Dangers in Your Fruit Salad? We'll give you all you need to know to keep YOUR family safe...") and two Mint Milanos were in front of her, uneaten except for the first bite.

The assignment had been to write about "a turning point." The basis for grading would be: 25% grammar, 35% story-telling technique, and 40% "voice." It would be a major part of this semester's grade.

A TURNING POINT

by Claire Pargito

She couldn't sleep anymore. She went through the days fat and crabby, barking at best friends, ignoring teachers, and stumbling through her classes. She couldn't even get angry at the others anymore. She was too tired.

He came into the room, like he often did. He was big and fat and smelled disgusting. He hardly ever showered. He grabbed her by the hair and stuck his thing in her face.

But something about this night, or early morning, whatever it was, was different. Like she had maxxed out. His stiff wanger was everything that was choking her, holding her back. She wouldn't be the good girl anymore.

She bit. Not it off, but enough to hurt, fast and deep.

His thing shrank immediately and he became this little pathetic yelping dog. Like a big stinking animal whose paw had been run over. She laughed, before standing up and punching him in the face. He was so distracted he fell over. She liked it.

She stood over him and wanted to spit.

Tonight someone would die.

Or had died.

Her teacher trembled. She picked up the phone to call the school psychologist at home.

She also had no idea what grade to give.

———✦———

Jose seemed to Peter to be the weakest of the three. His good nature melded with his simple mind and gentle-giant body. He allowed the kids to call him "Chico" and never lost his smile. Seen away from Brendon and Nolan he seemed unusually respectful of authority. Peter was pleased to see that he had saved the easiest for last.

Jose didn't want any calls made to his mother. Peter wasn't sure why. Probably something to do with fears about a green card, immigration, what-have-you, or just that the woman was overwhelmed with calls from the schools about Jose's four younger sisters and brothers. It was refreshing to see a boy so polite and compliant. Until the topic of Kendra Iatsik's pictures came up. Jose not only denied any knowledge of either Brendon or Nolan bringing those pictures in to school, he said he knew where they were really from.

"And where would that be?" Peter asked, nervously.

"From your desk. Right there."

"That's ridiculous. Not true."

"It is true, sir. That's where we found them."

"Brendon has already admitted bringing them in to school."

"But that's not true. He said that you pressured him into saying that or else you'd call Probation on him and would make things bad for his sister when she arrived here."

"I never said that, son."

"Yes you did."

Peter regarded him coolly.

"Is your family here legally on a green card?"

"How does that matter, sir?"

"Let me ask you this, son. Do you like it here?"

"How do you mean, sir?"

"Living in this country, going to a nice school like Hadleyville Falls High School?"

"Yes. Very much."

"Well along with enjoying the privileges that come with living in this country comes responsibility. I'm asking you to take responsibility for your role in certain events—which are already old news, and which carry little or no punishment—which led some people in this building to be very uncomfortable."

"We didn't bring those pictures in, sir. We got them from your desk."

"I know you believe that to be true."

"Because it is true."

"Look...Jose...here is your choice: You sign a statement saying that you, Brendon, and Nolan brought in those pictures and posted them and now feel very badly about it, or all three of you go for an official Superintendent's Hearing which could result in suspension from school for up to a year. You'd be entitled to a lawyer, but I doubt your family could afford one. By doing that you'd also be letting every teacher and administrator in this district know that you, and your little brothers and sisters, are nothing but trouble. They would get ready for them as soon as they saw their last name and realized that they were related to you. If you want them to get a fair shake here, son, you have to think larger than just yourself."

"Are you threatening me, sir?"

"I am telling you honestly about the way things work around here. Hadleyville Falls is a very small community. You don't want the community against you, son. And people talk."

"So you're asking me to sign something that isn't right?"

257

"You can be right, or you can be smart, son. Your choice."

Jose rose and walked out of the room without saying a word.

———•◦•———

The State Police, after consulting with the local Internet service provider and the superintendent, got a subpoena for all records, including log-ons, screen names, passwords, etc. relevant to the "stalking threat" made to Richie. They assured his parents that they had a suspect identified and would be questioning the suspect shortly. There was no reason to worry, as these things usually turned out to be adolescent "figures of speech," etc....If the parents really wanted to, the police could assign someone undercover to enter the high school. Both parents and Richie thought that would be overkill. They agreed to wait two days until a suspect had been questioned.

———•◦•———

Principal Epperschmidt was summoned to appear at Superintendent Elliot Greene's office at 11:00 a.m. on the last day of school. "As soon as possible," Mona's message-on-a-pad said.

"What's this all about?"

"No idea."

Mona usually knew.

———•◦•———

Claire refused to talk to Dolores Solomon. Dolores let it be known that the English teacher had contacted her with serious concerns. This was the first thing that turned Claire off; if she had wanted anyone to be "seriously concerned," she said, she would have asked. Which—no offense—she absolutely HADN'T, of this School Psychiatrist Lady, or whatever-her-title-was, since if she had anything to say she would say it to Mr. Mitchke, like she's been telling him most of the year, though she wasn't sure HE could be trusted either.

The second mistake Dolores made, according to Claire, was to have her English essay out in full view, with segments of it highlighted in lime-green. "If I had meant for it to have parts highlighted, I would have done it myself, and I wouldn't have used lime-green. Plus there was nothing in the assignment, you might notice, that said it had to be true. It just was supposed to be 'a turning point.' And nothing I wrote said it was true. So, number one: Who's saying it isn't fiction? And, number two: Who gave you the right to highlight it and rip it apart and criticize it like that, in lime-green? And, number three: If I had something to say I would say it to someone other than you in the first place. Plus you are making me miss class on the last day of classes, when people are signing yearbooks, which stinks." Claire gathered up her things and left.

Dolores called Alan doing her best to remain professional. He must see the girl today, she urged, and he should realize that the potential for a call to Child Protective Services—if not the police—was probably high. Claire hadn't told Dolores much, but one thing was certain: this girl had been sexually abused by someone. Dolores vowed that this one wouldn't slip through her hands.

Claire gave Alan five dates and times of having been sexually abused by Ronald Dubeck at her mother's home at 435 Butterlink Drive. "What are you going to do with this information?" she asked.

"Call CPS."

"And the cops?"

"Probably, yeah."

"Good. Can he get locked up?"

"I can't say. I guess so. Are you ready for all this? You'll have to repeat this stuff several times and testify in court, I imagine."

"I told you, didn't I?"

"But you didn't tell the psychologist."

"I didn't know her."

"You'll have to tell other people you don't know."

"What's your point?"

"If I go ahead with this it is no joke. These are serious accusations."

"Are you worried about you, or me?"

"Both of us, I guess."

"So...let's do it?"

There would be a thousand-dollar fine and a year in jail for failure-to-report; Alan made the call. CPS accepted the call for investigation. They wanted to question Claire before contacting the police. They arranged to come interview her at school.

It was a school policy that CPS workers questioning kids in school had to do so in the presence of someone representing the school. In this instance CPS insisted that it be her guidance counselor, not Mitchke, because the CPS worker felt a female counselor might be more comforting and appropriate. Claire's guidance counselor, a nice young brunette woman in her mid-twenties, was someone with over three hundred and twenty kids on her caseload, who had seen Claire twice in her high school career (once to explain why she couldn't enroll in Cosmetology until next year, once to explain why Phys. Ed. was a requirement and couldn't be dropped in exchange for a study hall—"…even if those bitches keep staring at me while I change??" asked Claire, never one to give in easily). She was more than happy to oblige and sit in on the CPS visit, even though it was the last day of school.

Alan waited downstairs for the call. It came about twenty-five minutes later.

"She denied everything she told you. Dates, times…all made up. She admitted she didn't like Ronald, but that was all. She went back to saying the English essay was all fiction and asked why everyone was so uptight about her exploring her imagination when the school encouraged her to do it all year long in English class in the first place. She made it clear that she wasn't writing in the first-person, because it wasn't really about her. It was about an imaginary someone else. She wanted to get back to class and sign yearbooks."

"Then why had she told me it was all true?"

"Maybe she's looking for more of a connection with you. She's very dramatic."

Alan slammed the phone down, cracking the plastic in two places. CPS had fucked up another one.

He called Dolores and told her. She was enraged. Dolores flipped through the student roster and scribbled down Claire's address—wrongly recorded as 435 Butterlink Drive, not the Group Home where Claire presently lived.

Dolores knew that Mitchke would screw this one up. Dolores would make this right. Today. After school.

———•——

State Police Sergeant Ross Barker scanned his planner and noted the kid-Internet-threat case. An exceptional performer in all areas of police investigative work, Sgt. Barker also had the distinction of being the first African-American to hold the position in Troop B.

It had already been determined that the computer threat came from the Group Home, located at 216 Bayview Court. The Group Home had confirmed the fact that only one girl— Claire Pargito—was on the computer during the hours in question. Sgt. Barker looked at Claire Pargito's school registration form and scrawled her parent's address – 435 Butterlink Drive—down on his pad.

———•——

The superintendent of the Hadleyville Union Free School District, Elliot Green, had Peter ushered in to see him without delay. The handshake was formal.

"Thanks for coming, Peter."

"No problem, Elliot. What do we have?"

"A number of things, Peter. I have to tell you, I'm extremely troubled by what I've heard about the way the investigation has been handled re: Kendra Iatsik."

"What have you heard?"

"That you bullied, lied, and threatened students to coerce 'confessions' to things they didn't do."

Peter had barely settled his weight into the chair.

"Why would I do that, Elliot?"

"That's a great question, Peter. Great question." Elliot stared at him.

Peter had nothing to say.

"The boy you picked on last—Jose Garcia—I spent an hour with him and his parents yesterday. His father is a fairly well-known actor, you know, he's been in projects with Edward James Olmos, people like that, and the mother is going for her Ph.D. in Cross-Cultural Education at N.Y.U. Jose's younger brothers and sisters are all top of their classes, exceptional students. Two of them are Peer Mediators. Jose is probably the goofiest of the bunch. He has good grades, despite hanging around kids who are trying to pull him down. So...I think you messed with the wrong family, Peter."

"How did I 'mess' with anyone, Elliot?"

Elliot reached into his top right drawer and pulled out a cassette recorder. He hit "Play."

<u>Jose</u>: "We didn't bring those pictures in, sir. We got them from your desk."

<u>Peter</u>: "I know you believe that to be true."

<u>Jose</u>: "Because it is true."

<u>Peter</u>: "Look...Jose...here is your choice: You sign a statement saying that you, Brendon, and Nolan brought in those pictures and posted them and now feel very badly about it, or all three of you go for an official Superintendent's Hearing which could result in suspension from school for up to a year. You'd be entitled to a lawyer, but I doubt your family could afford one. By doing that you'd also be letting every teacher and administrator in this district know that you, and your little brothers and sisters, are nothing but trouble. They would get ready for them as soon as they saw their last name and realized that they were related to you. If you want them to get a fair shake here, son, you have to think larger than just yourself."

Jose: "Are you threatening me, sir?"

Peter: "I'm am telling you honestly about the way things work around here. Hadleyville Falls is a very small community. You don't want the community against you, son. And people talk."

Jose: "So you're asking me to sign something that isn't right?"

Peter: "You can be right, or you can be smart, son. Your choice."

Peter was stunned. The kid had been wired. He couldn't remember why he hadn't ordered Santo to search the kid like he had Nolan. Brendon and Nolan must have prepped Jose.

"We've also done reinterviews with Nolan and Brendon. They both corroborated Jose's story and recanted their confessions. All three boys are consistent. The source of these pornographic pictures seems to have been…you."

"Not true."

Elliot pulled out the manila folder and set it in between them. Clearly visible, in permanent black magic-marker, in Peter's handwriting, was the word, "TROUBLE."

"Is that your handwriting, Peter?" Before Peter could stutter a response, Elliot cut him off. "Out of consideration for the good things you've done for our district in the past, Peter, I'm not going to let you answer that without legal representation. If I were you, I'd get a lawyer—fast—because you are being sued personally by the parents of each of the three boys for harassment. The District, as a whole, is also being sued. The only one who isn't suing us, it would seem, is Kendra Iatsik herself. You know why, Peter? Because she is over eighteen, and was over eighteen at the time those pictures were taken. There never was a legal issue regarding her consent to be photographed in the first place, Peter. No permission slips were needed. You never even checked that,

Peter? Her age was right on her registration and class schedule!"

"I told Mona…"

"Don't, Peter. Don't. Oh, and when you are looking for a lawyer, scratch Dominic Ippoliti off your list. 'The Duke' has been hired by the boys' families."

A heavy silence engulfed the room.

"You are being temporarily reassigned to the Intermediate School, as Acting Assistant Principal for grades 3-5 next year. Our internal investigation and hearings into your status may take up to a year to complete. In the meantime, I'd try to learn something about little kids if I were you, Peter. Please know that no one would blame you if you look for employment at the secondary level elsewhere. We would forward all the commendations in your personnel file but—under the new Project SAVE legislation—we have to advise any other school district of this little problem you've gotten yourself into as well. Some people in your situation might look to the private, or parochial school system as good alternatives."

"That's it?"

"That's more or less it. The other item is off the record."

"Well?"

"I would avoid having drinks in the Acropolis Diner in the middle of the school day if I were you. And I would certainly avoid doing that with any female staff members who are half your age for the near future. It makes a lot of people feel uncomfortable."

Peter stood to leave.

"Oh, one more thing: We'd be looking for you to take a Spanish language class over the summer if you choose to stay with us. We have more and more kids of Hispanic origin in our district, in the younger grades particularly, and—as Jose's mother pointed out—you are one of the only administrators who doesn't have at least a beginning-level understanding of the language."

"You can't mandate that."

"Goodbye, Peter."

———•·•———

Dolores waited an hour after getting off the phone with Alan before calling CPS herself. She spoke to Debbie Dunlop, the worker who had interviewed Claire earlier.

"Have you closed the case yet, Debbie? Did you write it up?"

"No."

"I know this is annoying, but I know that you've seen this a lot of times before," Dolores said. "Claire has changed her story again, back to her original claims. She's over her 'cold feet' and ready to talk," Dolores lied. "I know she can tell you everything if I can just get a few words of encouragement in first."

"We can't have you coaching her."

"Of course not. But I know she's ready."

"How do you know that?"

"She's ready to do a written confession, in the first person."

"Not the English class story?"

"No."

"Can you fax it to me?"

"If you go out to reinterview this girl after she talks to me for a few minutes, you'll get your written confession and I'll get the satisfaction of knowing that the right thing has been done, okay?"

"That's not the way we do things."

"I know! I know exactly how you do things. I'm asking you to do things a little differently just once to not let this predator slip through your hands, o.k.?"

"I have to talk to my Supervisor and see what other visits we've committed to for this afternoon." She put Dolores on hold. The music during the hold was a tinny version of "Somewhere, My Love." Debbie came back and said, "I can't do it. We have a lot of cases here which are still active."

"You just said you didn't write it up yet. This case is still active."

"You know what I mean. Cases where the kid hasn't denied what you say they told you before we arrived."

Dolores was beyond livid. "All right, how about this, Debbie: You give me what I want and I won't go to Dave Applefeld with many uncomfortable details about ways you and your colleagues have mishandled cases in the past four months...AFTER that little six-year-old girl your agency neglected to remove from her hellhole was tortured to death."

Debbie considered her words carefully. Dave Applefeld, a well-known writer for *The Hadleyville Falls' Gazette*, had recently been promoted from folksy, three-times-a-week columnist (where his specialty was "outrage-from-The-Little-Guy-in-five-hundred-words-or-less") to Executive Editor.

"That's in litigation right now."

"Yes, and the little girl is in a cold grave."

There was a silence.

"I sincerely doubt that you are in possession of any information that hasn't already been revealed to the police and attorneys."

"About that case? Maybe so. Maybe all I have is enough little details about non-returned calls—including two involving you—workers who couldn't care less, bad judgment calls, workers more-or-less advising parents on how to hit their kids without leaving marks…I'm willing to bet it could all add up to something in Dave's hands."

"That's neither fair, nor professional."

Dolores had deliberately called on a line she knew wasn't being taped at the CPS end. (The county was still getting around to upgrading all their lines to the same standard.) "You know what's neither fair nor professional, Debbie? That would be when your workers show up moments before the end of a school day, chewing gum, looking at their watches, to interview a kid who has been beaten at home— when we even had pictures of the belt buckle marks and purple bruises—and the first words out of your worker's mouth are, 'Okay, let's get this show on the road, we've got a bus this kid has to catch in ten minutes.' You just presume that everything you handle is a false report? Or you just don't care? Is that how that family was able to kill that little girl? Just a pattern of non-caring PLUS no supervision? How dare you question my professionalism, when there is nothing I've seen your agency do in the past two years which comes close to being professional. How about the time you didn't question for three weeks the mother who left her eight-year-old in a freezing car all night while she went out drinking and looking for new friends? Three weeks? Because 'she wouldn't return our phone calls.' That was YOU, Debbie. Not anybody else. Your agency is a joke, Debbie. You work for a joke, and the sooner everyone knows it, the better."

Dolores could hear her breathing.

"And if you're wondering how I know Dave: we're good friends. He goes to the same temple as I do. Temple Beth Jacob. And he'd be glad to keep my name out of it. You know, 'confidential sources tell us,' 'someone close to the investigation revealed.' I promise you one thing: It will be your name in the paper, not mine. And it will be big."

"Hold on."

"You want to go talk to your supervisor?"

"Yes."

"Good. Do it." (The hold-music was a string version of The Beatles' "And I Love Her.")

"O.K. We'll reinterview her. But it better be what you say. And you should know that a lot of people around here don't think highly of your reputation for getting facts correctly. We spend a lot of time chasing your cases which then are unproven."

"The day that I care about what CPS workers think of my reputation is the day you and I switch jobs, Debbie. So when are you coming to interview her?"

"Three-thirty to four o'clock."

"Fine, but school is closed then."

"Then we'll have to interview her at home. We don't like to do that."

"I know, but...get this done, okay?"

"Okay. We're going to need that new written statement. I'll be there. Wait—where am I going?"

Dolores shuffled papers on her desk and found Claire's schedule. "435 Butterlink Drive," she said.

"Fine. I'll meet you there. And you should know we are doing this because the facts seem to warrant review, not because you threatened us."

"Uh-huh."

"We don't respond to threats. We get them all the time. And...you should know that you aren't the only one who cares about children. Having a Master's degree doesn't put you in a different league. We're all in this together."

"Thank you, Debbie." Dolores hung up, took out a street map of Hadleyville Falls and tried to find Butterlink Drive. It was the far side of town, nearly four miles from the Group Home where Claire would actually be making brownies for group snack at 3:30 p.m.

ESCAPE FROM A GIRL'S CAR

Angel and Ninja Dave hunched over a street map of Grandville in the front seat of Dave's rusted Chevy Corsica, looking for Empire Avenue. There was a Dunkin' Donuts diagonally across from them, but the streets weren't matching the description given to them by Mighty Marky, reputed leader of the Grandville Crips.

"This is a girl's car, you know," Angel said.

"Hey, it was free from my uncle."

"It's blue."

"Yeah."

"Eggshell blue…It's butt-ugly."

"Where's Empire?"

"I'm looking."

"You think this is a setup? Like in the movies?"

"No," Angel said, squinting at the ten-year-old map. "I think you're a child. Start driving. Left. Yeah…that's it. Take it to Walnut, take a right on Walnut and we should be at the Payless Shoes he said to look for."

Dave did as he was told. Three seconds after making the right on Walnut they saw the red lights in the rear-view mirror. Grandview didn't have their own police; it was the State Troopers.

"Holy shit! You see that?"

"Yeah, it's no right on a red light in Grandville, bitch. What are you holding?"

"What?"

"What shit do you have on you?"

"We got the rocks in the back, I got six hits of 'E,' two Bart Simpson blotter acids, and a joint."

"You got to eat it. Gimmee the 'E.'"

Dave fished it out and handed it over fast as the cops gained behind him.

Angel divided it up, swallowed three doses and gave Dave three. "Swallow it. Fast."

He did.

"Now take the acid."

"No way."

"It's your funeral, homee. You're looking at felonies."

Dave licked the blotters fast; Angel reached over, grabbed the used blotters, and dove to stuff them in the front crotch of Dave's underpants. There was no way he could do this without making contact with Dave's dick and balls.

"You fucking faggot!!"

"Shut up. Eat the joint."

"You eat it."

"Okay."

Angel stuffed it in his mouth and swallowed it just as the sirens started.

"Keep driving a little. Don't speed up. Don't do anything stupid. These fuckers will kill you."

"What about the rocks?"

"They may not look. But if they do, how old are you?"

"Sixteen."

"Alright, then. Under the new rules you're still a youthful offender," Angel lied. "I'm eighteen. If you cop to it, we're both off. You get a warning and your record is sealed. If it's me, I get sent away. So we need you to cop to it."

Dave tried to think, as he pulled over to the side. The cop car pulled right behind, red light blazing and swirling. The cops parked at an angle so they could pull out fast and cut him off if he did anything stupid. Then they'd shoot him.

"Okay."

"You got it?"

"Yeah."

"The shit is yours. That way, we cool."

"Yuh."

Two cops opened their doors and approached. They were ridiculously tall and looked mean.

"License and registration?"

Dave produced them.

"This is a junior license. What are you doing out after nine o'clock?"

"We were going to see someone about buying a dog. A pit bull."

"A pit bull, huh? Nasty things. Now why would you want a pit bull?"

The second cop shined a flashlight directly in Angel's eyes. Angel felt like killing him.

"Get out of the car, both of you." The cops patted them down and searched for weapons and drugs.

"Mike, run the paper on this driver, please?"

"My pleasure." The second cop disappeared into his vehicle with Dave's license and registration.

"Whose vehicle is this?"

"Mine," said Dave.

"Who is this guy, then?" the cop asked, pointing at Angel.

"My friend."

"Can I see some identification, please?" he asked Angel.

"Sure." Angel took out the realistic-looking college-ID he had bought in Times Square for thirty-five dollars last year. The picture looked current, it was laminated and the proud seal of the University of Minnesota, Duluth campus hovered in the background. The birthday wasn't his, but it was close enough. Angel had just finished his freshman year in college, it would seem. It looked good.

"Angel...Garcia. You're a long way from home, Mr. Garcia, aren't you?"

"Mmmm-huh."

"Excuse me?"

"Yes."

"Came all this way to buy a dog?"

"Something like that."

The cop turned to Dave again. "I am requesting permission to search this car. Is that okay with you?"

Dave gulped ever so quietly.

"We can do this here, or we can take you in and run your prints. I'd rather do this here."

"Okay...yes. You can search."

It took the cops about a minute and a half to find the two rocks of crack-cocaine on the back seat.

"Whose is this?"

Angel looked at Dave.

"It's mine," Dave said.

"Oh really?" said the second cop.

"Yeah."

"You know what it is?"

"Yes."

"This what people use to buy dogs nowadays?"

No one said anything.

"What about Mr. Garcia here?"

"He didn't have any knowledge of it. It's mine."

"If we make an arrest and you both deny knowledge of it we have to charge both of you, you know."

"I know. He didn't know anything about it. It's mine."

"Okay," the cop said, shrugging. "Mr. Garcia, step over here please?"

Angel did, stepping out of earshot.

"How do you know this individual?"

"He's a friend of my cousin."

"Who's your cousin?"

Angel gave them Carlos' name. They had a working agreement.

"And what do you have to do with him today?"

"We really were going to buy a dog. Look, I know this kid has been in trouble before. My cousin asked if I would like try to help him out, be a mentor, be a Big Brother. I really am shocked about the drugs. He's...stupid, but I didn't think he was that stupid."

"He may very well be stupid, Mr. Garcia. But I'm not. My gut tells me that the stuff is yours."

"I can understand that."

"You can."

"Yes."

"Why?"

"Because a lot of kids who look like me never make it out of the ghetto and drug-dealing and you've probably run into them before and will run into them again and you're thinking I'm one of them."

"Wait here."

The two cops consulted privately.

"We're supposed to charge them both."

Dave made a move to whisper to Angel and the taller cop screamed at him to shut up and turn around.

"I know, but it's up to us."

When the cops' huddle broke up the shorter one stepped forward and addressed Dave.

"Son, we're bringing you down to the station to charge you with Criminal Possession of a Controlled Substance, Seventh degree. That's a CPCS Seven, depending on the weight of what you've got here. If you've got more, you get charged higher. But right now you're looking at a Class A misdemeanor. It is not a felony and it doesn't have to wreck your life. But I'm going to ask you one more time: Whose drugs are these?"

Ninja Dave held firm. "They're mine."

"And not his?"

"Not his."

"Fine. We don't have time for this kiddy-shit. You're both coming down, though, to run prints and take statements."

The cops read Dave his rights. He reiterated he'd be charged with Criminal Possession of a Controlled Substance. "You, you're just along for the ride. We're going to run your prints though, Mr. Garcia, and see if you're the Student of the Month you say you are."

The Ecstasy was without a doubt kicking in as the cops ran the prints. Dave wanted to hug everyone in the station.

"Surprise, surprise," the policeman said coming out of a little room with a computer printout.

"What?" Dave said, anxiously.

"I think we need to talk to this kid's parents, Mike. The other one—Garcia—he can go. You got his statement?"

"Yes."

"Cut him loose."

Angel gave Dave the most appreciative look he could under the circumstances.

What the computerized criminal background check had turned up, based on fingerprints and other ID, was this:

PETERSON, DAVID—age 16, PINS Petition (Person In Need Of Supervision), Diversion program, ref. Family Court, Judge Melamar, 2/12/03; felony assault, third degree, poss. of weapons (numchucks); Prob. Officer Jack Naylor; 1 x 2 weeks; Probation expiration date 7/12/05.

Now that Dave was sixteen he could be charged as an adult.

The criminal background check and fingerprint check on Angel Garcia turned up nothing. This was the first time in the system for this kid's fingerprints.

Angel's actual arrests in New York City—for felony criminal mischief, and aggravated harassment (graffiti-writing and bothering Rasheeda and her mother)—had resulted in Family Court appearances, due to his age. There were tons of fingerprints on file, but the files were sealed because he had been a youthful offender at the time and the prosecutors had agreed to reduce all charges to misdemeanors. The warrant out for him in connection with nearly killing Five-Dollar Bill was real, but good for nothing because, at present, he was Angel Garcia from Duluth, Minnesota, not Angel Rivera from New York City. Since Angel was eighteen he was released without a parent or guardian being called.

By the time Ninja Dave's parents came to the station—and found out that Dave had made statements claiming sole ownership of the drugs without having had access to an attorney—Angel was eighty miles away, in the direction of Allentown, Pennsylvania.

———◆———

Ronald Dubeck was on his third Scotch of the afternoon, staring hard at the 35-inch t.v. screen from his La-Z-Boy recliner (a Father's Day gift from his girlfriend), the talk-show clamor echoing through his skull. It was twenty-five minutes into some talk-show about "My Gay Stepbrother/Lover," with no one stepping forward from the audience to challenge the homos or snap their fairy necks in half like he would do a deformed chicken good. Nothing but cheers, catcalls, whistles. The young men crossing their legs slowly, hands fluttering to their knees, tears streaming down their fairy faces as they talked about the need for "acceptance" and "love, like everybody else." You had to listen real carefully to realize that these Oprah-rejects were actually boning their step-brothers and introducing them to the world of anal sex and disease. Which also wasn't being spoken about.

"Do you use condoms?" asked the fat-assed female talk-show host.

"Yes. Every time," said the swish named "Barry." "It allows us to be freer. We've gotten quite creative with it," he giggled, reaching out to hold the hand of his girlfriend-stepbrother, Mike. The audience hooted and applauded.

Well, there you go. Wrap it in plastic, get out the K-Y and go to it, you fairy-girls. Probably be on a talk show doing it for everyone to see next week.

Debbie Dunlap's car was the first to pull up to the bottom of Ronald's long circular driveway. It was a white Ford Escort with a huge green county insignia on it. She kept the motor running, listening to some incredibly crappy new Rolling Stones' song about "doing it all night, all right," eating a Light 'N Lively nonfat cottage-cheese with pineapple. This

278

was Dolores' show; there was no sense on knocking on any doors until the Calcium-Magnesium Lady arrived. This was what they called Dolores at Debbie's workplace, based on one case where a kid who was failing all her classes and being beaten for it at home regularly received Dolores' recommendation that she increase her intake of calcium and magnesium on a daily basis. The kid finally divulged the abuse to a Social Studies teacher instead of Dolores, despite the fact that Dolores had been seeing the kid every week for a year.

"Hey—maybe there's a job for her at The Vitamin Shoppe," Debbie's supervisor quipped, downing a Dunkin' Donuts Coffee Roll and a Vanilla Coolatta. "Or she could do infomercials." Everyone had laughed and returned to their paperwork with a new sense of camaraderie.

"Maybe she and that foreign-speaking psychiatrist could open a private practice together…"

"Yeah…The 'Nuts & Sluts Express'; free translations provided," Nancy Devane shouted out.

The whole Unit was laughing then. Tawny Breckton laughed until she started coughing hard, struggling with that phlegm that just never came up. Debbie remembered 'Nuts & Sluts' now and felt a little less alone, out here in front of the driveway of one of the county's likeliest creeps (whether this kid's story held up or not, a dirtbag was a dirtbag).

K96 was now playing a bad old 'N Sync song. Debbie's eyes drifted to the non-official "Stop" sign dug into the ground seven feet in front of her. Under the word "Stop" was hand-painted the words "Race-Mixing." The beat-up '89 Chevy Nova had a small, hard-to-read bumper sticker on it that said, in not-quite-deep-enough blue lettering, "America—Founded by White European People."

Debbie looked up to see Ronald's dog, George Lincoln (an eighty-five-pound German Shepherd), barreling down the driveway, his throat convulsing with fury, teeth gnashing, urgent barks filling the air. Instead of slowing down, the dog seemed to speed up the closer he got to the car, until the moment where he leapt up on the passenger's side, claws ripping against paint. His barking seemed to be a report in dog-speak back to the house: "Intruder! Five foot three, one hundred and forty-seven pounds, brown hair, female, alone, frightened! Advise now! Advise now!"

Ronald, having just sat down after letting George Lincoln out, stumbled sharply to his feet. The deer rifle was, thank Christ, only five feet from his chair, on a diagonal, and absolutely loaded. The weight felt perfect in his hand. Adrenaline rushed to the parts of his brain that weren't foggy yet, shoving aside the alcohol's effects for a few lovely moments. This was one of those moments that Ronald—more than anyone else in the county—was ready for.

Peeking out through a cleft in the scotch-plaid drapes of the front window he saw it—an official county vehicle, map of the county outlined in bright green, no doubt, taunting, announcing its intent: The day has come to take away your rights, hand over your guns. Then we'll take your land and build an Old Navy and gay hot-pants boutique and methadone maintenance clinic for migrant farmers from Mexico and a chapter headquarters for the N.A.A.C.P. He could hear it: "Take 'em, boys...and the ammo, too. Thank you, sir. No, you won't be getting them back without a court order. I'm sorry, sir, you'll have to write a letter to our Zionist Occupation Government and request an exception. Yes, sir; that should be addressed to Jerusalem, sir, not Washington. Correct, sir."

Not likely. As they said, "You can pry it from my cold dead fingers."

George Lincoln was around to the driver's side of the invading vehicle now, mouth wide, teeth dripping and gnashing, saliva streaking the window.

They would want him to fire first. They would draw him out, probably kill George Lincoln, get him to shoot first, then the helicopters, sharpshooters, and men in the woods would drop him. Clean shot to the head. Jew traitors. Poor Christian boys doing their work for them. Patrolling Iraq. Roadside bombs. Poisoning Yasir Arafat. Jews can't shoot, unless Israelis are brought in for the job. Which they frequently are.

Another car drove up, stopping a good eight feet away from George Lincoln. The dog ran to the passenger side of the gold Volvo wagon, jumping onto it, scraping and tearing in the direction of its driver. Dolores was shocked. She grabbed her cell phone, and dialed. She untangled the combination headset/mike that enabled her to avoid any radiation leakage from the unit itself.

In the moment that the dog was away, Debbie quickly rolled down the window on the passenger side, screaming out, "We're here for Claire! We don't want any trouble. We need Claire!"

Ronald smashed a window pane with his fist and stuck the big rifle out.

Dolores rolled down the window two inches on her side the next time the dog hurled himself at her Volvo. Holding the tall can firmly and taking good aim she pepper-sprayed the snarling creature, hitting him directly in the eyes.

The yelping moan of the animal in pain seemed to hot-wire Ronald's finger-brain connection. They were torturing George Lincoln before his eyes. The dog choked, then howled some more. Ronald took a breath and, calmly, fired two shots. They sailed at least ten feet above both vehicles in rapid succession, endangering no one.

George Lincoln ran blindly off to the woods, rubbing his head on the leaves, flinging himself on the dirt, rolling and moaning. It was similar to the wounded-but-not-yet-dying sounds Ronald had occasion to sample when he was shooting for sport. A horrible, helpless release into pure pain, with no promise of sweet death. He might have shot George Lincoln himself, in the heat of the moment, if he'd been able to line up half a shot.

Then he considered the two Jews.

He fired again. Just for the fuck of it. He shouted through the window, "Get the hell off my property. This is white, Christian property and I have paid my taxes. You are not authorized to be here. Leave while you can. You have one minute to leave."

"We want Claire. Let her go."

"What do you want her for?"

"We just want to talk?" said Debbie, her voice hoarse from shouting.

"I am not talking to you, or any of your United Nations' troops. I do not recognize the authority of any 'peace-keepers.'"

Dolores' call to 911 was well-organized and calm. "We are under fire. 435 Butterlink Drive, Hadleyville Falls. Armed man, likely to be Ronald Dubeck, is shooting at us; at least three shots have been made on our lives. We are sitting ducks in the driveway in front of his house. He may be holding his girlfriend's daughter, Claire, hostage. He refuses to allow myself and CPS worker Debbie Dunlop to question the girl. We have no verification that the girl is okay. Repeat—shots fired, 435 Butterlink, possible hostage situation, please help."

Sergeant Ross Barker's police unit was less than eighty feet away from the property, pulling up, as Dolores was on the phone with 911. He had heard the shots. He was well-trained. He knew that every second was life or death now. His car screeched to a fast halt, angled so the driver's side was away from Ronald. Sergeant Barker quickly ran out of the car, gun drawn after urgently calling for backup.

The dispatch of additional State Troopers to the scene, along with the county's as-yet-unproven SWAT team, a hostage negotiator, EMTs and an ambulance, would take another four and a half minutes.

Ronald watched, in disbelief, as an armed black man pointed a gun in his direction.

"Put down the gun, sir. Surrender your weapon."

There were no words.

"Surrender your weapon now, sir."

They wanted him to shoot at the invading Negro. He'd be cut down in a hail of fire. The Negro had more rights than he did, even on his own property.

"This doesn't have to be like this!" Debbie screamed in his direction.

George Lincoln cried hard, pawing at his eyes.

"Surrender your weapons, sir. Throw them out to me and this is over," Sgt. Barker said.

Siren screams in the distance came closer. Ronald thought he heard a helicopter. It would be the black helicopters. (The K96 Traffic Copter was monitoring the afternoon commute when it got word of an "incident-in-progress" and tried to give its listeners the latest.)

Before they could stop Ronald saw the glint of the sun as the Volvo's door opened on the passenger side.

"I'm opening my door," Dolores shouted. "I'm Dolores Solomon, I work with your girlfriend's daughter at school. I'm a School Psychologist. Please let me talk to you without any weapons. You have us cornered; we can't hurt you. Only you can hurt us. You have the power here. This is not a trick. I want to stand up and get out now. May I?"

Ronald caressed the trigger, unsure of tactics.

A tall Jew woman stood up. "I'm standing up. I have no weapons." She raised her hands. "We want to talk to Claire Pargito. That's why we are here. Nothing more."

Before she could finish the sentence four siren-screams blazed out of the distance toward them. The four vehicles appeared, screeching to a halt at the semi-circle across the bottom of the driveway. Doors opened and slammed.

It was a Jew-trick.

Ronald shot, half-remembering where he was last focused.

The bullet tore through Dolores' left shoulder, dropping her in half a second. A large chunk of blood, cartilage, and bone was thrust through to the back of her blouse. Dolores' half-scream was swallowed by silence as she lay backwards on the gravel.

"You crazy fucker!" screamed Debbie.

He could hear more door slams and the sounds of scrambling into position.

Ronald switched weapons. Throwing the deer rifle to the side, he picked up his AR-15. It could do a hundred rounds in seconds. If they were going to kill him, they would die. "Don't Tread on Me."

"If you come out now, sir, there will be no more shooting," promised the armed Negro.

"Give us Claire," screamed another voice.

Ronald remembered Ruby Ridge. They would be looking for the head shot. Ronald remembered Waco. They might burn the house down. He would not burn to death. He ran to get a wet rag, his AR-15 with him. The SWAT team, viewing him through a scope, saw him run to the kitchen. Two officers ran, unseen, to the sides of the house. Crouching low, they met at the back door just as Ronald shoved his weapon out the front window again. On signal from their commanding officer, they kicked down the back door and ran in just as Sgt. Barger was talking again: "Surrendering your weapons will bring a quick and peaceful resolution to this, NOW, sir."

"NOW" was the "go" code.

Ronald heard them coming. Mossad. Al-Qaeda. The Passover Plot. Angel of Death. Rabbi Meir Kahane. From behind. He whirled, firing, and was met with a line of fire that threw his torso into an uncontrolled fall as his knees disappeared under him. Smashed into bits by a horizontal line of bullets, his legs were useless. Another bullet, scraping by his head, tore a part of his lip off.

One of the Jews was standing on his hand, digging his boot into the soft part of his wrist as the other kicked the gun away from him.

"Where is the girl!?" they screamed. "Where is the girl!?"

"What have you done with her?"

Ronald laughed. His head was slammed into the ground, breaking four teeth immediately.

He was alive. He had not surrendered. He was bleeding, but unbowed. Overwhelming Zionist firepower. Won the battle, they'd lose the war. The first skirmish. Look how many of them it had taken.

He blacked out, blood seeping from his legs and mouth.

Dolores Solomon was airlifted to University Hospital, where she recovered strongly from her wounds. She attributed the rapid recovery to her lifelong habit of taking Co-Q10 supplements, along with mega-doses of Calcium/Magnesium, Vitamin E, and garlic with soy lecithin.

The headline story in *The Hadleyville Falls' Gazette* the next morning was, "Hero Shrink: Hail of Hater's Bullets in Vain."

Claire—impressed by the action, and particularly by the shooting of Ronald—gave them every word of the deposition they needed. From the safety of her Group Home she gave them the five incidents and threw in another three. She even offered Debbie Dunlop brownies she had made.

Ronald, being technically bankrupt, was appointed a Legal Aid Society lawyer—Irving Itzkowitz—who, in addition to being a lifelong resident of the county, happened to be Jewish. Irving ended up putting together a somewhat lackluster defense for Ronald, which resulted in a sentence of sixteen years with no possibility of parole. In state prison, having been identified as a member of an Aryan Nation prison gang by a member of the black Five Percenters, a fellow inmate smashed Ronald in the face with a piece of furniture during recreation hour in his second month of confinement. Stitched up, but unable to receive state funding for reconstructive surgery beyond the minimum, his petition to be transferred to another prison denied, Ronald remained jumpy and nervous through the remainder of his first year. The guards had a betting pool about the date and time of the next bloody attack on him.

THE LAST SERMON OF FATHER MARK, JULY 14TH

God does not expect us to be perfect. In fact, God knows we will sin. Not just make "mistakes," but sin.

It is part of the picture, part of our makeup, as sure a fact as Eve yielding to the Serpent in the

Garden of Eden. We had Eden and we threw it away. We are sinners.

But sinners-with-a-Plan. God has given us a roadmap.

It is not an easy map to read. There are complicated turns, merges, divides, and sometimes the speed limit seems too fast. But we are not alone on this long trip. If we were, we would despair.

That is why we were sent His Son. To keep us company on the drive.

The essence of the Jesus mystery, when you come down to it, is a story of *rejection*. If it simply had been the case that Jesus was a brilliant man, an intelligent, sensitive Rabbi of his time whose ideas caught on, became popular, and led to a higher level of discourse and better human conduct, he would have been a fine Jew and that would have been that. We would have had, perhaps, a better Judaism, but there would be no Christianity, no Mother Church, no personal path to Salvation.

But that is not what happened. What happened was that Jesus was *rejected* for his teachings, mocked, conspired against, led through a false trial and destroyed. He was a sacrifice—a Paschal Lamb.

This is The Path: Suffering, rejection, defeat and sacrifice. This is what makes our faith unique. To death and through death.

Because death is just a moment, a tollbooth on the highway back to God.

To atone before the moment of death gives us a reprieve from the fires of hell. And then defeat isn't defeat. It is coming home. To a big hug and a "job well done" and a glass of lemonade and eternal peace.

Coming home.

Father Mark took a last sip of Smirnoff. He listened as Glenn Gould played the "Goldberg Variations"—an aria and variations, numbers 1-30—in a recording made in 1970. No one had understood why Glenn Gould rerecorded these pieces, when he had so masterfully recorded them the first time as a young man in 1955. Gould's explanation— something about arithmetic and its correspondence with the music—made no emotional sense. Father Mark thought it was as simple as refusing to believe that perfection lay in the past and that the future held only decline.

He slid the gun across the desk, confident of its weight, anxious to pass through death. He looked into it and pulled.

The blast from the .357 did blow apart a large piece of Father Mark's head. But because he significantly flinched as he pulled the trigger he missed major brain tissue while shattering the physical structure of his head. Doctors at Westchester Hospital, following up on the excellent medivac work done in the first few minutes after the shot, were able to complete what they referred to, in a press release, as a "major medical miracle" in saving Father Mark's life.

"He is a very lucky man," Dr. Peter Birnbaum, Chief Surgeon said to CNN after three hours of surgery. "It's too early to tell but it is possible he will have at least partial eyesight in one eye, stable breathing function, and some of his autonomic nervous system functions. The next few hours will be critical, but we are hopeful he will live. This is a time for your prayers."

Father Mark knew he was flinching as he did it. Pulling the trigger, his last conscious thought—which would echo forever to the end of all words— was *I am a coward.*

Following a long recovery, unable to speak, the right side of his face having been reconstructed three times, Father Mark was moved, drooling, in his wheelchair, to Our Lady of Most Precious Blood long-term residential living center. The state—with the victims having reached an out-of-court settlement with the Archidiocese (dropping lawsuits in exchange for an undisclosed financial settlement, while the Church acknowledged no guilt in each case)—dropped criminal charges. The Church would pick up the tab for the remainder of Father Mark's years. This settlement was reached on Father Mark's behalf by The Duke—who had even managed to produce an affadavit, signed two months before the suicide attempt, giving him "hard power-of-attorney, surviving disability" to represent Father Mark's legal interests "without exception," with no stop-date specified. The settlement came on the heels of a well-publicized lawsuit by The Duke against the Church itself, for "...failure to recognize a long-standing pattern of deviant behavior on Father Mark's part, failure to properly supervise him, and failure to remove him from a position where he would regularly interact with children." The suit asked for twenty-five million dollars. Citing the need for "closure" and "for healing to begin all around" The Duke settled for five-million-eight.

Father Mark spent his days expressionlessly watching t.v.

The Duke picked up thirty percent of the overall settlement—one million, seven hundred and forty thousand dollars—without having to go to a single day of trial.

THE SUBARU IN THE SUN

On a wide, tree-lined street in the small town of North Brookfield, Massachusetts, Father Ed Garagiopolus talked to the small group of teenagers at 10:00 on a hot July morning. They had gathered to join two construction workers in completing the building of the simple, but clean, new house for Rasheeda. She held her squirming two-year-old son, Nelson, closely. Habitat for Humanity was charging her nothing for this, but she had to help them build it. No problem; it was good to slam something.

The group—mainly young Catholic teenagers from Father Ed's parish—was rounded out by four eleventh-grade boys from Congregation Beth Shalom across town, two pagan girls who brought the new Dar Williams' CD for the boom-box, and a Muslim kid whose parents were both wealthy doctors. The group didn't declare its mission in any way. They just took out their hammers and built the house.

Alison and Elijah sprawled on their backs in the field behind the elementary school. A bright August sun baked them. They watched the fluffy clouds blow slowly their way, morphing from a giant bear with cubs into a 2005 Subaru Legacy Wagon.

Alison's head lay on his shoulder. The ground felt firm. Alison's hair smelled cleaner than clean. Elijah's summer tan made him look two years older, she thought, snuggling closer to his body. He had the scent of the sun.

A squirrel skittered across the lawn. They could hear his claws lightly pushing against the dirt. The sun suddenly seemed to get warmer.

She imagined Elijah and herself climbing through the clouds, riding in a forest green Subaru, windows all open, ascending...

"Tell me that again," she whispered.

"What?"

"The river..."

"Oh." It had been easier to say when they both were looking at the clouds. This time Alison's dark brown eyes held him steadily. "'Together we flow like the river, together we melt like the snow...'"

She closed the distance between their faces in an instant, her lips finding his and yielding at the same time as pressing. She pulled away, but stroked his hair.

"Who wrote that?"

"Steve Winwood. Jim Capaldi. Traffic. Before our time."

"Then how come you know it?"

"I heard it in the dentist's office when I was getting anesthesia for my wisdom teeth. I was floating. I was out of it. But I still knew," Elijah said.

"Knew what?"

"That it was about you."

"You mean 'us'?" Alison asked.

"Yeah. Us."

"That's really corny, you know."

"I know," said Elijah.

"Exceptionally corny."

"Yup."

"How's your mouth feeling?" Alison asked.

"Good."

She let the moment hold for half of forever. They fell into the next kiss, not caring to measure the rest of time.

Photo by Lauren Manoy

Jerry Sander has worked with inner-city, suburban, and rural teenagers as a Certified Social Worker in private practice, in agencies, and in schools for the past 19 years. He currently works in a suburban public high school. A graduate of Oberlin College and New York University he is married and has four children. He and his family live in New York's Hudson Valley. Jerry's second novel, **Unlimited Calling (Certain Restrictions Apply)** is nearing completion. Jerry believes in the calming influence of guinea pigs and the spiritual superiority of dogs.